S R DURHAM

Prey

Second edition

ISBN: 9798371622822

This book was professionally typeset on Reedsy.
Find out more at reedsy.com

Contents

1

Aaron

As the train rolled to a stop at another tumbleweed station, Aaron automatically reached forward and clicked his phone into life for what felt like the fiftieth time.

No signal. Still no signal.

He thought of trying his second phone – the burner handset stashed in his bag – but quickly decided against drawing any unwanted attention. He'd just have to be patient, bide his time. The annoying thing was that he'd always planned to call ahead and warn them he was coming, but as soon as his train left Piccadilly, the reception had been as unpredictable as the scenery scrolling past his window.

It hadn't been long before Manchester's glass and grey concrete vanished, replaced by red brick houses and tree-lined avenues, then thatched roofs, smoking chimneys, and even the odd working farm. Eventually, all he could see was fields and hills in every direction. No sign of human life, like travelling back in time.

Just as Aaron clapped his phone back down onto the table, he heard the old woman sat opposite him swear under her breath, her hands scrambling to clear an open packet of wine gums to rescue the cardboard coffee cup she'd just knocked onto its back. Aaron tried to push himself away from the stream of black liquid as it surged towards him, but there was nowhere to go.

He sucked air through his teeth as the coffee cascaded over the edge of the table and onto his lap.

"Bloody hell," the woman said, whipping a crumpled tissue from inside her sleeve and attempting to smother the coffee. "I'm so sorry, love. I... Oh God."

Aaron's knee jerk reaction was to glare at the woman, silencing her, but he immediately felt a pang of guilt when he saw the regret in her eyes. She was even wearing the same old lady style dangly earrings that his Gran used to. He did his best to twist his mouth into an awkward smile.

"It's alright," he said, his voice low and controlled. "No worries."

He stood as much as the baggage shelf above permitted, then brushed the last few droplets of coffee off his jeans and onto the greasy carpet.

"I just didn't... Oh God, I'm so sorry," the woman said.

"It's fine, honestly."

He pulled down his black rucksack from the shelf and patted it, as if to reassure her.

"Always got a plan B," he said, his smile more natural this time.

He shimmied into the aisle while another passenger leant

over to hand the old woman a fresh wad of napkins, then he turned and headed for the cramped toilet cupboard at the far end of the carriage.

Once inside, he dried his legs and dressed in a clean pair of joggers, then stooped to tuck the wet clothes into his bag and, as he did, caught a glimpse of the things he'd stashed at the bottom of it – his real 'plan B' kit – two rolls of duct tape, a bundle of zip ties, and the sleek, carbon-black form of his best knife.

He zipped the bag, then straightened up and looked at his tired reflection in the mirror. He stared at his dark-ringed eyes for a few seconds and tried to convince himself that his plan B was just that; a backup. A last resort. If the next few hours went to plan, he was pretty sure he wouldn't need any of it.

* * *

The train doors clunked open and the crisp, clean air hurried in, too impatient to wait for Aaron to come out and meet it. He stepped onto the platform and pulled his knock-off Beats away from his ears, resting them around his neck so he could stand and listen. It was silent, except for a few frozen commuters clinking up the steps and over the rusted railway bridge, allowing him take in the eerily familiar view undisturbed.

To his left, a sheer cliff face shot up behind a row of cottages for hundreds of feet, while a boulder hill reared up in front, its back turned like the sidelong figure of a sleeping giant. Far off to the right was a peak that rose so perfectly out of the early evening fog that it looked almost fake. It made Aaron think of a moonscape on grainy film or a woodblock print of a Japanese mountain; wonders that people like him shouldn't be able to see in the flesh.

He stood captivated for a few seconds longer as the train snaked away into the gloom, then fished a pack of cigarettes from his inside jacket pocket. He shook the pack from side to side, so the contents arranged themselves at its edge like soldiers falling in line, then took a quick head count; five cigarettes and three skinny looking joints, as well as an emergency book of matches slid in between the foil and the cardboard.

He briefly stared at one of the joints, then thought better of it and took out a cigarette. Although the weed would surely help to settle his nerves, he couldn't risk turning up at the house visibly stoned or – worse still – in the middle of a full-blown para. He took a disposable lighter from the same jacket pocket and lit his cigarette, the first plume of smoke hanging over his shoulder like a lonely spirit.

Aaron crammed everything back into its place, pulled his headphones on, and made his way over the bridge, onto the quiet housing estate at the other side. He'd only visited here half a dozen times in his twenty-one years – the last of them when he was still a boy – but he was confident that he was supposed to turn right and continue down the hill, towards the main road.

He looked around as he walked in an attempt to pick out something memorable, some kind of landmark. Even though the fog and the fading light were both working against him, it was clear that the place had changed drastically over the years.

He passed a row of sandstone bungalows, spotless 4x4s on their drives. They were the kind of vehicles townies might buy the second they moved to the 'countryside' to combat the single-track roads, potholes, and – God forbid – few days of snow that might disrupt their commute. They all looked like the hardest thing they'd faced since they rolled out of the factory was a steep set of speed bumps.

As Aaron reached the end of the lane, he stopped to stub his cigarette out on a lamppost and drop the filter into a nearby bin. He looked across the road at a Conservative club whose doors were still bolted shut, then at a few shops further down to his left. His brow furrowed as he tried to remember if the house was near anything as sophisticated as a chippy or a butcher's shop, then decided it wasn't and started in the opposite direction.

The pavement quickly became so thin that he was forced to keep one hand on the wall to his left for balance. The stone felt scarred, sharp under his fingers, and was occasionally interrupted by moss that was cold and wet to the touch.

He was close now, he knew he was, and the sights were becoming more familiar with each step. He recognised the chest-high garden wall – which had looked more like a castle wall when he was a boy – and the bare fields that stretched downhill and the huge oak trees flanking the stone gateposts up ahead. As he reached the gate, he craned his neck around to read the letters that had been chiselled into a slab of granite on the right-hand side: OWLGREAVE HOUSE.

* * *

Aaron took his time shuffling down the long driveway, almost in denial of the whole situation. The intimidating possibility of the worst-case scenario just around the corner. The chain of events – however far-fetched – that could call his plan B kit into action.

It was like his feet were telling him that the longer it took to get to the door, the more likely it was that something miraculous would happen in the meantime to make the whole thing go away. His mind was more forceful than his feet, silently shouting at him to turn and run. To go scrambling straight back to the station and jump on the next train that pulled up. It wouldn't even matter where it was headed, as long as it was headed somewhere that this moment wasn't happening. Even going back to his bolthole flat in central Manchester started to feel like a refuge by this point.

Despite the arguments going on inside his already crowded head, he soon found himself at the end of the drive, the old farmhouse and its adjacent barn the only places left in front of him. He took off his headphones and stopped for a second, staring on while scenes of childhood memories projected faintly in front of him like ghosts caught in a loop.

He could almost see himself as a child; his grandfather steadying his small shoulders as he struggled with the tin bucket overflowing with food scraps, wobbling slowly over to the pig pen in the corner. It was empty now, wreathed in shadow.

Another image, of an older Aaron this time, crossed paths with that little boy and his bucket, sneaking around the corner of the barn to smoke a cig stolen from his mum's handbag.

A translucent car pulled past him then; a memory of the one and only time his mother had plucked up the courage to bring one of her boyfriends to meet her parents. The relationship didn't last, of course, but the bloke had been alright, he remembered.

Aaron watched intently as he waited for these memories to fade away, for the visual loops to disintegrate like worn-out tape. He breathed a heavy sigh, then walked over to the main house's back door.

Although the four concrete steps leading up to it still looked steep, they'd seemed unbeatable to him when he was a boy, almost like those endless mountainside causeways designed to humble Buddhist pilgrims. The outside light clicked on as he approached, brightening the driveway, which was empty except for a pile of scrap metal next to the barn – machine parts and iron railings and broken appliances all bleeding rust into the gravel.

Aaron took a deep breath, then bounded up the stairs to land three solid knocks on the door. He stepped back down to ground level and waited, readjusting the rucksack's straps on his shoulders and fidgeting with the headphones around his neck.

The two panes of glass in the door lit up, then a broad silhouette appeared to block them. Locks and bolts snapped undone, then the door swung open to reveal a man in his seventies. He was dressed in an open-collared pinstripe shirt with the sleeves rolled up to his elbows and a pair of olive-green corduroy trousers. To Aaron – who wasn't used to seeing people in anything but black tracksuits and the odd bit of grey camo – the old man's clothes were alien. They made him look almost uncanny, like one of those soulless mannequins at a museum dressed up to look like a medieval peasant. His monolithic stillness did little to counter this impression.

Although the light from inside the house was dazzling in the near-dark, Aaron was certain that this was the right man. The man he'd come all this way to see.

7

2

Aaron

"Can I help you?" the man said, glaring down from the top doorstep.

Aaron readjusted the headphones on his neck again as he started to mumble, glancing around the driveway as if he expected to see an autocue there to help him start the conversation. He'd rehearsed this introduction – or reintroduction – hundreds of times over the past 24 hours but, now that it had arrived, he felt like he'd forgotten how to speak altogether. Every phrase that his mind conjured up sounded cheesy and childish. He felt like his maturity was draining from him the longer he stood there and squirmed.

He steeled himself and looked back up at the man, assessing him for a few seconds. Once he was sure that this definitely was his grandfather, the *great and powerful Charles Mortimer*, he cleared his throat and tried again.

"Sorry... Grandad," he said. "It's me-"

"My God... Aaron?"

Aaron smiled, more out of relief than anything else. He'd

spent so long laying his cards on the table that Charles had simply reached out and taken them.

"What are you... How did-"

Aaron silently scolded himself again for not calling ahead, at least giving the old man some kind of warning.

"Would you like to come in?" Charles said eventually, stepping back into the hall.

"Oh, yeah. Thanks. Ta."

Aaron took hold of the iron bannister and hauled himself back up those mammoth steps to the threshold. As soon as he entered and stepped past his grandfather, the smell of the house was unmistakeable. The combination of musty furniture, muddy boots on old carpet. The faint, almost sickly, hint of potpourri and his grandmother's floral perfume. He stood and waited for Charles to close and bolt the door, then pressed himself against the textured wallpaper to let him past.

"Your Gran has just gone upstairs for her bath," Charles said as he led the way into the kitchen.

Unlike the new build estates Aaron had passed on the way to the house, the kitchen looked exactly as he'd remembered it. The terracotta tiles he used to skate over in his socks were the same, and the paint flaking from the ceiling in the corners suggested the room hadn't seen so much as a paintbrush in the intervening years, or any kind of brush, for that matter.

He knew that the open door in the back corner of the room led to the stairs, then onto a pair of sitting rooms, while the closed door in the middle of the room led down to a damp, mouldy cellar that was barely more than a cobweb-covered storage cupboard.

The kitchen's far wall was still lined with the same old pots and pans, all hanging like artefacts from brass hooks buried

9

deep in the plaster. Below it was the cream-coloured range cooker, the sight of which was enough to overlay Aaron's vision with memories yet again; him standing by his grandmother's side as she knelt to take fairy cakes and apple pies from the oven. That blast of hot air and the smell of golden pastry, a reward for whatever outside work Charles had given him to keep him out of trouble.

"Will you have a seat?" Charles said, gesturing towards the long oak dining table in the centre of the room.

It was already set for two with crocheted place mats, knives, forks, and spoons, and a jug of water and two glasses in the middle. The smell of meat roasting in thick gravy told him that dinner was probably bubbling away in the oven as they spoke. Beef hotpot, maybe. Perhaps even some roast potatoes too.

"Sorry, I didn't realise you'd be getting ready to... erm," Aaron continued to look around as the apology stumbled out of his mouth. He placed his rucksack on the floor by his feet, his stomach stirring as he heard the faintest clink of its contents threatening to give the game away in the first minute.

"I wanted to call ahead but it was, you know... the signal was a joke, basically," he said, forcing a laugh. "I did try."

"Not a problem," said Charles, having apparently gotten over the initial shock of seeing his now-adult grandson. He went to stand behind the chair at the head of the table and gripped the back of it, the wood complaining against the tiles as it took his weight.

"So," he said, his voice barely more than a rumble. "To what do we owe the pleasure?"

Aaron let out another nervous laugh, his hand going up to fidget with his headphones again of its own accord.

He was going to set off talking about how he was 'just in the area' – trying to be as casual as possible – but as soon as those first words had been said out loud, he knew how far-fetched it would sound, especially to a man as perceptive as Charles. He allowed his eyes to flick up and meet the old man's scrutiny, though he couldn't hold that lion-eyed glare for longer than a few seconds.

"Everything's been pretty mad recently," Aaron said. "You know, with work and stuff and doing bits for Mum... so I just thought I'd, well, just come out here and visit you guys, you know. To see how you were first, obviously, but to see if... you know, see if I could try and get my head straight too. Try and slow down a bit."

"I see. And how is your mother?" said Charles, the apathy in his tone suggesting that he already knew the answer. "Is she still–"

He trailed off. Aaron considered firing a few helpful phrases at him – 'a pisshead', 'a loser', 'a scrounger' – but the last thing he wanted to do was invite that elephant into the room if it wasn't totally necessary.

"She's good... well, ok, I guess," he said, showing mercy to the old man. "Still got a place in town and stuff. Renting it. She's kind of in between jobs at the minute, like... But, yeah, pretty good."

It wasn't true, obviously. She was still getting drunk on a daily basis, when she could afford it. Still spending the rest of her days slobbed on her moth-eaten sofa in front of daytime telly with whichever bloke was her latest 'mate from the job centre'. Aaron knew he would do anything for her – she was the reason he was here, after all – but it was hard to make her case on character alone, particularly to the same man who had shopped her to the police multiple times for stealing from him over the years.

Aaron looked up at Charles again, to try and better gauge his mood, but he was as inscrutable as he was intimidating. All Aaron knew about him for sure was that he was uncomfortable talking about his daughter. Very uncomfortable. He wasn't sure whether this was because the thought of her suffering upset him so much, or that he simply didn't enjoy acknowledging her existence. Once Aaron signalled the end of that particular conversation with a shallow smile, Charles straightened up and let go of the chair.

"How's Gran?" Aaron said eventually, nodding towards the staircase.

Charles sighed again. From his reactions, it seemed like Aaron was accidentally taking him on a tour of all the subjects he'd rather avoid.

"Unfortunately, she's not... well, these days," Charles said. He leant forward slightly to stare at his wife's place setting, which veiled his eyes and mouth in shadow. "I don't want to distress you, but there's a good chance she won't remember you, not straight away, at least. She has good days and bad days but, more often than not, she seems to get confused with new people. Obviously, you're not new, but-"

"No, no, I get it. I'm probably about a foot taller for a start," Aaron said. They both smiled for a second, not quite comfortable enough to laugh together yet. "Will be good to see her anyway."

"Yes, well. Don't expect too much from her," Charles said eventually. "It's... hard, at first."

"Sorry Grandad," Aaron said, almost under his breath. It was the only thing he could think to say, though he was suddenly struck with how strange it was that people apologised at times like this, even when the shitty thing in question had nothing to do with them.

"Thank you," Charles said. He looked lost. "But not to worry. She's a strong woman. We have help too, for the time being. A young woman called Liana."

"That's good," Aaron said. "She like a carer or something?"

Charles looked back up. "Of a fashion. She's been a lifeline for us, really. I'm not sure what we'd do without her."

Charles fell silent for a few seconds, then nodded to himself and walked around the table to where Aaron was stood.

They both listened as the pipes rumbled and groaned above, the walls beginning to tick as the water drained from the bath. Aaron thought that it would've been the same free-standing tub that he used to soak in as a boy, before clambering out and taking a cloud-soft towel from the airing cupboard and swaddling himself in it like a newborn.

"Can I take your coat?" Charles said eventually, though the deference in his tone seemed unnatural to him.

"Cheers," Aaron said, shrugging out of his black bomber jacket.

Although he'd been old enough to smoke for a few years – and had done for a long time before that anyway – he suddenly became conscious that his cigarettes could drop out of his inside pocket as he removed the jacket. He carefully folded it in half, lengthways, and handed it to Charles, who took it with a gentleness that was a stark contrast to his shovel-sized hands.

Aaron smiled, but was immediately shocked into action when Charles stooped to pick up the rucksack by his feet.

"No," Aaron said, unable to keep the panic out of his voice. "No, no... I-It's cool, I'll get that."

13

Aaron shot out a hand, snatched the bag up by one of its straps, and swung it up onto his right shoulder. He gave his grandfather a goofy grin, trying to soften his stern gaze. He eventually conceded and led Aaron to the coat hooks by the door.

"You can hang it here," he said, before striding back towards the kitchen. "Can I get you a drink?" he said over his shoulder.

"I'd love one, ta."

Aaron walked back into the kitchen to see Charles sliding a dusty bottle from the rack that stood against the side wall. He placed it in the middle of the dining table, next to the jug of water, then went over and took a pair of crystal wine glasses and a corkscrew from a nearby cabinet. Aaron gulped as Charles uncorked the bottle, bracing himself to force down an entire glass of red wine.

It wasn't that bad, as it happened. It was so different from anything he'd tried before that the first few mouthfuls were almost worrying. The initial flavour of tart cherries was mixed with something more earthy, almost like stone, and this strange combination soon shifted into a swirling, mouth-drying aftertaste of cinnamon and wood smoke. It was interesting, moreish, and the thought of soon being able to touch a piece of that rich, fat-marbled beef to his tongue made his stomach growl.

It was at this moment that Aaron realised he hadn't eaten since his boss' ultimatum almost 24 hours ago. Since then, he'd been distracted from his hunger by constant forward motion, the fear and anxiety driving him on like coal being shovelled into a steam train's firebox. Now, in this room filled with comforting smells of his childhood and the warming alcohol that was making his vision swim; his racing heart finally began to slow.

"Are you working?" Charles said after a few sips.

"Erm, not really... at the moment. Doing stuff here and there, you know."

Aaron knew he had to stay vague about his lack of official employment and even considered distracting Charles by moaning about the welfare system or the government. Just as he was about to speak, he noticed the stern look on his grandfather's face and remembered how little time he had for that kind of weakness.

"Stuff," Charles said, more of a statement than a question.

"Yeah," Aaron said. "Doing what I can, you know. Not a lot of opportunities around at the minute. Just gotta wait and see what-"

"You should create your own opportunities," Charles said. "It's like building anything from scratch. If you make something for yourself, you know how it works, you know how to handle it. That's what I did, there's no reason you can't. If you're given opportunities you're not equipped to handle, they're often wasted. Just look at your mother."

Aaron took a mouthful of his drink to hide from Charles' words. People often referred to having rich parents as having a head start or a leg up, like it was some kind of automatic advantage. For Aaron's mum, Michelle, it had been more like a stone around her neck. It forced her to strike out on her own and move to the city where no one knew her, to get away from her controlling father, and ultimately get swallowed by it. Of course, Aaron had only known her side of the story, but the way she told it, it was no wonder she was eventually overwhelmed.

"I suppose you're right," Aaron said, trying to push thoughts of his Mum to the back of his mind. "You gotta take what you can get, even if the world don't want you to have it."

Charles raised an eyebrow but seemed almost proud of his grandson's swagger.

In truth, Aaron made decent enough money doing what he did, better than half the people he knew. Obviously, he couldn't tell Charles that he did this by dealing weed to students and layabouts, just like he was too embarrassed to admit that he spent the rest of his time sat playing video games.

Until recently he'd been doing so well in his job that he thought it might soon be able to take a step up the ladder, maybe even start looking after his own patch. That was before last week. Before he made the fuck up of all fuck ups. As a result, his prospects were looking a lot more uncertain. Everything was. After all, his fuck up was the only reason he was sat across from his grandfather now.

He was here because he was getting ready to beg to the only person left who had the power to help him.

3

Aaron

Aaron was leaning over to have his glass refilled when his grandmother, Phyllis, shuffled into the kitchen. Her carer was steadying her with one hand on her elbow, and one behind her back, guiding her opposite shoulder.

Phyllis was wearing a grey towel dressing gown and a pair of tired old slippers. Her hair would have most likely reached the nape of her neck, had it been combed or styled in any way. Instead, it stuck out in all directions, as if she'd had her hands on a plasma ball. It reminded Aaron of that poster first year students would sometimes have up in their halls when he stopped by to make a drop; the one of Albert Einstein sticking his tongue out.

Although the thought of this image would have usually made Aaron smile, seeing what his grandmother had become in the years since he'd last visited Owlgreave was a punch in the gut. She'd always been petite, barely over five feet tall, but now she'd shrunk to the size of a child. Her shoulders were hunched, her head bowed. The only skin Aaron could see was a few pale inches of her lower leg and ankle, and they looked more like the legs of an origami bird.

The other woman, Liana, was everything Phyllis wasn't. She was slender, but she had the poise and strength of a dancer, a ballerina even. Her limbs were solid, her back was straight.

As Aaron stood, his chair screeching across the terracotta tiles, Liana's huge blue eyes flicked up to meet his. Her stare was intense and alert, like a fierce mother standing in between a predator and her children. Phyllis was still too preoccupied with putting one slipper in front of the other.

Aaron raised an awkward hand and smiled. "Alright," he said. "Hiya Gran."

Liana didn't react until Charles stood and spoke. "This is Aaron," he said. "My daughter's son. Our grandson, of course."

Liana helped Phyllis struggle into her seat at the dinner table, then stood and smiled at Aaron, though it was a clipped, dutiful expression.

"Hello," she said. "It is good to meet you."

Her accent was heavy but measured, and she gave a slight bow of her head as she spoke.

"You too," Aaron said. "My Grandad says you've been awesome, helping my Gran and that. How are you doing, Gran?"

Phyllis looked up this time, albeit in slow motion, and met his eyes. And in that moment, Aaron's heart sank. His grandfather was right; he could have been anyone as far as she was concerned.

"I'm... very well, thank you," she said, struggling to hide her confusion at the name he'd given her.

"Phyllis, this is Aaron, Michelle's son," Charles said. Despite the fact that English was clearly not Liana's first language, he spoke to his wife with a lot less familiarity, enunciating every word carefully in his booming baritone.

"Oh, how lovely," Phyllis nodded, an oblivious smile on her face. She turned back to Aaron. "Nice to see you. Are the family all doing well?"

All Aaron could do was smile and nod back. "Yeah... all good ta."

Once Phyllis was seated, both men joined her at the table while Liana floated off towards the back of the kitchen, un-hooking a pair of oven mitts from the wall on her way. Aaron quickly realised that she was expected to switch from carer to chef when needed, and probably anything else that Charles was unable or unwilling to handle, day-to-day. The advantages of having money, Aaron thought.

Liana disappeared immediately after dinner was served, despite Aaron voicing his confusion that she would walk away from a meal that she'd clearly spent hours preparing. Even so, she was reluctant to stay at the house, leaving the three of them to eat in silence.

As Aaron had anticipated, the meal was indeed his Gran's famous beef stew, served with roast potatoes, pickled red cabbage, and slices of crusty bread slathered with salted butter. It was rich and soothing, just as he'd expected it to be, though there was still something unusual about the taste. He couldn't be certain, as so much time had passed, but there was a good chance that it was even better than his grandmother used to make it – the meat more skilfully seasoned, the potato skins even crispier – but that didn't matter. Better still meant different.

After they'd loaded the dishwasher – the first new addition

the house that Aaron had noticed, besides Liana – Charles helped his wife up the stairs to bed, promising to return in a few minutes. Although it had been good to see his Gran again after so many years, Aaron couldn't help but breathe a sigh of relief as she said her goodnights.

He fished his personal phone from the pocket of his joggers and illuminated the screen. Now that he'd been in one place for long enough, the patchy rural signal had finally manifested, causing his phone to buzz erratically as the notifications flew in. They were mostly WhatsApp groups and spam flooding his emails, as well as a few text messages, like one from his flatmate asking "where the fuck" he was.

He smiled as he typed and sent a reassuring but vague message, then went into the hall to unzip his bag and check his burner phone.

"Fuck."

He had four missed calls and a message from 'ice cream man' – the code name for his boss, Eastside Dave – which simply said, "ring me".

Aaron zipped up the bag and stood and popped his head into the kitchen to check for any sign of Charles, then ducked back into the hall, and crept out of the door. His breath caught in the freezing air as he strode up the drive, white clouds billowing over his shoulders like a translucent cloak.

Aaron stopped once he was out of earshot of the house and looked at Dave's number on the screen, his shaking thumb poised over the 'call' icon. He wasn't sure if it was the adrenaline or the cold that was causing him to shiver, but either way he had to compose himself before he spoke to his employer. He closed his eyes and breathed, then jabbed the icon, sparking the screen into life. Even the sight of Dave's code name above the word 'calling...' was enough to turn Aaron's stomach. After three rings, the phone clicked, and a hoarse Mancunian voice answered.

"There he is, about fucking time... Lord Lucan."

"Dave, it's me... Aaron."

"I know who it is, you soft arse. Where are ya?"

Aaron took a breath, unsure of what to say to diffuse the situation as quickly as he could. In that instant, he was mystified as to how he hadn't thought to prepare for this exact question.

"I'm just... out at the minute," he said, as evasive as a teenager out past his curfew.

"Out? Fucking hell... Ok, try again. Where are you, exactly, right this second?"

"I'm, erm... just in town, like-"

"Look, right, let me stop you there," Dave said, his voice hardening. "You know what? I'll do you a favour right, I'll tell you where you are. Or, should I say, I'll tell you where you're not. You're not in fucking town, mate. You are not. So don't fucking start this off lying to me, yeah? You are not in fucking town. You know how I know you're not in fucking town? Because my boys saw you getting on a train to fucking Sheffield."

Aaron let out a flickering breath, then screwed his eyes shut as if that'd somehow protect him from the voice on the other side of the phone.

"Is that right? Or are they lying to me an' all?"

"No," Aaron said, his voice feeble. "No, I did. This afternoon. I'm coming back though. Coming back soon."

Dave let out a spiteful chuckle. In the brief pause, Aaron could hear the sound in the background on Dave's side of the phone. Toys clattering, high-pitched voices – children's voices – in the next room, even the exaggerated enthusiasm of cartoon animals shouting at each other from a TV.

"That's a fucking good call," Dave said eventually. "I told 'em you would. They said, 'Dave, he's done a runner' and I said 'no fucking way man. No fucking way my boy Azza's that thick. Not when I know his little mammy lives just down the road'. And they said 'oh yeah, you're right Dave. We forgot that'. I know she's a fucking mess lad but she doesn't deserve to pay for your fuck ups as well as hers. You should make sure you look after her, you know what I mean?"

Aaron clasped his phone in both hands and touched it to his forehead. What started as a few frustrated taps against his skin quickly turned into heavier strikes, though he stopped as soon as he realised Dave was still on the line.

"You still there lad?"

"Yeah, sorry," Aaron said through gritted teeth. "I'm just... Look, I'm working on getting the money, I promise. That's why I'm here. I'm working on it right now, I swear down."

"You're not telling me porkies again, are you?"

"No... Look, I swear. Just, please, don't do anything like... It's nothing to do with her, yeah? It's my mistake, I get that... just don't do anything to her. Don't hurt her."

"Hurt her?" Dave said, incredulous. "What do you think I'm gonna do, kill her? Look mate, I don't know who the fuck you think you are but, trust me, I'm not getting sent down just to teach you a fucking lesson about hanging onto gear. I don't have to. I'll just get one of her skag head mates to do it. Probably only take a few grams."

Aaron tried to think of something else to say, some kind of promise that would get him and his Mum off the hook, but his mind was frozen by fear. All he wanted to do was hang up the phone and sink into the ground, deep into the soil where he could try and hide long enough for this all to stop happening.

"Helloooo?"

"Yeah... Yeah, I'm here."

"Fucking hell lad, what are you being so morbid for? You sound like you're gonna start fucking skriking. This should be easy for you. Man of your means."

"I told you I'll get it. I'll sort it."

"There you go," Dave said, a triumphant note to his voice. "Now look, I've got a meet with O'Brien a week tomorrow and I can't afford to turn up short, you know what I mean? He's the one you wanna watch out for, not me. Right sicko, he is, the big man. Dread to think what he'd want to do to settle up."

Aaron's jaw was starting to judder like the exhaust pipe on a beat-up car.

"Yeah, c-course," he said, though he'd lost all track of what day it actually was. "Is that W-Wednesday, yeah?"

"Tuesday. And you don't make a bloke like O'Brien wait, you get me?"

Aaron whipped the phone away from his ear and checked the time. Confirmation that the last few hours of Monday really were ticking away. Seven days. That was enough time. He could still make all of this go away.

"I'll get it to you before then," Aaron said. "I swear down, just..."

"Yeah, yeah, yeah, whatever mate. Look, don't you worry about me or O'Brien, just worry about getting that fucking money, yeah?"

"Yeah."

"Good lad. Don't fuck it up."

The line went dead, and Aaron slumped against the fence behind him, slowly sliding down until he was sat on the cold gravel. He cradled his head in his hands, scrunching further down until felt small enough, and hidden enough, to let the burning tears burst free.

4

Aaron

The warmth of the house, combined with the lingering smell of gravy and rosemary spiked olive oil, was almost enough to thaw the aching cold that had seeped into Aaron's bones while he'd cried and sworn and smoked, pacing the empty driveway. It had surprised him at first how easily the tears came – he couldn't even remember the last time his emotions had boiled over like that – but he'd decided to blame it on the wine. It was new, after all, and the strength of it had hit him like a sucker punch as soon as he rushed out into the fresh air.

Either way, he'd hoped that a few minutes of silence would help steady his nerves, but all it had done was give him time alone to stew on his own self-made bad luck, making the idea of firing up one of the joints in his cigarette packet even more tempting than it was before.

He closed the door behind him, then hung up his jacket and kicked off his trainers, immediately noticing his rucksack still propped against the hallway wall. He'd rushed outside so fast, with his eyes glued to his phone, that he'd completely missed it. He swallowed dryly and inspected the bag, making sure the zip was still in the same position it had been when he stepped off the train. Surely, if Charles had gone through it and found the tape and the zip ties and the knife, he would have marched straight outside and demanded an explanation.

Aaron shook it off, convincing himself it was just paranoia, and went into the kitchen to look for his grandfather. The room was empty, so he headed towards the dimly lit hallway just visible through the door at the back of the room. The staircase, which climbed in three, right-angled flights, was almost invisible in the gloom, the bannister just catching the moonlight as it filtered through the high, arched window that dominated the left-hand wall. Aaron stood at the foot of the staircase and listened for a few seconds, but all he could hear was the distant rumbling of the dishwasher in the kitchen.

Just then, from one of the two doors to his right, came a sharp snap. Fresh wood being piled onto a roaring fire, Aaron thought.

He followed the sound and found Charles in the closest room of the two, just moving to take his seat as the fresh log was being licked at by hungry flames.

"Oh," he said. "I thought you'd left."

"Left?" Aaron said, letting out an uncomfortable laugh. "I've only just got here, haven't I?"

"I suppose so," said Charles, groaning as he stuffed his wide shoulders inside the wings of a beaten leather armchair. "Are you planning to stay the night?"

Aaron took a couple of steps forward, trying to get a better view of his grandfather's expression so he could work out whether the question was a genuine offer or just a formality. He peered around the wing of the chair to see Charles staring

26

straight at him; his lean, wolflike face as inscrutable as ever.

"Is that ok?" Aaron said.

"Of course. You have some things in that bag, I presume? Fresh clothes?"

Aaron's eyes widened. Even hearing his grandfather acknowledge the existence of the bag was like a bucket of ice water down his back. He smiled as naturally as he could, though it felt more like he was about to throw up right onto the thick sheepskin rug at his feet.

"Yeah," he said.

"Good, not a problem. If you're coming in, would you mind?" Charles said, gesturing towards the open door at Aaron's back.

"Oh, yeah. Sorry."

"Thank you."

Aaron closed the door, then padded over and stood patiently while Charles trickled golden-brown liquid from a crystal decanter into a heavy bottomed tumbler. Once he was satisfied, Charles placed the decanter onto a thin, wooden side table, then rested the glass on the chair arm; his fingers like an eagle's talons clasping the rim.

"Would you like another drink?" He said, though being this sociable looked to be physically uncomfortable for him. Even the word '*another*' seemed to imply Aaron was already wearing out his welcome.

"Yeah," Aaron said. "Why not. Ta."

He stayed on the spot while Charles took another tumbler from underneath the table and filled it, then held it out and shook it as if it was scalding his hands.

Aaron stepped forwards and took it gratefully, then looked over his shoulder at the softer, friendlier armchair opposite Charles', its drab, corduroy upholstery draped with a che-

27

quered woollen throw. His grandmother's chair, he remembered. He looked over for Charles' nod of approval, then reversed into the chair, careful not to spill a drop of his drink as he did so. The chair swayed gently as it took his weight, the rocking mechanism hidden inside still going strong after what must have been decades of ownership. Going stronger than its owner, Aaron thought.

"Is this brandy?" Aaron said, giving the heady liquid a sniff.

"Scotch."

Another new experience, Aaron thought. He took a shallow mouthful and did his best not to wince at the burn of it, like drinking oak-smoked napalm. Charles didn't seem to notice, his gaze fixed on the flames.

The two men sipped their drinks quietly for a while, the droning silence only broken by the occasional snap of burning firewood or the creaks and groans of the house as it settled itself for the night. The room was in darkness except for the fire and a tall, stained glass lamp in the far corner, though Aaron knew the layout well enough to pick out most of the things he'd remembered from his childhood.

The mantlepiece was crowded with a trio of carved wooden lions, a series of intricately painted clay bowls, and a brass-handled elephant whip. Aaron knew all of these to be mementos from various trips his grandfather had taken to Africa and Asia. This was also true of the waist-high statues of wide-mouthed, red-lipped tribesmen that flanked the bookshelf, and the stuffed eagle perched austerely on top of it.

"Do you think you'll go on any more trips?" Aaron said. "You and Gran?"

This caught Charles just as he was about to take a drink. He sighed and lowered the glass as he thought about the question.

"I very much doubt it."

Aaron nodded, then took a sip of his own drink – wincing slightly less this time – before continuing.

"Must be hard when you were so used to it," he said, still glancing from one antique to the other. "Like... me, I've only ever left the country twice, and both times it was just to France with Mum so she could get wine and cigs. Like, I don't know what I'm missing, you know what I mean? But you... You've been everywhere."

"Hardly," Charles said. "Your grandmother and I would usually take our holidays in The Lakes... North Wales. She didn't like to... doesn't like to fly."

Aaron continued to appraise his collection of trophies.

"So, this was all when you used to go away for work?" said Aaron.

"That's right. When I was working for Mr Blackwood. A few other trips after that."

Aaron had heard plenty of stories about Charles' old employer and mentor, Mr Blackwood. As far as he could remember, the man was loaded and had owned a massive estate about an hour's drive from Owlgreave. At the time, Charles and Phyllis still were newly married and lived in a small cottage on the grounds.

"What was it you used to do there?" Aaron said. "Hunting or something?"

"Gamekeeping, yes. Originally," Charles said. He stared back into the fire, as if he could see his memories playing out in the flames. "I stalked deer for Mr Blackwood. Then, after he passed away, I ended up working for a group that owned several estates nearby."

"Wow," Aaron said, blinking with surprise. "Mental that

29

someone can end up owning that much... stuff. You know?"

Charles just grunted, as if the question was so inane that he couldn't muster the energy to reply to it. "They had property all over the country, thousands of acres. Near wilderness, some of it. Completely private. Occasionally they'd become bored with hunting game on their own land, so they'd go on trips further afield. If they asked me to, I'd go with them; help liaise with the locals, let them know what was expected and so on."

Charles drained the rest of his drink, then immediately refilled it, glancing over to monitor Aaron's glass as he did so.

In truth, Aaron was struggling with his whisky. The red wine had been manageable, even enjoyable after the first glass, but this was a different proposition altogether. The only experience he'd ever had with spirits at all was in his early teens when he'd siphon small portions of his mother's stash into a plastic bottle, cover his tracks with judicially applied tap water, then take it to the park with his friends after school. Even then it was all topped up with Lucozade, Cherry Coke, or Fanta Orange, and invariably ended up tasting like fruit-flavoured petrol.

"Do you still get up to anything?" Aaron said as he shuddered from another mouthful of the whisky. "Any hunts or anything like that?"

Charles scoffed. "No, I'm far too old for that, much as I'd like to sometimes. There isn't the work to be had these days anyway. The way things are going, it won't be long before anything vaguely resembling English tradition is relegated to the history books... Most likely be replaced by-"

He cut himself off mid-sentence and turned to face Aaron. It was like he suddenly realised he was about to express a genuine opinion in front of his grandson and lost his nerve. That would be too real for him, Aaron thought. Too familiar.

"Do you remember teaching me? To shoot, I mean?" said Aaron, allowing a wry smile to creep onto his lips.

Charles cocked his eyebrow, half turning to acknowledge the question. "Shoot what?"

"That air rifle you had... you not remember? Shooting wine bottles down the bottom of the garden? I got pretty good to be fair. And that time Mum came down and went mental when she found out what we were doing. I used to do her head in asking for toy guns from the paper shop after that. Those ones with a Lone Ranger mask and a Sherriff badge."

Aaron chuckled to himself, but all Charles did was take another sip, then let out a long sigh and look back into the fire.

The quiet started to gather again as the conversation died, like darkness closing in around a guttering candle. On the face of it, a quiet drink by the fire was the perfect opportunity for Aaron to confess the real reason he'd arrived on his grandparents' doorstep, but every time he looked over to Charles and opened his mouth to speak, all he could imagine was the worst-case scenario.

After all, £14,000 wasn't a small amount of money under any circumstances, and the kind of questions a loan of that size would invite were uncomfortable to say the least. Charles barely knew him now and Aaron still hadn't decided how much of the truth he was willing, or even able, to admit. On the train, he'd been toying with the idea of saying the money was for a deposit on a flat, or for a university access diploma or something. Anything that allowed him to preserve even the slightest morsel of dignity in Charles' scrutinous eyes. The possibility that Charles would outright refuse, or, even worse, that his response would dictate the introduction of Aaron's 'plan B' kit, was unthinkable, even after Dave's threats over the phone.

Aaron reassured himself by looking around the room again, reminding himself that he was sat in a huge old house, full of expensive antiques, at the end of a long drive, deep in the countryside. Surely, for a couple who were able to live in this kind of luxury – with their own private carer and housemaid, no less – parting with a few grand would be little more than an inconvenience. A justifiable investment in their only grandchild's future.

These thoughts whirled inside Aaron's mind like go-karts on a track, buzzing wildly as they flew past, only to come around a few seconds later, just as loud and obnoxious as they were before. The alcohol wasn't helping. His head was swimming as he tried to focus on distant picture frames or a particular stuffed animal. He was already craving another smoke, silently cursing himself for not shelling out for fresh pack before he got onto the train. He'd make the trip to the newsagents first thing, he thought – if there was one.

"I think I'm gonna go out for a smoke, if that's alright?" He said. He felt like he was asking a terrifying teacher for a pass to go to the toilet.

"Alright," Charles said. He leant back in his chair as he savoured the last of his drink, then gripped the armrests and hoisted himself to his feet.

"I'll say goodnight then," he said. "I'll see you for breakfast, I suppose. You remember which room you're sleeping in?"

"Yeah, I think so. Uncle Dan's old room?"

Charles hesitated for a second, as if he was thrown off by the mention of his late son's name.

"That's right," he said eventually, then cleared his throat. "Liana will be back again first thing, so you can... just come down when you're ready."

"Will do. Thanks Grandad. I really... you know... Thank you."

Charles nodded, then stuffed his hands in his pockets and waited by the fire until Aaron left.

5

Aaron

Aaron awoke to the light of a blinding grey morning streaming through the window next to his lumpy single bed. He'd clearly been so exhausted that he'd forgotten to draw the curtains before passing out in his clothes, though the joint he'd eventually given in to probably had something to do with it too.

The bed groaned as he sat up onto his elbows, long-forgotten springs jutting up to reintroduce themselves as he rolled.

As he massaged his eyes with the heel of his hand, the white noise coming from the open door began to form into distinct sounds – a burst of water from the tap, the clinking of cutlery on plates, the thud of cupboards being opened and closed. He patted along the windowsill until he found his personal phone, then checked the time and his notifications; *8:15, no missed calls, no messages.*

He whipped off the covers and sat up, pulled his rucksack from space underneath the bed, checked the burner phone (also no messages) and retrieved his phone chargers. He plugged them in and attached both phones, then slid the bag back into its hiding place, careful to let the duvet hang down and conceal the gap.

As he stood and looked around the cramped, cluttered room, more long-forgotten touchstones from his childhood began to introduce themselves.

He walked over to a set of drawers at the far end of the room, which supported a row of books held at either end by the letters D and M, wrought from iron. He immediately recognised a few of the books, not just by their design, but by each tear and scuff belonging to that particular copy of that particular volume. He let out a shallow laugh of recognition, like seeing a long-forgotten friend, as his fingers grazed the pale blue spine of *The Chronicles of Narnia*, then skipped to the tattered brown binding of *The Tales of King Arthur*. He could practically hear his grandmother's voice reading the words as he thumbed through the vanilla and almond-scented pages of *The Wind in the Willows*.

As he replaced the book, he caught a glimpse of a thin poetry collection that suddenly reminded him of his grandfather. He took it out and sat on the floral pillow of the rocking chair in the corner and read the first poem, *The Lion and Albert*.

There's a famous seaside place called Blackpool
That's noted for fresh air and fun
And Mr. and Mrs. Ramsbottom
Went there with young Albert, their son
A fine little lad were young Albert
All dressed in his best, quite a swell
He'd a stick with an 'orse's 'ead 'andle;
The finest that Woolworth's could sell

Although he hadn't been aware when he started reading, he suddenly remembered that the poem takes a dark turn when the Ramsbottom family arrive at Blackpool zoo and young Albert decides it's a good idea to jolt a sleeping lion into life by jamming his horse-headed stick into the animal's ear. As is to be expected with such an allegory, the beast turns and swallows the young boy whole, leaving his parents powerless and distraught.

While this was all familiar to Aaron as he read, he began to feel uneasy as he realised that the moment he had been anticipating – the lion miraculously spitting young Albert out, his lesson learned – was never going to come. The ending of the story, although laced with dark humour, was depressingly bleak. He scowled as he read the last few lines:

The Magistrate gave 'is opinion
That no one was really to blame
And 'e said that 'e 'oped the Ramsbottoms
Would 'ave further sons to their name
At that Mother got proper blazin':
"And thank you, sir, kindly, " said she–
"Wot, spend all our lives raisin' children
To feed ruddy lions? Not me!"

Aaron stared at those final words for a few seconds longer, almost incredulous at the fact that he'd heard the poem so many times and still managed to forget that it ended so hopelessly and taught such a harsh lesson; that the world was a violent, indifferent place, and the humans within it were no safer from its brutality than any other species.

He slapped the book shut, then stood and slid it back in place beside its dust-caked companions and stepped out into the hall, towards the sounds of the awakening house below.

* * *

Aaron walked into the kitchen to find his grandparents sat in their customary chairs around the table, with Liana at the range cooker, hovering over a frying pan that had to have been filled with bacon. The warm, greasy smell almost knocked Aaron off his feet. He couldn't remember the last time he'd had anything other than cereal for breakfast, which was quite often eaten dry, straight out of the box.

Charles glanced up from his newspaper as Aaron entered, assessing him over half-rimmed glasses perched on the end of his nose.

"Morning," he said. His voice, still groggy from sleep, boomed around the tiled room.

"Morning. Morning Gran," Aaron said, laying a gentle hand on her shoulder as he walked behind her chair. She wasn't reading anything, just sat staring straight ahead with her fingers coiled around the handle of an empty teacup.

"Phyllis, this is Aaron," Charles said. "Michelle's son. He stayed here with us, last night."

"Oh, how lovely," she said, her smile and nod at no one in particular.

Maybe she's blind too, thought Aaron.

"Would you like some bacon?" Liana said, carefully sliding a steaming plate behind Charles' paper. Aaron glimpsed scrambled egg, black pudding, and baked beans alongside the still-sizzling meat, and six slices of brown toast were already stood in a rack in the centre of the table, waiting patiently to

37

be taken out and buttered.

"Please," said Aaron. "Looks amazing."

Liana smiled dutifully, then turned and glided back towards the stove.

Charles swung his paper shut, then folded it and tossed it onto the table in a single, fluid movement.

"So," he said to Aaron, taking off his glasses and placing them on top of the paper. "Do you have plans for the day? Anywhere to be?"

His eyes darted between his cutlery and his plate as he spoke, though his hunger was clearly no match for his well-honed manners. Aaron shrugged.

"Not really. Was going to see what you two had planned... see if you fancied, I dunno, getting out somewhere, maybe?"

If he was going to get his hands on the money he needed, Aaron would have to take his time, put in the hard work to re-earn his grandfather's trust.

Charles arched one eyebrow, his smouldering gaze flicking between Phyllis and Aaron, then Liana as she arrived with two more plates. She set a full fried breakfast in front of Aaron and a small portion of scrambled egg in front of his grandmother. The warmth and the smell of the food rushed up to greet him as he looked down, noticing fried potatoes and onions in amongst the components he'd already identified on Charles' plate. He swallowed quickly to drain the saliva filling his mouth.

"I'm not sure your Gran will be up to that," Charles said, wrenching Aaron from his reverent silence. "Liana usually takes her down to the bottom of the garden and back, so it's not really-"

"You could come with us, if you like?" said Liana from the chair opposite, a steaming mug of coffee clasped in her hands.

38

Aaron looked over at Phyllis, who was still wearing the same absent smile.

Although taking what would most likely be a slow stroll around the garden with his grandmother wouldn't help Aaron broach the subject of money with Charles, it did give him the excuse to hang around that he'd been struggling to come up with a few moments earlier.

"Course, yeah," Aaron said. "Sounds good. As long as that's ok?"

Charles nodded, though he made a point of shooting a stern glance towards Liana before turning his attention back to his breakfast. He didn't seem angry exactly, Aaron thought, but he certainly wasn't becoming more congenial either. If this conversation was going to happen, it had to happen at the right time; not too soon, but not so late that Charles' straining etiquette failed him altogether.

* * *

The air outside was crisp and clear, but noticeably thin. It was both rare and rarefied to Aaron's exhaust fume-fuggy lungs, like breathing in high definition, and was a far cry from the cloying smog of the city he called home.

The wind shrieked as it barrelled over the house's sprawling back lawn, sending leaves tumbling down the slope to the bottom of the garden, where high walls served as a barrier to the tangled bracken beyond.

All three of them had wrapped up against the wild weather – Liana and Phyllis in matching grey overcoats and coloured bobble hats, and Aaron with his hood pulled tightly over his head – though the rafts of charcoal cloud above them looked ominous enough to make even these multiple layers wet and useless within seconds.

They set off down the hill joined at the elbows; a chain of three with Phyllis the weak, tottering link at its centre. Aside from the youngsters at either end occasionally checking in, they walked on in silence.

In this void, the sounds of an almost-forgotten world were allowed to step forward and reintroduce themselves to Aaron, just like the dusty books in his uncle's bedroom had. First came the clatter of crows fleeing their bare-branch perches, then further out – away from the cloistered garden – came the din of a factory, the whir of a tractor, even the muted two-note trumpet of a distant train; all husks of ageing metal heaving their way through the sunless Northern winter.

"So, how long have you worked for my Gran and Grandad?" Aaron said as they began to pick up speed. Liana seemed startled, apparently keen to let all of this task be completed without any unnecessary small talk.

"Oh, I, er... almost two years," she said. "It's just part time, now." It seemed as if her accent had thickened now Charles was not around, like she was nervous to be alone – almost alone – with Aaron.

"Right," he said. "And you came here before that? Around here, I mean?"

"Yes. I studied near here for three years... Physiotherapy at Sheffield University... but I wasn't-"

"You couldn't find a job there?"

She gave a sad, almost apologetic smile. "No."

Aaron sighed. "I know how you feel. Well, not having the degree and that, but... you know, finding enough work.

It's hard. And for students too. I know loads of 'em in Manchester... some who've dropped out halfway through... or they've finished, and they can't find anything. It's shit, man."

Despite Aaron's genuine sympathy, Liana was apparently still too on edge around him to commit to any kind of outward emotion, other than professional courtesy. He looked over his grandmother's bobble hat at Liana and was suddenly struck by how young she appeared, how innocent. It was just like some of the international students he'd encountered on his deliveries to halls at both of Manchester's universities. That reluctance to even make eye contact, lest they be somehow transfixed by his corrupt English influence. He imagined Liana must have hidden in her room for the entire three years, now she was hiding here.

"So... you don't sound like you're from Sheffield?"

"I'm not. I am from Slovakia," she said.

"Oh ok, cool. Whereabouts? Like what part?"

"You wouldn't know it. And it doesn't matter anyway. There's nothing there. Nothing to see, nothing to do. No opportunities."

"Even compared to this?" Aaron said, gesturing at everything and nothing in particular.

Liana looked around, first at the distant factory, and its chimneys rising up from behind the woods, then further on to the hills behind it.

"This is England," she said eventually. "It is so beautiful, like an old movie. And there is opportunity for me here. It is an easy first job for me, and Mr and Mrs Mortimer are very well connected," she squeezed Phyllis' forearm. "I like it here very much."

"But you don't live here, at the house?"

She shook her head.

"Did they not want you to, though? Thought that'd probably be easier for you to help my Gran and that?"

"It's none of my business," she said, a nervous laugh rippling beneath her words.

Aaron craned his neck around to catch Phyllis' downcast eyes. "Are you alright Gran? Do you want to have a rest?"

"Oh, no... of course not," she said, patting his forearm. "I'm not as old and frail as all that, you know."

"We can sit down under the tree, Mrs Mortimer. Like always," Liana said, pointing towards a wrought iron bench partly concealed by the yew tree at the bottom of the hill.

"Oh, how lovely."

The three of them sat side by side on the bench, looking up at the house. It looked immovable from its vantage point on top of the ridge, its sandstone tarnished almost black and the empty windows appearing darker still. There was a degree of shelter for the three of them under the yew tree's stooped branches, both from the cold of the wind and the din of its screaming, though this only served to amplify the silence between them. To Aaron's surprise, it was Phyllis who broke it this time.

"It's an ugly old thing, isn't it?" she said, to no one in particular. Liana and Aaron shared a confused smile.

"The house?" Aaron said.

"Yes, just look at it. Looks like it hasn't been cleaned for a hundred years. Someone should buy it and fix it up, instead of leaving it to go to ruin like that."

Aaron wasn't sure if she was talking about the fact that the house had taken a back seat to her and Charles' years and her illness over time, or whether she was genuinely under the impression she was looking at some abandoned property in need of a facelift. Aaron met Liana's eyes briefly, in the hope of nudging her into some kind of professional platitude, though she looked just as unsure as he did.

"Do you not like it here, Gran?" Aaron said, resting a gentle hand on the old woman's shoulder.

"Oh, I can't complain," she said. "It's a bit grey but the air's lovely and fresh isn't it... What do you think?"

"Yeah," Aaron said. "Could be worse. I'm just glad to be here. I've not been here for a long time, you know. I used to come here with my Mum, a long time ago when I was a kid."

"Oh, that's nice," Phyllis said with a smile. "How is she?"

Aaron flinched slightly; his brow furrowed again. He had called her 'Gran' a second ago, maybe she'd held on to that long enough to put two and two together, he thought. Was that even possible? Is that how it works; you can get your memories back if they're all spoon fed to you in a short enough window? With this in mind, he decided to press on.

"Yeah, she's good, thanks," Aaron said. "She misses you and Grandad loads, I think. She wouldn't believe I'm here with you now. Bet she'd love to be here, if she was... you know, if she could be."

Phyllis looked up at Aaron and smiled broadly. "You give her my best, will you?"

"Course," Aaron said, his voice quivering slightly as his surprise erupted into elation. "Yeah, I'll see her soon, hopefully. She could come up here soon, even. Would be good to get everyone together again."

"Oh yes," Phyllis said. "Very good."

Liana reached over and worked her index and middle fingers in the gap between Phyllis' sleeve and her woollen mitten, feeling the old woman's skin for a second.

"You're getting a bit chilly, Mrs Mortimer. Shall we go inside and get a cup of tea?"

"That sounds wonderful. Lovely."

"Is that ok with you, Aaron?" Liana said, struggling with the pronunciation of his name.

"Course, yeah. Hang on."

Aaron pushed himself up from the bench, then turned help hoist Phyllis to her feet. The smell of her floral perfume engulfed him as he leant in and slid his arm under hers, memories of so many childhood hugs hello and goodbye.

"You all good?" he said.

"Ready, yes," Phyllis said. "Thank you, love."

* * *

After practically carrying Phyllis up the hill back to the house, Aaron helped Liana to settle her in her rocking chair next to the fire, where he agreed to wait while Liana went to boil the kettle. Just as the conversation was beginning to gain momentum, the door creaked open and Charles leant through.

"Can I have a word please?"

Aaron's stomach leapt up into his throat. He pictured the bag, hopefully still hidden under the bed, and his phones on charge in the corner. Could Charles have given into his suspicions and searched the room? Had he seen the contents of the bag? Or a suspect message previewed on one or both of the phones' lock screens?

"With me, you mean?" Aaron said eventually, his voice wobbling despite his best attempts to sound casual.

"Yes."

"Oh... I was just gonna wait here with Gran until Liana-"

"Phyllis, I'm just borrowing Aaron for a moment," Charles said, his eyes never leaving his grandson's.

"Oh, that's alright. See you later, love. Thank you."

Aaron tried to smile, but the adrenaline was thundering through his body now. He almost slipped as he stood from the chair arm, then gave a weak wave to Phyllis and followed Charles out into the hall.

6

Aaron

After leaning back into the room to say something else to Phyllis, Charles led Aaron further down the hall, the floorboards groaning under his weight, until they reached the next room along. Aaron knew it was the second sitting room; the one that was slightly larger and usually served as the after-lunch version of the after-dinner lounge they had just left.

Dull grey light streamed into the hall as Charles opened the door and stepped inside, turning on his heel to show Aaron over to the chairs by the French doors. He did as he was bid, taking some kind of reassurance in the fact that this conversation was still beginning on an ostensibly amiable footing. After all, Aaron thought, surely Charles wouldn't be inviting him for a private 'word' if he'd seen weapons, duct tape, or an incriminating text message upstairs?

Aaron took the chair on the left of the pair, stared out thorough the net curtains onto the back garden, which was still being pummelled by the bracing wind. Charles closed the door and came over to take the seat opposite him.

"Everything ok?" Aaron said.

Charles sighed and hunched forwards, his elbows on his knees and his fingers steepled and pressed to his lips. He assessed Aaron for a few seconds, then straightened and eased himself back into the chair, adjusting the pleat of his trousers as he crossed one leg over the other.

"I'm going to ask you a question, and I would like you to answer me honestly. Can you do that?"

Aaron popped out his bottom lip as he nodded. This was reassuring, he thought. Perhaps even a problem unrelated to Aaron at all. He tried to smile.

"Yeah, course. What's up?" Aaron said, his eyes darting to the wall that separated them from Phyllis. "Is it something with-"

"No," Charles said, anticipating the question. "I know... I apologise if this seems callous, but I'm not in a position to make time for any kind of uncertainty at the moment. There's a lot going on and I just need to know the truth.... The absolute truth. Then we can deal with any... consequences in the appropriate way. Do you understand?"

Aaron nodded.

"Good," Charles said. "So, with that in mind..."

Aaron swallowed hard, dug his nails into the embroidery of the chair arm.

"You mentioned you were out of work... that your mother was in a similar position. I know she has her own... issues. And, of course, I've not seen either of you for a long while, so I may have misunderstood... But I'm still struggling to see any other reason for this visit of yours, other than money. So... my question, I suppose, is... is that why you are here? For money?"

Aaron leant forwards, all but mirroring his grandfather's

47

pervious mannerism, except for clasping his fingers on his head instead of steepling them at his lips. The subtle difference between thoughtfulness and exasperation. He swore under his breath, then looked up to meet his grandfather's burning gaze.

"I'll take that as a yes," Charles said. "I thought as much. Fortunately, I can spare you the indignity of having to give me an explanation as to why you need it, because there is a very simple answer."

"Look, it's not like that," Aaron said, his hands held out in contrition. He tried to remember which one of his fabricated back stories was the least pathetic. "I just need some help with starting this-"

"Aaron," Charles said, the bass of his voice stopping Aaron mid-sentence. "Save your breath. I have nothing to give you."

"I get it, I totally understand why you would say that, but I promise it's not what you think."

"Aaron," Charles said, his gaze still unerring. "We. Have. Nothing."

Aaron sputtered out an incredulous laugh. "Come on," he said. "I get it. You think I'm a waste of space, like Mum... or you think it's for her or whatever, but it's not, I swear."

"Aaron, listen to me. It is not that much of a stretch to say we are practically destitute. After I stopped working... your grandmother's care, and the bills, and house upkeep, and everything else. It has bled us dry. There's almost nothing left. Even if I wanted to help you... I can't. At present, I don't even know how we are going to help ourselves."

Charles stood and started slowly towards the door, leaving Aaron dumbstruck, staring at his grandfather's empty chair, waiting for something to happen. It was as if he thought he could have another go at the conversation if he waited around for long enough, like waiting for a free play on a vacant arcade machine. Charles lingered for a second at the door before he opened it.

"Now that you know," he said, his head bowed. "I don't see that there's anything more for us to discuss."

He disappeared into the hall, but Aaron wasn't ready to follow him. He was still transfixed by the empty chair, slowly being engulfed by the sound of Dave's threats in his ears, the looming spectre of his meeting with O'Brien. The flickering image of his Mum's face. The rucksack full of gear he jettisoned to help him get over that wall and away from the police. The fourteen grand that seemed even farther away now than it had then.

* * *

Aaron crossed paths with Liana on the way up to his uncle's old room to collect his things. She was burdened with a floral tray of tea and biscuits, a glass of water, and some kind of medication packet, and although she seemed unaware that Aaron had been all but asked to leave, they exchanged a courteous smile as they passed one another. Aaron climbed the stairs, then padded along the carpeted hallway; his mind a flurry of ideas and possibilities.

He passed his grandparents' bedroom – only the corner of one of the two double beds in there was visible through the crack in the door – then passed his mother's old room and the main bathroom, which still had the same sickly, off-green tiles that it had since he could remember.

His uncle's bedroom was at the very end of the hall, but

49

before he reached it, he had to pass a small corridor that branched off and led to another room around the corner. He stopped as he reached it, his eye caught by the dim light that was streaming through the open door and reflecting off of the matte white walls.

It gave him the second for another memory – another grainy, ghostlike version of himself – to come tottering past, his grandfather at his heels.

"Not in there, young man. That's grandad's office," Charles' ghost said.

Aaron – driven by the recollection of what his younger self was just about to see – followed the memory towards the office door. He gave it a solid push, so it glided over the thick, beige carpet, and stepped inside.

Unlike every other room, the office had no taxidermy or oil paintings on its walls, or anything to add any character at all. No antiques on the desk or the shelves. No animal skin rugs on the floor. In fact, the whole place looked far too bland to have anything to do with Charles or Phyllis or their grand old house. The only thing of note was that the room was so overfilled with papers, books, and cardboard boxes that it looked like it could collapse in on itself at any moment. Aaron glanced at the door behind him and imagined it being slammed that little bit too hard. Even that was probably all it would take to bury him alive and seal the exit for good measure.

He moved forwards and scanned the room until his eyes landed on it, tucked away in the far corner. Its very existence confirmed the validity of all of his other Owlgreave-related half-memories, like a rubber stamp on the front of a parcel; his grandfather's safe.

It wasn't a chunky metal cube with a dial at its centre,

like you'd see cowboys trying to crack on Saturday afternoon westerns, but a tall green cabinet with a metal handle in the centre and a digital keypad at around chest height. Still more than enough space inside to store plenty of valuables.

Aaron tried to remember the layout but wasn't sure he'd ever been allowed to look inside. He reached out to try the handle, more to make it official than out of any real hope. While it had a little play in it, the safe was most certainly locked. He imagined shelves at different heights within, smaller strongboxes and jewellery cases and stacks of cash. Maybe even some kind of contraband smuggled home from Charles' international travels.

Aaron stepped forwards, shook the safe with both hands to feel its weight, then nodded, now sure of his next move.

* * *

Aaron ducked into his uncle's old room to retrieve his phones and his bag; snatching the latter from underneath the bed before wheeling around for the former, stuffing the chargers into the bag's side pocket as he walked back into the hall.

He clicked his personal phone into life as he did so, stopping dead at the sight of his Mum's name next to bracketed double figures showing twelve missed calls.

"Fuck," Aaron said, tapping the call button with his thumb. He crept down the hall and leant over the bannister to check the hallway below as the line blipped its way to a connection. He started walking back towards the end room, though he stopped when his Mum picked up before the first ring had even finished.

"About time," she said, her voice already slurring despite

the time.

"Hiya Mum, what's the matter? You alright?"

"Alright? I wouldn't say that," she said, coughing loudly down the phone. "I went down to the corner shop this morning and there were these two lads – two white lads dressed all in black – hoodies and trackies and big coats. I saw them waiting outside the shop when I was in getting some fags, then I saw them again when I came out."

"Right, and what do you-"

"Then I went round to Darren's for a bit, you know, round the corner? Anyway, I came out after few hours and they were both there, again. Followed me all the way to the flat."

"Shit... did you call the feds?"

"What do you think?" she said wryly.

"Ok, fair one. But it could still be something and nothing. You do live in a rough part of-"

"They weren't from here. They were from town. Could tell that just by looking at 'em. All expensive gear on and that. I reckon it's something to do with you."

Aaron let out a long exhale, dropping the bag and reaching up to pinch the bridge of his nose with his free hand. He moved his lips to form the breath into a silent, drawn-out curse.

"So, what is it? What have you done now?"

"Mum, it's nothing, I promise you," he said, his voice barely above a whisper.

"Where are you? You at home?"

"Nah, I'm... I'm out. Took the train to come and see a mate."

"Oh? Alright for some. So, I'll just stay here and clean up the mess, shall I? Like a good mother should?"

"When was the last time you cleaned anything, Mum?"

"You what?"

He knew that was a step too far. No matter how selfish she could be at times – especially if drugs, alcohol, or men were involved – Aaron knew she had always wanted the best for him, even if her execution was a bit ham-fisted sometimes. He thought of all the kids whose mums had missed school plays or football matches, quite often because of a more socially acceptable reason like working weekends or running late at the office. No matter what, Aaron's Mum would always be there to watch him do whatever he was doing, even if she was half-drunk from a long afternoon in Wetherspoons.

"Nothing," Aaron said after an awkward pause. "I'm sorry... Look, it might be me, I dunno, but it's complicated, alright? I'm sorting it now anyway. It'll all be over in a few days. Why don't you go and stay at Darren's for a bit?"

"Darren doesn't want me there all the time, getting in his way when he's-"

"Right, ok... one of your mates, then or... whatever. You shouldn't be walking around there on your own."

"Oh, you're really worried about your old Mum now, are you? When's the last time you came up here, anyway?"

Aaron flinched. Since he'd left home, she seemed to have gotten worse; apparently happy, now that her work was done, to spend her days doing nothing but getting fucked up and hanging around with other, like-minded wreck heads. If he was honest, he could have visited her more over the last year or two, but the truth was he didn't want to. He felt like he barely knew her anymore.

He sighed, switched the phone to his other ear. "You were passed out last time I came round, Mum, you know that. And I'll come as soon as I'm back, alright? Could even go cinema or something, go for some food. Soon as this is sorted. My treat."

"Sounds lovely," she said with a snort. The venom in her tone made him wince.

"Right, well just try and keep-"

The line went dead, it's droning dial tone line like a flatlining heart monitor. Aaron slapped his phone in between both of his palms and swore again, this time putting his neck into it.

"Fuck. Fucking-"

He held the phone above his head, ready to hurl it to the ground. He hesitated, swore again through gritted teeth. He thought about the other phone in his pocket, the burner phone that had a direct line to the very man who he felt like he wanted kill, this second, with his bare hands. Dave.

"Shit," he said again, lowering his main phone and stuffing it into his pocket.

No matter how painful it was to stand by and watch as mistakes slowly consumed every part of his life, trying to coerce Dave with threats of physical violence would only serve to speed things up; like trying to fight a house fire with buckets of petrol. He breathed heavily for a while longer, slumped against the hall's noisy, textured wallpaper, then slid down it until he was sat on the carpet.

* * *

Aaron stayed there unmoving for a while, his eyes closed and his head spinning. The cold sweat and the nausea and the flickering breaths, all combined to make him feel like he'd taken a bad pill. After a while he bolted into the bathroom to be sick, then, after splashing cold water on his face and drying it with one of the crusty, ancient hand towels, he stepped back into the hall and exhaled up at the ceiling.

The objects at the bottom of his bag – his plan B kit – were practically screaming his name by now, though not for the purpose he originally intended. He strode over and grabbed it, fumbling at the zip as he strode back towards the office.

By the time he stormed inside, he'd taken the blade from its sheath and closed the bag back up. He closed the office door as quietly as his adrenaline-bulging limbs would allow, then dropped the bag and went over to the safe. He checked the door again, listened for any signs of life in the hall, then slipped the carbon black blade in behind the hinges and started to pry.

7

Aaron

Aaron's initial persuasion of the hinges came to nothing, so he quickly set to work on the handle itself. The longer he stabbed into its keyhole, occasionally moving back over to try the hinges again, the closer he knew 'plan B' was coming to initiation. He could almost feel it behind him, its hot, wet breath on the back of his neck, taunting him.

"Come on... come on you piece of-"

The safe rattled and clattered as he stabbed at the handle. It wasn't the first lock he'd forced – even with this particular tool – but it was by far the most stubborn. Sweat dribbled down the side of his forehead as he strained, the blade and the lock both somehow resisting the urge to snap. He relented, doubled over and exhaled in frustration, tapping the butt of the knife against his knee as he tried to figure out some kind of strategy. One more try, he thought. All he had to do was make use of his anger, his fear. Pour it into his aching muscles like fuel and break his way into this tired old safe and make good use of the neglected valuables within.

He straightened up and slid the knife back into place behind the top hinge and leant towards the safe, bracing both hands on top of each other as he put all his weight behind it. Just then, partly muffled by the din of rattling metal, the door to the office swung open behind Aaron.

He stopped what he was doing and spun around, the blade still lodged in place, to see Charles' wide shoulders almost filling the doorway. All Aaron could focus on were the whites of his grandfather's smouldering eyes, the twitching of the muscles at the hinge of his jaw. He looked as if he was about to explode.

"What the hell are you doing?" He said. His words slow and solid, almost but not entirely masking his rage.

Aaron yanked the blade from the door and turned to face Charles, suddenly very aware that what he was now holding had now become a deadly weapon, and not a safe-cracking tool. He turned that handle over in his fingers, its rubber already drinking the sheen of his sweat.

"Look, I told you it's not-"

"Give me that," Charles said, stepping forwards.

Suddenly, instinctively, Aaron's arm shot forwards, the point of the black blade level with Charles' barrel chest.

"Wait," Aaron said, his voice shrill with panic. "Just wait... stay there, I need to-"

"Lower that knife and give it to me, now," Charles said through gritted teeth.

Aaron's shuffling retreat had left his back pressed against the wall, his knife arm still locked out in front of him.

"Aaron. The knife. Now."

"No. No just wait. We need to," Aaron's free hand was rubbing furiously at the back of his neck. "Look, I need to explain, I need to-"

"Give it to me!"

"No, please, I can't. Just, move back. Back into the hall."

"I will not be threatened in my own house by a boy with-"

"Just fucking back up, yeah? Back into the hall, give me some space. Go."

The room felt like a prison. The sweat and the heat from Aaron's reddening face causing his head to spin again. It felt like heresy to bark orders at his grandfather, but violence would surely be seconds away if they stayed this close for any longer.

"Back away, the hall," Aaron said.

Charles stood and seethed for a moment, then straightened and stepped backwards into the hall.

"Ok. Where's Gran?" Aaron said between ragged breaths.

"Where you left her," Charles said, his teeth still on edge.

"Liana too?"

He nodded.

"Good. Keep going then. Downstairs, to the kitchen. Go. And don't try anything. I'm not playing anymore, this is serious."

* * *

"You're making a mistake," Charles said as Aaron led him over to his chair at the head of the kitchen table. Despite the fact there was a knife pointed squarely at him as he spoke, Charles' tone remained as measured as ever.

"I've made plenty of mistakes," Aaron said. "One more isn't gonna hurt."

"This one will, I assure you."

Aaron dropped the rucksack onto the table and began digging around inside, his eyes never leaving his grandfather's. Charles' stern expression remained unmoved, even as Aaron eventually produced the roll of duct tape and stack of zip ties.

"What are you doing?" Charles said.

"I've had enough," Aaron said. "I wanted to do this the easy way, but you had to try and act hard... Mum always said you were a fucking bully."

Charles scoffed, then squared his shoulders and turned his head to one side, almost inviting Aaron to do his worst.

Aaron was becoming more flustered the longer he rooted around for the final few zip ties he knew were inside the bag. He'd only brought enough for two people. With the knife still in one hand, he took eight of the ties and strode over to his grandfather.

"Put your hands behind your back, behind the chair."

Charles did as he was told and Aaron bound his hands together with a pair of zip ties, though the thickness of his wrists made things fiddlier than they should have been.

Aaron had only done this once before, when he'd reluctantly agreed to accompany a senior member of Dave's gang, Tyson, on a targeted mugging in Manchester city centre. The guy had been a jeweller who'd been bragging loudly about a successful deal over champagne in Cloud 23 – the panoramic bar of the Hilton hotel that towered above the city – and one of the staff had overheard and sold the tip to Dave.

Aaron and Tyson had watched him for a couple of days, waiting for the jeweller to slip up and go for his customary drink before dropping off his wares at the hotel. One lucky day they followed him over to one of the bars on Deansgate – briefcase in hand – then grabbed him in the toilets, tied him up in one of the cubicles, and taken everything he had. Although he'd been just as cooperative as Charles was being now, the man's jabbering pleas for his life made the whole situation truly stomach churning. Aaron had vowed that was the first and last time he'd steal for his own personal gain, but this was different. It was about more than money.

His mind had been plagued by thoughts of what could happen ever since Dave's call, and now the stakes were even higher, his anxiety was practically screaming in his ears.

"Right, ok," Aaron said, tugging on the makeshift cuffs on his grandfather's wrists. "Feet, one at each leg."

He crouched and placed the knife on the tiled floor, then pulled Charles' right leg tight to that of his chair and slipped another pair of ties around it. He sealed the ties with a length of duct tape, just as he had at Charles' wrists. As Aaron set to work securing the left leg, Charles let out an almost exaggerated sigh.

"Am I boring you?" Aaron said as he picked up the knife and came back around to meet Charles' gaze.

"You're very close to the point of no return," he said, his menace still somehow unaffected by his restraints. "You need to think very carefully about your next move."

"There are no moves... This ain't a game of chess," said Aaron, turning and pacing the length of the table as he spoke. "Look, this is all... It's only because I don't have any choice in this. You've no fucking... Just trust me this is the only way. There's no other option, you get me? People are in trouble, you... You wouldn't let me explain before."

"What could you possibly say to justify this-"

"Honestly.... You have to help me Grandad, please. This is my life, Mum's – your daughter's life. How is that not enough for you? Just tell me the code to that safe and this can all be-"

Charles' forced laughter cut Aaron off.

"Save your breath, boy," Charles said. "I don't believe a word. And even if I did, what exactly did you think is up there? A safe full of money? Full of jewellery... gold and silver?"

"Don't fucking laugh at me, yeah?" Aaron turned on his heel and marched back towards Charles, raising the knife slightly from where it had dangled at his side. "Look, you're the one tied to the chair. And it's your wife and-"

"Do not!" Charles barked. It was the first time in this whole situation that the old man had shown his true emotions, or a glimpse of them at least. He closed his eyes briefly as he swallowed the rage down. "Do not even think about it," he said, composure already regained. "Phyllis will not be able to comprehend this, as you well know. If you choose to involve her in this it could... it could exacerbate her condition. Or worse. You cannot involve her in this."

"If she walks in here, or Liana does, and she kicks off and calls the feds then all this gets even worse. No, I'm sorting this now."

"The feds," Charles said with a shake of his head, his voice dripping with scorn. "Look, Aaron you're running out of time here. You won't-"

Charles' voice was cut off Aaron passed from the kitchen into the hall. Despite the gravity of what he was doing, since the very beginning he had been wary of letting the worst-case scenario – plan B – become anything other than a means to an end. He knew, if emotions ran high, there was the potential that it could become some kind of delayed payback for the way Charles had treated his mother over the years, or the pain caused by the sheer indifference he seemed to feel towards anyone on earth but his wife. He had to keep this professional.

61

Aaron grabbed a chair on his way out, then walked down the hall to the first sitting room. He opened the door and popped his head in, just like Charles had done earlier on, careful to keep the chair out of view. Liana was sitting across from Phyllis, both of them enjoying a cup of tea by a freshly crackling fire.

"Oh," Liana said as she noticed him. "Hello."

"Hiya," Aaron said, forcing an awkward smile. "I'm just having a chat with my Grandad in the kitchen but it's kind of... private, so I need you two to stay in here, ok? Is that alright? Gran?"

"Of course," said Liana. "We are just having tea."

"Cool. That sounds good. Well, enjoy and kind of... Just stay here, yeah? Just this room, ok?"

"Ok," Liana said, though her furrowed brow betrayed suspicion.

Aaron shut the door again, then took the chair and wedged it underneath the doorknob. He knew that this clunking around would arouse Liana's suspicions even further, but it was all he could think of. The original plan to restrain both of his grandparents had gone out of the window as soon as he realised how fragile Phyllis was, and the introduction of Liana – a young, able bodied woman – into the mix was another complication he didn't need.

Satisfied the door was braced, Aaron walked back into the kitchen to see Charles still staring ahead at nothing, his rage seething beneath the silent, motionless surface.

"They're locked in the sitting room. They don't even know. Let's get this done quickly and they'll never have to, alright?"

"I've already told you, there's nothing in that safe for you."

"Grandad, listen to me!"

Aaron slapped the knife onto the table and hopped up beside

it, pulling a free chair forward to use as a footrest. He leant forwards onto his knees, only inches from Charles' face now.

"I lost something, or had to lose something, that belonged to a very dangerous man – a very spiteful, violent man – and he wants it back. He wants the money from me in by the weekend, and I don't have it... and if I don't get it he's going to hurt me, he's going to hurt my Mum. You have to help me. I know you're ashamed and I know you probably think I'm even more of a fuck up than my Mum, but this is serious. Literally, life and death. Please, Grandad, help me with this and you'll never see me or Mum again, if you don't want. I swear."

Charles sighed again. "I've already told you. We. Have. Nothing."

"Don't fucking bullshit me!"

Aaron kicked the chair away and jumped down from the table, barging past Charles to stand, then crouch, in front of the oven. He kneaded the heels of his hands into his eye sockets as he screamed through gritted teeth, frustration practically boiling the blood that thundered through his temples. He felt his stomach lurch again, but there was nothing left other than a straining dry heave. He walked back around to Charles.

"How stupid do you think I am? You expect me to believe that you, in this house, have no money? I only need fourteen grand. That's nothing to you. I know it's nothing to you. You don't think I remember all the-"

"It's gone. I have told you this numerous times. I do not need to lie to you."

"What are you on about?"

"Listen very carefully to this, because I am becoming tired of telling you. After I retired and your... After Phyllis became ill... it all went on her care. On the house, on our debts. There is

63

virtually nothing left. I've spent the last few months trying to figure out how we are even going to afford Liana for the rest of the year, let alone the one after that. Believe me, Aaron, there is nothing left to give you."

"Are you serious? Nothing? Not even a few grand? Maybe if I give this guy something, he'll give me more time, or-"

"There is nothing," Charles said. "And even if there was, I wouldn't give you a penny of it."

Aaron stared up at the ceiling and ground his teeth together until his jaw ached. He could feel burning tears collecting in the corners of his eyes.

"What's in that safe?" he said, head still tilted back.

"No money. Just a pair of my old guns, a few boxes of ammunition. That's what it's designed for, not valuables."

"Fuck's sake," Aaron said, more to himself that Charles. "So how much would I get for all of that, do you think? And the Land Rover out back?"

"It doesn't matter. You're not taking any of it."

Aaron growled his frustration again and swiped the knife from the table.

"Do you not understand how serious this is? Do you not think I've got the bollocks to use this?" Aaron's breaths were becoming more and more ragged in between yells. "You do realise I've been keeping them out of this to try and do you a favour?" – pointing the knife back towards the sitting room – "This could get really bad really fast, you understand?"

The last syllable fell to a near whisper at the sound of crunching gravel, the distant sound of an engine getting louder, closer.

"What the fuck?" Aaron hissed under his breath.

He ducked instinctively, then rushed towards the window at

the back of the kitchen so he could get a look at the driveway. He rubbed the condensation away with his sleeve, the circle of clear glass revealing a white van rumbling down the path towards the house. He dropped even lower, so his eyes were level with the windowsill, and watched in terror as the driver pulled up at the back steps and killed the engine.

8

Aaron

It was a young woman who emerged from the driver's seat of the van – probably no more than 18, Aaron thought – with a stern looking, make-up free face and mousy hair braided in loose pigtails. Although the fleece, faded jeans, and high wellies were almost standard dress in this part of the world, the dark apron and long white coat she wore over the top made her look almost comically out of place at Owlgreave.

She'd spun the van around before parking, which meant Aaron was unable to see what she took out of the back before slamming the doors closed and walking up the steps to pound on the back door.

Before the third knock had even landed, Aaron had already turned – wide-eyed – to meet Charles' gaze. Although his grandfather didn't look as if he was about to start screaming the house down, Aaron drove a stiff index finger against his lips as he walked back to grab the duct tape from the table.

"Do I have to use this, or are you going to keep quiet?" Aaron said, his voice a crackling whisper.

"It doesn't matter, she's here for me."

"What do you mean? Who is it?"

Charles sighed. It felt to Aaron as if he was far too busy to be explaining this kind of thing to his thick-headed grandson, like the whole situation was little more than an inconvenience.

"It's Tess," he said. "The butcher's girl. She's making a delivery. The same one I take every week. She'll know something is-"

Aaron ignored him, turning on his heel and striding towards the hallway.

"No money but you can afford butcher's meat delivered to your door," he muttered as he went.

Aaron poked his head into the hall and immediately wrenched it back at the sight of the girl's silhouette swaying from side to side, one hand raised to her eyebrow like it would help her to peer through the frosted glass.

"Fuck."

Aaron took one more look at Charles, then rested the knife on the windowsill and stood for a moment while he took a few deep breaths.

He immediately noticed that it wasn't the same flavour of adrenaline that had coursed through his veins when he'd tried to break into the safe, or even when he'd been chewed out by Dave or guilt-tripped by his Mum. It wasn't frustration or rage he was fighting. This adrenaline was less frantic. More concentrated, more precise; the kind of adrenaline a lawyer might need before giving his closing speech in a big murder case.

Three more knocks, heavier this time.

"Ok, come on," Aaron said as he strode towards the front door. The girl stepped down as he opened it, then scowled as she moved down again, her confusion and apparent disgust at the sight of Aaron clearly evident from the outset.

"Alright," Aaron said, trying his best to smile through the nausea. "Is that for... here? For my Grandad?"

He gestured to the Styrofoam tray that was tucked under her left arm, the deep red hue of steak and racks of lamb and pork chops visible through layers and layers of tightly wrapped cling film. The girl had the sleeves of her white coat rolled up to her elbows, revealing the muscular forearms beneath.

In fact, the longer Aaron looked at her, the more he realised that she was built like a bull herself; thick arms and broad shoulders that made her fleece bulge at hits seams.

"Yeah," she said, more of a grunt than a word. "For Mr Mortimer."

Her jaw clenched as she attempted to peer past Aaron into the dimly lit hallway. Aaron stepped aside to block her view.

"He's just... helping my Gran at the moment. I can take it," Aaron stepped down and held out his hands. "I'm Aaron, Michelle's son, if you know her? I'm staying here for a bit."

The girl hesitated, her eyes barely more than slits in her pallid, pancake face. She looked over Aaron's shoulder again and, apparently satisfied, shrugged the tray out from under her arm and held it out. As he leaned down to take it – with both hands from her one – Aaron was hit by that unmistakeable smell of a butcher's shop; surgical steel and cold, dead chunks of animal flesh. There was no blood on her apron, but the sickly smell seemed to emanate from her as if she had been bathing in it.

Aaron grimaced as he turned to head back inside, shouting a dismissive thanks over his shoulder as he reached the door. He turned to close it and found her still stood in the spot where she'd handed over the meat.

"You alright? I need to pay you or something?"

The girl nodded, her face still scrutinising his every move.

"Ok, cool. You just... don't move. Just one sec and I'll go and ask him where he keeps it. One minute, cheers."

Aaron partially closed the door behind him and strode back towards the kitchen, throwing the cold, stinking meat box onto the oak table at the first opportunity. He snatched the knife from the windowsill, nervously tapping the blade against his leg as he approached Charles.

"She says she needs paying," Aaron said. "Looks like you're going to have to tell me where your money is after all."

Charles rolled his eyes. "The money is in my wallet, next to the armchair."

"Which armchair?"

Charles grinned, a humourless, hyena's grin, then said: "The one your grandmother's sitting in."

Aaron let out a laugh, then shook his head.

"Course it is."

He leant to the side to look through to the far corridor. The flat of the blade was still tapping furiously against his thigh as he mulled over what the best course of action was.

"He's got a knife in his right hand," Charles said, his voice low and forceful.

"What did you say?" said Aaron turning back to face his grandfather.

The old man allowed himself another grin. "I was just making sure she knew."

"Making sure who knew what?"

Aaron spun around to face the far end of the kitchen and was met by Tess' wild-eyed face, no more than a few feet from

69

his own. By the time he'd realised what she was holding, the rusted chunk of iron sliced through the air towards him and smashed into the side of his face.

9

Charles

Once he was certain that Aaron had survived the blow, Charles helped Tess to carry his grandson's unconscious body down to the cellar; although the girl, in truth, took most of the weight.

In recent years, Charles had gradually been able to come to terms with the fact that he wasn't quite as agile, or quite as quick, as he used to be, but the way that even his brute strength was now apparently starting to fail was almost unbelievable to him. It had always served him well – from settling disagreements in smoke-choked pubs to hauling richer men's trophies across whichever game reserve he'd been ordered to accompany them to – yet now, just like his house, his wife, and everything else in his life; his muscles were slowly succumbing to decay.

Even so, between them they managed to wrestle Aaron down the creaking wooden steps to the cellar and, using his remaining zip ties and duct tape, bound his hands around the thick iron pillar that stood in the centre of the room. It ended up being so awkward to thread the zip ties by the glow of the single bare lightbulb that Charles had delegated that job to Tess as well.

She made light work of it – just like she had of Aaron – and seemed to relish the opportunity to rubber stamp her dominance with multiple layers of duct tape.

Charles loomed over her as she worked, watching as his grandson was bound up tight like a felled deer, his skin pale but for the dark blood trickling from his temple. With Aaron's expression so helpless, his features softened by the dim light, Charles thought he saw a glimpse of the boy he once was, before his brown curls were shaved to the skin and his features were set in a permanent scowl.

Charles had always worried what would become of Aaron after being raised in that broken, hopeless city with only someone as hateful as Michelle to guide him, but he never expected he'd one day have to face down the monster the boy eventually became. Even if this situation wasn't his fault in the grand scheme of things, Aaron's mistakes were made now and, unfortunately for him, they were irreversible.

Tess stood and handed Charles the roll of tape, then immediately crouched back down and started patting at Aaron's legs until she heard the tap of his phones. She unzipped his pocket and fished them out, then stood and handed them to Charles.

He nodded his thanks and examined the handsets; one a sleek black smart phone and the other a chunky clam shell.

"Two?" he said.

"He's a drug dealer," said Tess, like a classroom snitch stood next to the teacher's desk. "Only drug dealers need two phones."

"Really?"

"Yep," she said. "My cousin Ryan told me about it. One for

them, one for their customers and all the dealers and that. I bet he is, you know. I bet that's why he was trying to rob you."

Charles examined the phones for a moment longer, then pocketed them and touched Tess lightly on her rock-solid shoulder. "I won't forget this."

"Don't mention it. Just glad I got here when I did."

"Would you mind keeping an eye on him... until he comes to?"

"Yeah, no worries. I'll shout if he wakes up."

"Good, thank you."

Charles thought he saw her face change in the dim light, something almost resembling a smile, but there was no joy in it. More like an animal baring its teeth. He left her looming over Aaron's motionless body, still stood close enough to smash him straight to the ground if he made any mistake as stupid as waking up.

It had been a long while since Charles had even set foot in the damp cellar – he was quite often too saddened by the sight of Michelle's old bicycle or Daniel's boxed-up football kits and subsequently reminded of the distinct paths they had taken to self-destruction. He knew it was selfish to think this way, but the real reason that they hurt him so much was not because he grieved for his dead son nor wanted to help his dropout daughter, but because their belongings reminded him of his own failures.

Charles had expended so much effort, and caused so many tears, trying to toughen his children up to face the outside world – just as his father had – but in doing so, he had also failed to prepare them to combat their own demons. After all these years, he finally understood that, but like many of the realisations he'd made in later life, when everything slowed down and he'd time to think; the damage was already done.

Charles ascended the steps, and as he did so he felt relieved to leave the damp and dark behind him and emerge back into the warmth and light of the kitchen.

He shut the door behind him and headed straight for the sitting room, his aching limbs given fuel by the sight of the chair that was sealing Liana and Phyllis inside. He wrenched it from under the doorknob, pushed it to one side, and burst into the room; startling both women to the point where they almost dropped their teacups and saucers to the carpet.

"Mr Mortimer... is everything alright?" Liana said, setting her cup down on the side table and standing from the armchair. "Aaron came in and then the door rattled and we couldn't get out. Is something wrong?"

"No," Charles said, only able to hold a smile in place for a fraction of a second. "Are you both alright? You don't need to go to the loo, do you Phyllis?"

"Oh no, I'm quite alright thank you. Do you?"

Charles smiled, edging over to Liana until he was close enough to whisper.

"There's been an... incident. I can't really explain but all I... well, I might need you to stay here tonight, with Mrs Mortimer... if you're happy to, of course. We can add it to your time sheet for the week."

Liana nodded. "Yes, of course. Do you need me to-"

"No, it's fine. Just keep Mrs Mortimer busy in here, or next door if you can. And don't come in the kitchen until supper."

"Ok... I mean, yes, Mr Mortimer. Thank you."

"Not at all. Phyllis?" he said, his voice back up to full, booming volume. "Phyllis?"

"Hello?"

74

"Yes," Charles said, coming to stand by her side. He touched her on the shoulder as gently as he could, though the adrenaline was still coursing through his veins, and she turned and looked up at him. Even though her eyes were rheumy and hooded by baggy, tired lids, the sparkle in them was reignited the instant she flashed her smile.

Beneath the paper thin, wrinkled skin, Charles could still see the full cheekbones and delicate chin of the girl who had set his young heart ablaze. The one who would look across the pillow at him with adoration while they huddled away cold winter nights together in his gamekeeper's lodge. Despite the warmth in her expression as she looked up at him, he was almost certain that he was the only one of them who could recall that time or resurrect any of the true happiness they both experienced then. Was this how it was to be, until the end, he thought? Dwelling forever on thoughts of death, and the death of memories, until one or both of them came to embrace it?

He scolded himself, feeling wretched at wandering to those dark places at the simple sight of her smile, though – ultimately, deep down – he knew it was inevitable. That, after all, was the reality of living with someone cursed with Phyllis' particular affliction. He was forced to confront the impermanence and fragility of life on a daily basis. Soon both of them would die, and along with them all of the singular moments in time they shared. However torturous this thought was to him though, Charles knew he would happily live like this for the rest of his days, rather than face the thought of waking up one day without her.

"I have a few things to attend to. You enjoy your tea with Liana and I'll be back shortly."

He leant down and kissed the very top of her forehead, where her skin and wispy hair met, and turned to leave. His face dropped the instant his back was to his wife, and his eyes shot towards Liana.

"I won't be long. Here, or next door."

"Yes, Mr Mortimer."

* * *

Tess was already back upstairs when he walked back into the kitchen, leant against the dining table with both hands gripping it firmly. She looked, to Charles, like a child with her favourite toy, terrified it might be tugged away from her at any moment by a jealous sibling.

"Is everything alright?" Charles said. "I thought I asked you to stay down there?"

"You did," she said, straightening up and turning to face him. "I'm sorry, I just... He's still out cold. I'll go back down if you like, but it's... I had an idea."

"An idea?" Charles said. He walked towards the table and – instead of taking his usual seat, which still had severed duct tape and zip ties strewn around it – walked around to the opposite side and mirrored Tess' original stance.

"Yeah," she said, retaking her place. "What are you going to do with him?"

Charles sighed. "To tell you the truth, I've no clue."

"Is he really your grandson?"

Charles cocked his right eyebrow, then pushed himself away from the table and began pacing back towards the stove. "By blood."

"Ok," she said, biting her lip. "Maybe not then."

Charles stopped and turned to face her, then leant back onto stove and folded his arms. "Try me."

Tess gulped and looked away, puffed out her cheeks.

"Go on, girl," Charles said, nodding at the chair. "You've dug me out of one hole already, why not another?"

She whipped her head back around to meet his gaze, though her permanent squint made reading her eyes almost impossible.

"My dad's away for the night on Thursday. He's taking meat for a big do at Barden Hall – for Samhain, I think."

Charles scoffed.

"Sorry," Tess said. "Did I not say it right?"

"No, it's not that, it's... sorry. Go on."

"Oh... so, yeah, he misses my dad's lamb chops, he says, old Mr Reeves," she let out an odd-sounding giggle. "Anyway, there's this do and then – the next day – he says there's going to be a special hunt. Like a clean boot, only with..."

She trailed off as Charles sprung from his perch and leant over to make sure Liana and Phyllis were still comfortably out of earshot. He approached her slowly, his voice barely audible.

"I know it," he said. "They've happened for many years. Last I heard, the... risk was becoming too high."

"Well," Tess said, looking down at her ragged boots. "It's happening. I've even been to a couple myself. My dad wants me to help him this year with the-"

"Alright," Charles said, holding his right hand up to her in a dismissive gesture. "That's alright. So, what are you suggesting? Aaron, as-"

"This was when I thought he was a burglar, not now he's your grandson."

"He's always been my grandson."

"No, I... That's not what I meant. Look, I shouldn't have-"

"No, it's fine. I understand. I see why you... Thank you."

Charles made sure he added a note of finality to his words, refolding his arms and waiting for her to leave.

"Ok. Do you want me to..." she said, cocking her head towards the cellar door.

"No, I'll take care of it. You've done more than enough already. Your father should be extremely proud of you, Tess, you're a credit to him. Thank you."

This brought a smile back to her round face. She basked in the compliment for a second longer – apparently it was her first for some time – then she turned and headed for the hallway.

Charles stayed where he was, studying her as she walked. He could almost sense that she had left something unsaid; the tension in her muscular shoulders looked like she was bracing for a blow to the back of her head. Sure enough, she ground to a halt just before she reached the door out of the kitchen, waiting for a heartbeat before facing Charles again.

"My dad said that you've been struggling recently... because of Mrs Mortimer and the house and everything. Not gossiping, just explaining why you were sometimes late to pay or... you know."

The girl's hands were balled tightly at her sides, as if the words were causing her physical pain. Still, she continued.

"The only reason I say so is that – this hunt, the one this week. Well, it's a big one, I think. So, I think they're paying a lot for... you know, contributions. Runners. If you were to..."

Charles clenched his jaw, embracing the pain that erupted from his creaking molars as he ground them together.

78

"Paying how much?"

"I'm not sure," she said. "I don't even think my dad knows for sure either... but he said it's a lot."

10

Charles

After he saw Tess out, thanking her one final time, Charles headed straight upstairs to use the phone in his office. He sat down on the rickety swivel chair and dialled; his eyes fixated on the scuffs Aaron's blade had made near the hinges of the safe. As Charles waited for the phone to connect, he couldn't help but imagine what might have happened if Aaron had actually managed to open the door and make use of what was inside. It could have turned into a bloodbath, particularly if Tess hadn't been as adept with a metal bar as she turned out to be.

"Hello, Sutherland Reeves & White, how can I help you?" came an uninterested voice on the other side of the phone.

"Matthew Reeves, please."

"And who can I say is calling?"

"Charles Mortimer."

"Just one moment please."

Rather than unleashing a tide of bile-churning hold music, the line simply went dead, static occasionally blipping like a pot of soup on the boil. After almost two minutes, a familiar voice finally oozed through the silence.

"Mortimer, what a lovely surprise."

It'd been many years since Charles had spoken to Matthew Reeves – the overindulged son of Charles' one-time employer, the renowned barrister Sir William Reeves – but even the oily tone of his voice was enough to make him feel like ending the call then and there.

"Matthew," Charles grumbled. The thought of affecting any kind of disingenuous affability with this man was felt like a hair shirt on Charles' back, but he steeled himself as best he could. "How are you?"

"I'm absolutely bloody fantastic, thank you. More importantly, how are you?"

"Fine, thank you. I had something-"

"I must say I couldn't believe my ears when my receptionist told me who I was being summoned by," he snorted at his own turn of phrase. "To what do I owe the pleasure... the honour?"

Charles ignored his theatrics. "I'm calling to discuss something with you, something... sensitive."

"Oh Christ, Mortimer you bloody tease, you. Go on, out with it then."

"It's about... your father. His estate. I've been informed you're holding hunts again. This week, in fact."

"Well, of a fashion," Reeves said with an exaggerated sigh. "We still hold them sometimes, usually at the end of the month, when we can, but it's not like it was. It was fine for a while after you 'retired', shall we say... but it all became so bloody difficult with trespassers and the like, that there was even talk of putting it all to bed. You know these old buggers though, there's-"

"Trespassers?"

81

"Yes," Reeves said, the word sounding more like a sneer. "Bloody eco-terrorists and the like, turning up in masks and combat fatigues, thinking we were hunting foxes. If only they knew, eh? Only one or two of them have ever caught sight of anything but, still... Very risky to hold the hunts anywhere else but my father's place now. Even then, they caught a bloody journalist there a few weeks ago."

Sir William's estate was only around twenty-five miles from Owlgreave, but its surroundings made it one of the most secluded pieces of property in the whole country. Although there was a wide driveway and a few manicured lawns at the front of the house – which itself was a relatively run-of-the-mill English Baroque hall – the rest of the estate was concealed by a sheer cliff face on one side and a thick wooded area on the other. Another, smaller wood protected the back of the property, which terminated on the banks of a large reservoir. This meant that the only way in or out (on foot or by car) was the front gate, which made the rest of the grounds perfect for indulging in the kinds of unorthodox interests that enthralled Reeves and his associates.

"My God," Charles said.

"Too right. She'd been taken up onto the ridge by one of these hunt saboteurs and was snapping away like the bloody Dickens. God knows what would have happened if the groundsman hadn't been switched on."

"Who caught them?"

"Old John Swire, apparently. Still going strong."

"And were they..."

"Oh no, not yet. They're still there. Being held until this one coming up, the big one. Obviously it's been difficult with the girl's disappearance being on the news, but-"

"So, it is true then?" Charles said. "There is a hunt?"

"Of course. Everyone's practically champing at the bit for it," Reeves let out a little snort, which made him sound like he was a small boy doing his best not to laugh in a school assembly. "There's a big bonfire the night before – you know what my father is like – then we hunt first thing Friday. Well... maybe second thing, depending on how sozzled they get. I must admit, a small part of me hoped that you were calling to say you were thinking of making a comeback. Last I heard from the old man you were in dire straits."

"How much is it," Charles said. "The buy in?"

"Therein lies the rub, Mortimer. Inflation has taken its toll since your day, you know."

"How much?"

"Twenty grand," he said. It was almost as if he was trying to mimic Charles' severe tone.

"And the pot?"

"Aaah the pot," he said, letting out a whistle for emphasis. "Well, that will also be a bit of a shock to you, I imagine. I'd say it'd probably be up to... I don't know, most likely a comfortable seven figures."

All of the blood drained from Charles' head, he almost felt as if he was about to topple from his chair onto the bland office carpet.

"Seven figures?"

"Indeed. Nice little prize pot for whoever wants it. Have you come into some money then?"

"No. But I might have a buy in," Charles said, his voice as firm as marble.

"Bugger me," Reeves said, huffing down the phone. "Now we're talking. Go on."

"We were burgled, this afternoon. Luckily Tess, Mac Benton's daughter... she was around and she helped me to subdue him."

"Your buy in is the burglar?"

Charles grunted his assent.

"Bloody hell, how old?"

"Early 20s. Lean, fit. No injuries, bar a good blow to the head."

Charles winced as the line fell silent. He could practically hear Reeves salivating on the other side of the phone as he processed the information.

"I was not expecting that from you, Mortimer, not one bit. Sounds ideal. I can't wait to hear what the old man says about this little revelation. So... does that mean I can consider you bought in to compete?"

Charles allowed the chair to swivel to the left, turning him to face the window that looked out onto a small garden area at the side of the house. He sat there for a few moments, watching the exposed branches of the apple tree swaying in the wind. In years gone by Phyllis would have gathered the apples every few days, eventually baking them in pies or strudels, topping them with custard or fresh cream. Now, since the illness had taken her, the apples stayed where they fell; helplessly exposed as they were torn to pieces by the birds or simply left to rot and collapse into the earth.

"Mortimer?" Reeves said, rudely tugging him back into the present.

"Yes," Charles said. "Yes, you can."

"Well, that does it then," Reeves said, chuckling to himself again. "I'll make the calls, get you added to the roster. They already have a full host but I'm sure they'll be accommodating when they know who it's for."

"Thank you."

"Thank *you*. I look forward to it. Get your guns dusted off and... I'll be in touch."

11

Aaron

Aaron came to with the taste of wet dirt and copper on his tongue, the uncomfortable sensation of dried blood caking at the corners of his mouth. As he raised his head – wincing as a shockwave of pain rushed out from the spot where the bar cracked into his skull – all he could see was a pile of junk and a bare stone wall, dimly lit. Boxes sagged with damp, broken appliances, and old furniture barely concealed by mould-spotted dust sheets. Owlgreave's cellar, he thought. He was in the cellar and they must have carried him down here, Charles and that tank of a girl.

He tried to push himself up off the ground, but his hands wouldn't move. He looked down to see them tied together, on the other side of a thick iron pillar, with his own zip ties and duct tape. He gave a couple of tugs to test them, but his heart wasn't in it; he knew deep down that Charles would've left no margin for error.

"Fuck," he said, though his voice was so hoarse that it wasn't much more than a whisper.

He rocked himself into a sitting position and looked around

the room. Other than dust sheeted junk that lined the walls and the wooden staircase in the far corner, it was completely empty. The floor was bare stone – as were the walls – and the ceiling was rough timber joists, chipboard, and wads of itchy yellow insulation.

It was still possible for him to stand but he didn't see the point. He decided to let his lungs do the work instead.

"Hey!" he shouted. "Grandad... Liana..."

No response came. He closed his eyes and took a deep breath, new pains appearing in his ribs and jaw as he did so. Most likely injuries from the fall that followed the blackout, the thought. He gritted his teeth, then tried shouting again. Alongside names he decided to throw in the occasional "Hello?" or "I'm sorry". None of it worked.

Occasionally he'd hear some creaking or shuffling above, and once he was sure he heard a short ripple of Liana and Phyllis' laughter, though it was so muffled that it could have been anything, or nothing.

After coming to terms with the fact that no one was going to hear him, he pulled himself towards the pillar and attempted to claw at the zip on the pocket of his tracksuit bottoms. It was only after managing to open the zip – using his index and middle finger like a pair of chopsticks – that he realised his phones were both gone.

"Fuck. Fuckers."

No help was coming from those inside the house, and apparently none would be coming from those outside either. He planted his feet either side of the pillar and yanked again, every muscle straining, waiting for the satisfying snap of broken plastic that he knew would never come.

Exhausted, he slumped down onto his knees on the cold floor

and buried his throbbing head into the crook of his right arm, whispering curses in between ragged breaths.

Just then new light flooded into the cellar as the door to the kitchen was pushed open, then immediately slammed. Aaron looked up to see Charles' scuffed boots thumping down the stairs, the wood creaking under his weight. He was alone. Aaron stood as his grandfather approached, though the old man knew to keep his distance.

"You're awake," he said, easing his hands in the pockets of his corduroy trousers. Even with Aaron bound and beaten, Charles stood with his feet firmly planted and his shoulders square, ready to repel any attack that was launched at him.

"What the fuck is going on?" Aaron said. He was unsettled by the definite slur that had appeared in his speech.

"You don't remember?"

"I remember getting jumped, yeah... by that fucking 'roid-head bird. What the-"

"Tess."

"I don't care what her fucking name is. Let me out of here, now," Aaron tugged at the restraints again as he spoke.

"You know I can't do that," Charles said, briefly glancing back up the stairs to the house. "Too much has happened. It can't be undone."

"Look, you know I can't stay here. If I don't get that money by next week, they're gonna hurt her... they're gonna hurt Mum. And fuck knows what they'll do to me."

Charles said nothing, staying rooted to the spot and staring that burning stare.

"Grandad, please. Look, I know I fucked up... I panicked, and I shouldn't have done that, and I'm sorry... but you can't keep me here forever. I need to get out, try and find this money. I know a lot's happened but I'm the only one who's been hurt... I'm happy to forget that if you can... and you'll never see me again. I'll never come back here again."

Charles sighed. "It's too late. It's been decided."

Aaron's brow furrowed, his bloodied face like a Halloween mask in the stark light from the bare lightbulb.

"What do you mean? You called the police?"

"No."

"What then?"

Charles inhaled hard through his nose and took a step forward.

"What is it?" Aaron said, his tone becoming more and more frayed. "What's going on?"

"Listen to me, Aaron. You are the one responsible for this. It was you who arrived here with the intention of-"

"Hey, I didn't come here to-"

"Let me speak," Charles said, the force of his voice like a bomb exploding in the silent cellar. "It was you, more so than us. You who created this... impossible situation. I don't want to involve the police any more than you do, but your actions – your intentions – are indefensible. You would have held your grandmother and Liana and me hostage until you got what you were after, what you thought I had. How far would you have gone? Would you have used that knife on me? On your Gran?"

"I'm not here for me! I'm here for... her."

"Would you have used it or not?"

"No!"

Charles snorted.

"Liar," he said, striding over into the corner of the room as far as a dusty old mountain bike sticking out from under a sheet. "You're just like your mother."

89

"You don't even know me. You don't-"

"Of course I do," Charles said, running his thumb over the exposed handle bar. "No one's problems are equal to yours, are they? And it's never your fault. Just bad luck... the cruel world-"

"That's bullshit. You don't know-"

"-it's not surprising you're happy to betray your own family to get what you want."

"It's not what I want, for fuck's sake. Are you deaf? They're going to hurt Mum, or worse. I just needed that money and I'd have been gone."

"I've heard it all before from her," Charles said, walking back around to the bottom of the stairs. "And I always made the same mistake. Thinking it would change things. It never did. All those fond memories you have of visiting us, every time she brought you here under one pretence or the other... they're all lies. Every time it was always because she was here to beg or to steal. To feed her own selfish habits. Clearly you're no different."

He started up towards the house, grinding to a halt at the feeble sound of Aaron's voice.

"What are you going to do?"

Charles sighed and looked up the stairs. Thin beams of light bled through gaps in the door framed his face in gold like a regal portrait in a museum. His face barely moved as he answered.

"Everything I've told you about money, about the way I've been fighting to keep this house standing, to keep your Gran standing... it's all true. You're not the only one desperate for money. You tried to get yours and you failed... But you can still help me to get mine."

Charles carried on, muttered something about food and

water, then stepped into the blinding light of the house, slamming then locking the door behind him.

* * *

Aaron was awoken by the sound of heavy footsteps down the stairs, immediately shocked by the fact he'd managed to accidentally fall asleep in such an awkward position. He rocked forwards onto his knees and winced as the pain burst from the side of his head again like a surge of lightning.

He opened his eyes as the pain subsided, to see the girl from the butcher's shop stood at the foot of the stairs with a glass of water in one hand.

Aaron tried to ask her what the fuck she was doing here, still squinting as his eyes adjusted to the light, but it came out as a jumble of unrelated, nonsensical words. She must have given him some whack with that bar, he thought.

"Charles had to go to out," she said, having apparently understood anyway. "He told me to watch you. He said you might be thirsty."

As much as he wanted to tell her to fuck off, the sweat he'd given to try wrench his hands free – combined with the hangover from the previous night's alcohol – had left him deliriously thirsty. He had his pride, and he had his anger, but not so much of either that he wouldn't lap that crystal clear water from her bare hand like a grateful dog if she let him.

He nodded and she edged over to him, her free hand already balled into a hammer fist just in case. Although the thought of swinging a knee or elbow at her did cross his mind, he knew that it wasn't much more than a fantasy. He didn't have the energy for a fight, nor the will to take another blow to his already aching head.

He tilted his head back to let the water pour over his raw lips. He was so grateful for it that it tasted like something more than water, something better. Like the difference between seasoned and unseasoned meat. It tasted so good that it took him a few seconds to realise Tess had her other hand at the back of his neck, cradling his head. The stink of raw meat was like a cloud around her.

He wrenched away from her, water cascading down his chin as they parted. She scowled in confusion for a moment, then stepped back out of harm's way and put the glass down on the floor, leaving her hand next to it until she was sure it wouldn't topple over.

Aaron was unsettled by Tess' newfound compassion; it didn't match up with the apron-wearing brawler who had sparked him out with a single blow only a few hours before. He slurped the last few drops of water from his lips, then sat back down on the floor.

He sighed, swore under his breath. "Is that it then?" he said.

"I dunno," she shrugged. "I've never done this before."

"What, and you think I have? I still don't even know what I'm doing down here."

"Because you tried to rob your own grandparents, that's why," she said, folding her arms. "You think you can just get away with something like that?"

"I didn't even... I wasn't even gonna do anything. You haven't got a fucking clue."

"You had Charles tied to a chair," she said, incredulous. "Your Gran and that other girl locked in a room. You had a knife when I walked in. What do you expect?"

"Why not call the feds then?"

"Because," Tess said, cocking her head. "You can be more useful than that."

"What the fuck are you on about?" Aaron said, pulling himself to his feet. "That's what *he* was saying... What's he gonna do with me?"

Tess' lips curled into a spiteful grin, which was more gums than teeth. She really was a strange looking kid, Aaron thought. Almost alien in her features, her tight pigtails making her look like an oversized child.

"You'll soon find out. And it's your own fault. You shouldn't have come here to do that, it's... wrong. It's wrong to steal, especially from your own family. Good thing we look after each other around here."

Aaron forced a chuckle, though it was obviously hollow. She stepped forward, apparently starting to enjoy herself now.

"So... I bet you're hungry, aren't you?" she said.

Aaron looked up and stared into her little pig eyes, like two pencil holes in the featureless skin of a bongo drum. He *was* hungry, but it was the water he'd been craving, and she'd allowed him to have more than he expected. He was pretty sure he could last for a few more hours on that – and she was obviously under orders to leave him alone, for the time being at least – so he decided now was as good a time as ever to speak his mind. He narrowed his eyes.

"Fuck off, you ugly little cunt."

Although it looked a lot more of a struggle this time, she eventually wrenched her mouth into another grin, though it vanished as soon as she stooped to pick up the glass and turned away.

"I'll remind you of that, next time I see you," she said as

she shuffled over to the bottom of the stairs. She climbed the first few, then stopped and ducked to stare underneath the bannister at him, that tiny toothed smirk on her face again. "And I will see you, I think. Or bits of you at least."

12

Charles

Charles could already smell the food as he approached Owlg-reave's back door, chicken and leek pie; one of the many staples from Phyllis' recipe bible. He had plucked the book from the back of the larder as soon as Liana started mentioning chilli and noodles and anything else that, however nutritious, was far beyond his restricted English palate. Way back when, he'd even taken to lining his suitcase with tinned Fray Bentos pies if he knew a safari was going take longer than a few days.

Phyllis, Liana, and Tess were all sat around the kitchen table when he entered, boxes of rifle bullets and shotgun shells clutched under one arm, his cheeks ruddy from the cold.

"Evening all," he said, setting his things down on the kitchen counter. He saw little point in hiding them out of sight. "Tess, can I have a word please?

"Is everything ok, Mr-"

"Not to worry. I'll be back in a moment."

Charles showed Tess outside onto the steps, then shut the door firmly behind him and folded his arms.

"Was everything... alright?" he said. His voice was low, condensed by the crushing silence of the open air.

"He was fine. Gave him some water. Then left him alone."

"He didn't... Try anything?"

Tess shook her head, the ends of her pigtails brushing her cheeks as they swung from side to side. "No, she said. "He's not very nice though, is he."

"Well," Charles said. "If you were tied up in a cellar, you probably wouldn't be very nice to the person who put you there either."

She smirked. "I suppose. He was pretty wound up. Asking about what you were going to do to him."

Charles scowled. "You didn't say anything?"

"No. I wanted to... Especially when he called me a horrible name... But I didn't. Are you still thinking of-"

"I don't know. To be completely honest, I'm not even sure what the alternative is now."

Tess became sheepish, looking over her shoulder at her van. Charles felt around in the dark for the door handle.

"I can pay you," he said. "For your time."

"Oh no, no. Don't be silly it's fine. I just wanted to help."

"And you're sure?"

She nodded. "Yeah. He shouldn't have done what he did," she said. "I know he's your grandson and everything, but... Well, he's made his bed now, hasn't he."

Charles opened the door, his eyes still fixed on hers. He'd always thought she looked quite strange, almost like a clone of her burly father, but in the near darkness she looked downright odd. Charles tried to smile, but he could only twist his usually downturned mouth into something resembling a neutral expression.

"Well," he said. "Thank you. Again."

"Pleasure... Again. I suppose I'll see you at Mr Reeves' estate, then?"

Charles sighed, clenched his jaw as he thought. Now caring for Phyllis had gone from a part- to full-time commitment, Liana was more indispensable than ever. Charles was not going to risk turning Aaron in to the police and somehow becoming incriminated himself.

Letting the boy loose would be even more dangerous. Then there was a chance he could come back, perhaps even with associates or renewed intent. No, taking Aaron as a buy-in for the hunt was a single − albeit unpleasant − solution to two separate problems, and the more Aaron showed his true colours, the easier the entire process was becoming.

"I expect so," Charles said eventually. "Thank you, Tess. Goodnight."

* * *

As usual, Liana's cooking was an impeccable take on another of Phyllis' signature dishes, perhaps even superior in many ways. Even so, Charles was always aware that it was different. That it wasn't made by the hands that had cooked his meals for decades. He and Phyllis had so rarely gone out to eat in the final few years before her decline, that he'd more or less forgotten what cooking other than hers tasted like. Not that it mattered. Now, picking at the creamy, rich chicken on his plate, he would have given anything to taste Phyllis' food again, to sit down for a meal with the person she used to be.

He was a passenger through much of the dinner conversation

– Liana had agreed to stay and help get Phyllis up to bed – and he was dreading having to reveal the truth of the situation to the young girl before she left.

After all, he needed to have her in the house most of the day, every day now, and virtually nothing more to give her. Of course, she was a good person – one of the kindest hearts he'd ever encountered, in fact – but even Liana must have been starting to worry that she'd never save enough money to go onto bigger and better things elsewhere, once Charles and Phyllis were gone. If he thought it would be anything other than an albatross around her neck, he would have left her the house in his will. It was either that or leave it to Michelle, or – until this week – Aaron, both of whom would surely do nothing but renounce it or leave it to crumble, once they realised how difficult it would be to sell the ramshackle old place.

Just as Charles was mopping up the last few streaks of sauce with his pie crust, Aaron's voice bellowed up from the cellar.

"Hello? Grandad? I need to speak to you... Grandad!"

All three of them were startled by the violence in his shouts, silver cutlery screeching against porcelain.

"Goodness me," said Phyllis. "Is that here?"

"It's alright," Charles said, kissing her on the crown of her head as he slipped past her. "Liana, would you?" he nodded towards the stairs.

"Of course. Shall we go up for your bath Mrs Mortimer?"

"But I've not quite finished yet, dear. I don't know if-"

"I'll put it in the oven for later, don't worry. Come on, let's get up here. There you go."

They were still shuffling around as Charles unlocked the door and rushed down the stairs, the wood creaking with each step of his descent.

"What in God's name are you doing? Your Gran's having supper up there and you-"

"What do you want me to do?" Aaron said. He was stood as close to the stairs as his restraints would allow. "I need to talk to you."

Charles grabbed hold of the bannister as he shakily dismounted the stairs and kept hold of it as he stood and assessed his grandson. Although the bare lightbulb accentuated the shadows under his eyes, he looked exhausted. Pale and shellshocked. There was a dark patch on his tracksuit bottoms, which started at the crotch and spread down the inside of his left leg. If Charles hadn't been so incensed that Phyllis had heard Aaron's shouts, the sympathy he was beginning to feel for him earlier may have even begun to develop further.

"What is it?" Charles said, finally letting go of the bannister and stepping forward.

"I need my phone."

Charles let out a humourless laugh. "Are you serious?"

"What do you think? I need to talk to my Mum. I need to tell her to... I need to warn her."

"Warn her about what?"

Aaron winced in apparent exasperation. "This is what I've been trying to tell you... you weren't bothered. It's my boss, the one I owe the money to. He's threatened her if I don't get the money to him by next week. If I don't make it then she needs to know... I need to tell her to run."

Charles folded his arms, cocked his head to the side. "Out of the question," he said.

"Come on," Aaron said. "I promise I won't piss about, no code words or anything. I won't say anything. I just need to tell her what's what before it's too late. Please, Grandad."

Charles shook his head, then turned back to the stairs.

"Grandad?"

"No. And that's the end of it."

"Grandad, please?"

"If you shout like that again I'm coming back down with the tape."

Charles waited for a moment, then carried on upstairs.

13

Aaron

Aaron had never even seen a commode chair before, let alone used one. After clattering down the stairs, Charles had wheeled it over and parked it next to him, then turned to leave like it needed no explanation. Even after Charles' clipped instructions (and the unexpected gift of a fresh toilet roll), knowing what to do and actually being able to do it – all while zip tied to a metal pole and fully clothed – were two very different propositions.

He'd managed it, eventually, but quickly added 'shitting in a commode' to the long and growing list of things he never wanted to experience again. He replaced the vinyl seat cover on the chair and took the weight off his legs for a while, but even then, the smell was too strong; all that rich food and alcohol, he thought. Even after he'd pushed the chair into the corner with his foot, the smell still hung in the damp cellar air; a sickly reminder of the utter misery in which he found himself.

He was slumped back on the floor, attempting to sleep against the pillar with one of his aching arms as a pillow, when the door opened gently and a pair of feet – much lighter than his grandfather's – descended the stairs.

Liana stopped when she reached the bottom, staring open-mouthed and clutching a clean commode pan to her chest. She was still wearing her self-imposed uniform, though she had her sleeves rolled up to make room for the length of a pair of yellow marigolds.

Aaron guessed that Liana had the situation, or some of the situation, explained to her, but her awkward, twitching expressions told of a quiet trauma occurring within.

"Could he not do the job himself?" Aaron said, making her jump.

Her expression barely changed. She just scanned the room for the chair, then bowed her head and shuffled over to it.

"Oh, right. Silent treatment. Fair enough," Aaron said, more to himself than anyone else. "Are you in on it as well? Like that fucking Tess. She made it sound like my Grandad's gonna have me chopped up and sold to the butcher's. You reckon that sounds like something he'd do? Nice old Mr Mortimer?"

She said nothing, continuing to work with her back to Aaron, the sound of metal and plastic clinking together as she changed the used pan for the new one.

"Liana? Come on, I need your help, please. I'm sorry... and I know I've fucked up – massively – but you need to help me. It's my Mum... She could get hurt if I don't get out of here. Like really hurt. And she's done nothing wrong. I swear, it's... Liana, please?"

Once she'd replaced the seat, Liana pushed the commode chair back over to the pillar and turned to leave. Aaron called her name one more time, which stopped her instantly. She turned her head towards him but kept her eyes glued to the concrete floor.

"Tess told me what you did to Mr Mortimer, and to Mrs Mortimer and me. What you were going to do. She said you're dangerous, and you can't be trusted anymore. She said you're like an animal; like a dog who bites the master he's supposed to protect."

Liana finally screwed up the courage to meet Aaron's gaze, though her eyes were filmed with glistening tears and her mouth turned down at the corners.

"I can't help you, Aaron."

* * *

After Liana left, Aaron pulled the chair back over with his foot and did his best to get some rest. He'd tried a few different techniques, but eventually settled on nudging the seat cushion onto the floor and using it as a pillow, though the freezing cold of the concrete that seeped up through his clothes made sleep virtually impossible.

Even when he was able to drift off briefly from pure exhaustion, a searing cramp in his bound arms or the thunderclaps of his aching head would bring him screaming back awake. Each time it would take him a few seconds to readjust his eyes to the dim light, to realise his hands were zip-tied together at the other side of an iron pillar. To realise he was alone, and beyond help.

He'd sit up and scan the crumpled boxes and the discarded furniture, too battered to even give away, then look longingly at the stairs and wait for nothing. With no phone and no windows, he had become totally blind to the passage of time.

He had an idea of when that first night had passed, when the house began to creak awake again with his grandparents' movements, but he'd barely managed to sleep.

He heard Liana arrive and go straight upstairs, presumably to help Phyllis out of bed, then came back into the kitchen and startled clattering around with pots and pans. He heard the bass of Charles' voice, but his grandfather clearly had no intentions of coming down to make small talk.

The cellar door did eventually creak open, letting the sounds and smells of the kitchen flood in, but it was Liana again, this time with a bowl of honey drizzled porridge and a plastic bottle of water.

She put both items on the floor and waited for Aaron to stir.

"What time is it?" he said, his voice hoarse.

"Just after 10," she said. She had her hands clasped in front of her, her fingers drumming madly against her skirt like she was stood in a hallway, waiting to walk into a job interview. "Would you like help with the porridge? Or the water?"

Aaron wrapped his fingers around the pillar and hauled himself to a seated position, then shuffled backwards until he was sat on his commode seat pillow. He nodded.

"Water, please."

He could hear how fast her breathing was as she knelt and picked up the water bottle, her fingers clumsy at the cap as she fumbled it open. She held it towards Aaron's mouth – careful to stay as far away as her slender arm would allow – and touched it to his cracked lips and poured.

Just like when Tess had fed him that first glass, Aaron found himself prioritising water over oxygen, slurping greedily at the bottle until he was forced to pull away, gasping for air and soaking the front of his hoodie. He recovered, then went back in for more, though he managed to control himself better the second time.

"Thank you," he said between ragged breaths. "Can I?"

He inclined his head towards the steaming bowl of porridge, staring at it like a feral animal as Liana screwed the lid back on the water and put it on the floor. She kept her distance as she fed Aaron his breakfast, one mouthful at a time. Usually, the experience of being spoon-fed a bowl of sweet slop was reserved for the very young or the very old, Aaron thought. There was a particular kind of strangeness – a rareness – to the fact that he was receiving this kind of treatment in the prime of his life, which made him feel oddly privileged.

He didn't waste any time blowing on the porridge, choosing instead to draw air into his half-open mouth as he wolfed it down. It burned his tongue as he ate, but he didn't care. To his mind, after almost 24 hours of the freezing air and the damp seeping into his bones, too hot was still better than too cold.

After another slug of water to soothe his blistering tongue, Liana collected her things and disappeared back upstairs without another word.

14

Charles

Charles was kept busy throughout Wednesday – the day before he was due to travel to Barden Hall – and he was eminently thankful for that fact.

First, he took the Land Rover to the mechanics, heeding the hastily scrawled ghost of an 'M' on the back of his hand. Unfortunately, the visit was over as soon as it had begun when the owner, Bruce, told Charles he was much too busy to fit him in on such short notice. Bruce did attempt to make amends, confirming that the Land Rover looked "fine" from where he was standing (10 feet away), but that did little to subdue Charles' creeping anxiety. Ever since he'd noticed the rattling engine, he'd been plagued by visions of the it failing him en route to Reeves' estate, leaving him stranded on the roadside with two guns on his back seat and a duct taped prisoner in his horse box.

After rumbling out of the crowded mechanics carpark, Charles then headed back to Paul Arrowsmith & Sons to purchase some more ammunition.

Although he was sure the three boxes of two seventy Winchester would be more than enough for his rifle, he realised (after double checking to the safe in his office) that his shotgun shells amounted to little more than a few odd cartridges loose on the shelves. It was a fitting metaphor for the house itself, he thought; a hard-wearing skeleton protecting nought but emptiness within. Concealing it from prying, judgemental eyes.

Owlgreave looked ominous as Charles returned, almost black against the pale whale skin sky. A rectangle of blinding yellow in the house's bottom right corner was the only visible light; the kitchen, where he expected Phyllis would be sat at the table watching Liana as she cooked.

Charles considered pulling Liana aside for another private conversation, but the second he saw Phyllis' vacant smile as he entered, he realised it would be a waste of time. He sidled over to Liana, who was standing at the stove. She glanced over her shoulder and smiled, then turned back to the pot of vegetables on the boil.

"Soup tonight," she said. "If that's alright?"

Charles looked back at Phyllis, then leant against the cupboards next to Liana.

"Liana?"

"Yes? Is everything alright?"

Charles thought he felt one of Aaron's phones rumbling and instinctively clasped a hand down onto his pocket, before realising he'd smashed them both to pieces and scattered the debris into the canal. He folded his arms, keeping his eyes on Phyllis as he spoke quietly.

"Yes, thank you. I just... I'm going to have to ask you to do something for me. It's not usual, but it is necessary. I'm sorry if it puts you in an awkward position, but... I can't see any alternative."

"Ok," she said, stirring the soup with a long wooden spoon. "What is it?"

Charles breathed in deeply through his nose, inflating his enormous chest like a hot air balloon.

"I'm going to have to take a trip tomorrow. Overnight, for a couple of days."

He turned his head to assess her, but she kept her eyes fixed on the bubbling pan.

"What I'm asking is... Would you be able to stay here with Phyllis, look after her while I'm away? I'll pay you for your time, of course."

She stopped stirring, then tapped the spoon clean of the rim of the pan and set it down on the worktop. It was beginning to unsettle Charles that she couldn't bring herself to look directly at him. Her back was stiff, her face expressionless.

"Is Aaron... staying here?" she said.

"No. He's coming with me."

"Oh," she said, seeming to relax slightly. "Then... yes, I think that should be ok. I can always call Tess if I need–"

"Tess and her father will be with me. But her mother should be around. Just call the butcher's shop if you need anything, or me. I'll take the old phone with me, just in case. Is that alright?"

She nodded, then went over to the larder and opened it and took out the salt and pepper. She came back over to the pot and added a liberal amount of one, then the other, then took a teaspoon from the drawer and tasted the soup.

"Liana, is that alright?" Charles said again.

"Sorry," she said, forcing a smile. "Yes, that's fine."

"Good. Thank you," Charles touched her lightly on the

shoulder, then went over to join Phyllis at the dinner table.

"Mr Mortimer?" Liana said, the worried expression back on her face. "You said he's going with you?"

"Yes, why?"

"Is he... is he coming back?"

Charles looked over at Phyllis, then over to the locked cellar door. Liana stood there; the spoon clutched at her chest as if she thought it was about the blow away. After a few more seconds, Charles wrenched his eyes from the door and met her expectant gaze.

"No, he isn't."

15

Aaron

Aaron was torn from half-sleep, startled by the sound of heavy boots clomping down the cellar stairs. It wasn't just Charles this time either; at least one other person. He hoisted himself to his feet, turning to face Charles and Tess, who were both wrapped up in coats, scarves, and gloves. Charles was holding the roll of duct tape by his side, Tess clutching a hessian sack.

"What's going on? What are you-"

Aaron was cut off by the sound of ripping tape. Charles came straight for him and sealed his mouth shut then, as soon as he was clear, Tess came in and stuffed Aaron's head inside the sack and pulled a drawstring sealing it around his neck. He was still trying to speak through the tape as he was shoved this way and that. It seemed like there were four or five people jostling him now, hands appearing and disappearing at his wrists and his armpits, wrenching him free of the pillar.

For the few seconds his hands were free, they felt almost weightless.

"That hand, there."

It was Charles' voice, low and conspiratorial. Tess whispered something in reply, though the bag over Aaron's head was acting like a muffle as well as a blindfold. Four hands brought Aaron's wrists together, then fresh zip ties ended his temporary freedom, duct tape sealing it for good measure. One of them took hold of the makeshift handcuffs, while the other took his shoulder and put a firm hand in between his shoulder blades. The pair had so much muscle between them it was difficult to tell which one was which.

"One foot in front of the other," said Charles, from behind. "Alright?"

Aaron tried to turn to face his grandfather but was shoved back where he came from.

"Do not try to make this difficult," Charles said. His voice was hissed, the words clipped short. "This is happening, whether you like it or not. If you struggle it will just take longer. Do you understand?"

It was already beginning to get damp inside the bag, his nostrils flaring as they strained to pull in the air that his mouth couldn't. He could feel moisture – that could have been sweat or even some kind of condensation – dribbling from his forehead onto the bridge of his nose.

"Do you understand?"

Aaron nodded, then was propelled forwards; Charles' hand pushing him while Tess yanked him onwards like a disobedient puppy.

"Stairs," she said after a few steps.

The tips of Aaron toes found the first one, but he was unable to shuffle on properly, the front of his shin scraping down the sharp edge of the step.

Grunted curses exploded from his mouth – his body's

automatic way of dealing with the stinging pain – but still, they pulled and pushed, Aaron's shoeless feet scrambling to catch up with his hands, with Tess' firm grip. The dull blackness lightened slightly as they exited the cellar into the kitchen.

The bottoms of Aaron's socks were so wet that they slapped against the tiles with every step. It made him think again about skating over them to the oven as a boy to check on his Gran's apple pie. He wondered whether these damp, dirty footprints would be the last he'd ever leave on this floor.

As they marched into the hall, towards the door, Aaron wanted to tell them his shoes were still in the cellar, but it was no use. Soon enough it was dark again, and he felt the cold concrete – *slap, slap, slap, slap* – then gravel and mud. After a few more steps they brought him to a halt, and Charles' hands disappeared from his shoulder and back.

He could smell the air of a brand-new day, crisp and cool and unspoiled. Bolts clunked and metal ground against metal, then he was pulled forwards again and led up a corrugated ramp and into what sounded like a huge metal box.

It was even colder inside this than it was outside, like standing in a gigantic fridge. The metal floor bowed and clattered under the weight of their boots as they moved him further inside the box and layered even more restraints – coarse rope this time – around his wrists. Once he was secure, they did the same around his waist, then tugged at the restraints to check them.

"That alright?"

Voices.

"Yes, fine."

Charles and Tess.

"Ok."

112

Boots clattered again and Aaron felt the air change, suddenly becoming aware that he was no longer hemmed in by them. He tried to step forward but was firmly tied to the frame of the metal box.

Aaron's vision darkened even further as a door slammed shut, the echo still reverberating even as the boots crunched away, back towards the house.

16

Charles

They had been on the road for almost an hour by the time the sun started to rise; rose gold light spilling over the fields, casting long shadows. It wasn't that Charles had felt the need to travel under cover of darkness – the horse box was impossible to see into, thanks to his modifications – but the thought of getting up at the usual time and having to say his goodbyes to Phyllis and Liana, knowing where he was headed, was unthinkable.

The previous evening, he'd given Liana as full of a brief as was comfortable, then pressed all of the cash he had in the house into her reluctant, yet grateful, hands. He hadn't needed any assurances about the young girl's loyalty, but her diligence ever since Aaron's arrival had confirmed everything he already hoped; she would take care of Phyllis, no matter what happened to him. He just hoped he could return with enough money to keep her for as long as Phyllis needed.

The route from Owlgreave to Barden Hall was under 30 miles, and most of it was confined to A and B roads that wound through the hills without much interruption; save for the occasional village or hamlet that could be blown through in seconds.

Charles had made this drive so many times that he was able to channel all of his energy into making sure his right foot was as light as possible on the accelerator. He knew that it didn't take much for the speedometer to start creeping up on these kinds of roads, and he certainly hadn't put all of this into motion – and taken on so much risk already – just to have a busy police officer pull him over for speeding.

Just as Charles was beginning to feel comfortable in the warmth of the newly risen sun, it was snuffed out by the thick forest that enclosed the road on both sides. The chill was palpable again, as if they'd somehow passed into a different climate, in a different part of the world.

After a few minutes, he turned left off the road onto a thin track that was quickly swallowed by layer upon layer of fir trees, hedges, and bracken, all of which were dripping wet with morning dew. The Land Rover shook from side to side as it picked its way over cold-hardened potholes and gravel, though it complained less about its job than the horse box (and its disorientated passenger) that clattered along behind it.

The gates appeared up ahead, dwarfed by trees despite their size, while four men in dark winter coats and woollen hats stood in front the stone gateposts – two either side. They had ragged beards, grizzled expressions. Private security, Charles thought. Most likely men who'd gotten tired of being paid buttons to fight other men's wars overseas and decided to do something for themselves. It would have been easy money, most of the time, and if they were happy to turn blind eyes and deaf ears to everything that went on behind those gates,

Reeves would certainly compensate them handsomely for it.

Charles came to a wobbling stop as one of the men stepped forwards and held up his left hand; his right instinctively coming to rest on what was most likely a concealed weapon at his hip. He came over to the driver's side and waited for Charles to roll down the window, his tired eyes darting between the bags on the back seat and the blacked-out windows of the horse box.

"Morning," Charles said. "Charles Mortimer."

"Mortimer?" the man shouted over to his colleagues.

One of the men at the far gatepost produced a rubber-clad tablet from his overcoat pocket and started tapping and swiping the screen.

"What's in there?" said the man at the window, jabbing his finger towards the horse box.

Charles squinted slightly as he decided about how best to respond, sizing the man up. He quickly realised that, underneath the beard, this man wasn't much older than Aaron – late twenties, perhaps – though his eyes were harder and sharper, beneath heavy brows. Where Aaron played around with knives and drugs, and even looked to cheat and steal from his own family, this man was a different breed. He had seen the brutality of the world as it is, and he knew what was to come. The truth. In realising that fact, Charles also realised that he was now, finally, free of any obligation to deny that truth.

"Buy-in," he said. "One."

The man grinned, steam billowing from his mouth as he chewed loudly on a piece of gum.

Charles looked over to see the man at the gatepost peering in at him, apparently cross-referencing what he saw with something on his tablet. After a few more seconds of this, he craned his neck to confirm the Land Rover's registration number, then stuffed the tablet back in his pocket and stuck up his thumb to the man at the window.

"Happy days," he said. "You know where you're going?"

Charles nodded. "I do."

"Sweet," the man said, then he turned and walked back over to his place at the near gatepost, pulling a small radio from his pocket as he went.

Charles rolled up his window and watched as the gates to Barden Hall creaked open, welcoming him and his grandson.

* * *

It was another half a mile or so of rough track before the house appeared in the distance, its four sandstone towers standing sentinel at the crest of the bluff. As Charles drew closer, he saw that the thick mahogany door at the centre of the building – the maw of the beast – was still firmly closed, and the close-clipped lawns that were usually populated by staff and visitors milling from place to place were completely deserted. A towering stack of broken pallets and scraps of wood drew his gaze; most likely the bonfire that would be ignited to mark tonight's festivities, he thought.

Although the site had been used as a hunting lodge by the English nobility since the fifteenth century, the house as Charles knew it had only existed for around two hundred years. In this time, it had suffered partial collapses due to earthworks, leaks, flooding, infestations, and even a few fires; still it looked as solid and immovable as the sheer rock face that dominated the estate's eastern side. A powerful building to protect a

117

powerful family.

It had been over a decade since Charles has set eyes on his one-time employer, Sir William Reeves, and even back then, the man had seemed ancient. He was short and feeble, and quite often looked as if he had been dragged from his bed by a horse, rather than woken gently by one of his servants, if they had the temerity to wake him at all. He had always needed a cane to walk more than a few steps, quite often ran out of steam if he was required to utter more than a few sentences.

Despite all of this, the man exuded power and demanded respect. It was inherent in him, in his sabre sharp stare, in his carefully chosen words. It gave him a strange kind of advantage in the violent world he inhabited; Charles had always thought. The very fact that he was so physically weak forced him to use his brains and his words like weapons, at all times. He was able to instil genuine fear, whether it was a member of his household or his worst enemy, with little to no physical action. Charles had always thought of him as being like a well-timed spark into dry grass, that catches and feeds and grows into wildfire.

When Charles finally pulled up on the wide gravel forecourt, his eye was drawn by a pair of men standing by the red brick hut at the far corner of the house. They were both dressed in padded green jackets and flat caps, smoking and talking over cups of steaming tea. It was such an evocative sight that Charles felt as if he had stepped back in time, to when these grounds and the forests beyond were all his to manage, the hunts his to lead.

The men looked up to regard him at the sound of the slamming Land Rover door, their faces crumpled into suspicious squints. Charles shouted his greeting halfway to them, in an attempt to break the interminable silence.

"Morning," they said, with about as much enthusiasm as they might greet their dentist.

Both men were middle aged, though the darker-haired of the two was clearly more senior, given the flecks of grey in his stubble and sideburns.

"My name's Mr Mortimer, I'm here for the... for tomorrow. I have a buy-in."

"A what?" the younger man said.

"A..." Charles looked back at the Land Rover and its horse box, did his best to come up with some kind of suitable euphemism. Brazenly addressing the reality of the situation this early in the morning seemed odd, almost too matter of fact. "A buy-in for the hunt. I need to-"

"He's only pulling your leg," said the older man. He jabbed his colleague in the arm, forcing a mischievous chuckle from the younger man. "Daft bugger. You say your name was Mortimer?"

The man's foul breath wafted over as he spoke, like an olfactory companion to the sickening sight of his brown teeth.

"Yes," Charles said.

"Charles Mortimer?"

Charles nodded.

"Bloody hell," the man said. He dropped the roll up to the floor, then switched the steaming mug to his left hand and held out his right. Charles hesitated for a second, then reached out and shook it firmly.

"John Swire," the man said. "I worked under you here, for a few months before you left."

Although he came back a few times in the intervening years to visit Sir William, Charles had officially left the staff at Barden

Hall in the early 1980s, which meant – if this man was telling the truth – he'd not set eyes on him for the best part of forty years. He studied the man's face, tried to imagine it less wind beaten, without the lines and the grey stubble and the rotten teeth.

"Swire?"

"Aye... just 'that new lad John' to you back then, I'd imagine."

"Sorry, I..."

"Ah, never mind."

"It has been a while. Are you... head 'keeper now?"

"That I am," he said with a grin. "This is Danny. Danny Lees. One of the underkeepers."

"Pleasure," Charles said as he shook the younger man's hand.

"Sorry, I was only messing before," said Lees. "John's told me loads about you."

"Really?" Charles said, scowling at Swire.

"Well," he looked back at his younger colleague, almost bashful. "You were the top dog here when I started. Everyone knew it."

Charles smiled awkwardly.

"We've got a few here already," Lees said, nodded towards the house. "Buy-ins. Supposed to be a big 'un tomorrow, by all accounts. We can take yours in as soon as everyone's up and about."

"Sir William's tended to sleep in at the minute," said Swire, still clearly eager to make up for his colleague's disrespect. "Nothing happens until he's up. Do you fancy a brew while we're waiting? It's only in there."

He nodded towards the red brick building, the one they

used to call 'The Monkey House'; initially because of the rumour that monkeys had been kept in there by the original owner of the house in the early 1800s, and second because the gamekeepers used it as their makeshift headquarters and had proudly taken the sobriquet of 'monkeys' for themselves.

"The Monkey House is still standing, is it?" Charles said.

Both men sniggered. "Right you are," said Swire. "Nothing changes does it... Come and have a pew and we'll get the kettle on."

17

Aaron

Aaron was still blinded by the hood, and so cold now his legs and arms were made of pins and needles, but at least the swaying of his metal cage had finally stopped. His heart had slowed as the drive went on, but now he was sure the journey was over he felt like every cell in his body was in a frenzy, running in every direction to try and break out. He hung his head, fighting back vomit, and tried to breathe as deeply as the bag would allow.

He knew he had to clear the fog from his head, the fear would do nothing for him but stop him from paying attention to his surroundings. He'd heard slamming doors, crunching gravel, and the low voices of men talking, but other than those few useless clues, he had no indication as to where he was. The strangest – and maybe the most useful clue – was the crushing silence.

It was unlike anything he'd ever experienced. Even at Owlgreave he'd been able to hear some activity, like the far-off din of the factory or the echoing rattle of lorries as they barrelled down the bypass. Here there was nothing. No cars, no movement. Even the few birds chirping in the distance seemed miles away. His own ragged breathing inside the hood was louder by far.

After a while, maybe even half an hour, Aaron heard locks clunking, then what sounded like heavy wooden doors being swung open. Moments later, the crunching and muttering voices started up again, this time coming towards him, around to the entrance of his prison on wheels.

The metal clunked as more locks were undone, and the ramp groaned as it was opened and allowed to slam into the gravel. Aaron tried to call out, to ask whether his grandfather was one of the pairs of boots that were striding towards him, but the tape was still holding fast across his mouth.

He was grabbed then from both sides – two rough hands on each of his upper arms – while the rope was cut away from his waist. Whoever was holding him smelled unfamiliar, like stale sweat and cigarettes. The one on his right had the worst breath he'd ever smelled.

As soon as he was free, the two men – they had to be men – pulled him forwards and led him down the ramp and onto the gravel. He tried to let his legs go limp, to give them something to carry, but the one on the right drove a heavy boot into his shins, sending angry pain surging all the way up his leg.

"Stay on your feet, you daft bugger," a gravelly voice said.

Had he been sold, somehow, he thought? Sold to who, or for what reason, he wasn't sure, but it was the only possibility his misfiring brain could manage.

They ignored his mumbling, trying to ask questions through a thick layer of tape. Even inside his own head, Aaron's voice was jittery and fragile. He swallowed hard and gave up, doing

123

his best to refocus on his breathing.

After the gravel, he was hauled up a few steps and suddenly the floors under his socks were different. It was hard to tell, given the numb ache in his legs, but it felt solid and warmer than the wet gravel. Smooth, almost like varnished wood. Just as he was getting a feel for its texture, everything changed again, and he was being pulled up a carpeted staircase.

He realised that the staircase must have been a very wide one, as the two men stayed by his side the entire time they climbed, then turned, then then climbed higher again.

"You don't have to come all the way you know," said the gruff man on his right.

"It's alright," came a voice from behind them. Charles' voice. He was walking with them. "I need to speak with him first."

More voices started up, two more, from up ahead, then the hands ground to a halt and Aaron along with them.

He sucked in hair through his nose in surprise as the bag was whipped off his head, revealing Charles' wolf sharp features and a long empty corridor behind him. Aaron's breathing was so uneven and difficult now that he felt like he'd forgotten how to do it, like if he stopped concentrating his lungs would collapse inside his chest like empty crisp packets.

As the wooden floors and wide staircase had suggested, they were in some kind of grand old house, most likely in the countryside, given the silence outside. Aaron looked away from Charles, at the men who still had hold of his arms. They were both dressed like farmers, Aaron thought, or the kind of people playing farmers on TV, at least. The older one, the one with the horrible breath, was grinning at him, like they were all in on some kind of practical joke that was finally about to be revealed.

"Do you want the tape off?" the older man said to Charles.

"No," Charles said. "This won't take long."

Aaron tried to ask what the fuck was going on, his eyes bulging as he shouted into his gag.

"Listen to me," Charles said, his voice as low and controlled as always. "I had no choice in this. It's simply the only way some good can come out of this mess. The mess *you* made."

Aaron strained to speak again, and Charles nodded to the old man to rip the tape away. Aaron grimaced, tried his best not to scream, though is felt like a few layers of his skin had come away with the tape. He breathed deeply, licking at his raw lips, then met Charles' gaze.

"Grandad? What's going on? What are... where are we?"

Charles' mouth opened, as if he was considering how to word the explanation, but he sighed and closed it again, and nodded to the old farmer.

The men hauled Aaron around to the right to face two stocky men standing either side of a locked door. One of them produced a key and unlocked it, then the other took hold of the rope and pulled him away from the farmers.

"Aaron?" Charles said from behind.

The stocky man, Aaron's latest captor, allowed him to look over his shoulder and face his grandfather.

Charles cleared his throat. "I need you to remember that you did this. That you deserve it. That is the only reason you are here, and what happens next is the direct result of your choices. Your actions. The best thing you can do – the only thing – is accept it... with some dignity."

Charles turned and walked back towards the stairs, leaving the man to yank Aaron towards the door by his rope and push him inside.

18

Aaron

The slam of the door was still ringing in Aaron's ears as pushed himself up onto his knees. He looked up to see a room full of people silhouetted against the grey light streaming in through a pair of tall windows.

His eyes adjusted in stages. First came the geometric pattern of the wooden floor he'd been thrown onto, then the bare white walls and the sculptured stucco ceiling. Then came faces, bodies, clothes, the chairs they'd stood up from, most likely at the sound of the commotion from outside. Everything in the room – including the people locked inside it – looked tired and dirty and fragile, ready to come apart at the seams.

Aaron sat back on his heels and wiped his nose with the back of one of his bound hands, still staring open mouthed as the line of people edged towards him.

"Shit... Are you alright?" said the girl at the front.

She had short, dyed black hair, a strong jawline, and high cheekbones, almost like a runway model. Although she only had a pair of black socks on her feet, she was wrapped up in a thick black bomber jacket that was so oversized Aaron guessed it must have belonged to one of the men standing behind her. The one closest – a slightly overweight man with greasy brown hair much longer than hers – reached out and touched her on the shoulder.

"Hang on," he said. "Just stay back here. Just wait a sec."

She shrugged him off and stepped forward and knelt in front of Aaron.

"It's ok," she said, softening her voice. "We're not gonna do anything to you. We won't hurt you, alright? We're all in the same boat. Are you alright, do you want a drink?"

Aaron nodded vigorously, his tongue automatically darting over his cracked lips at the thought.

"Ok, hang on... Greg, can you get him some water please. Just wash my cup out."

The long-haired man hesitated for a second, then huffed and went over to the circle of chairs by the right-hand window and picked up a shallow plastic mug, like the kind from a cheap hotel tea and coffee set. Greg sauntered over to the left-hand side of the room and through an adjoining door into a darkened room.

As they waited, listening to the hiss as Greg turned on a tap, Aaron's eyes flicked from the girl – who was still knelt in front of him – to the other three people gathered around.

Just behind the dark-haired girl was a tall, skinny man with a long black beard that reached down to his chest, though his moustache was trimmed away to virtually nothing. Next to him was a petite, plump woman, who was clasping her hands in front of her thighs like she was waiting to be called into the headmaster's office. She had dark eyes, skin, and hair, and looked to be the oldest in the room, if only by a few years.

Next to them was a young, gaunt lad who couldn't have been older than sixteen or seventeen. He was stood further back, furiously chewing at the nails of his left hand. From his sunken eyes and the sheen of sweat on his pale face, Aaron guessed he was an addict who had been forced into going cold turkey by being imprisoned here.

The long-haired man, Greg, reappeared and strode towards Aaron, oblivious of the water spilling from the overfilled cup.

"Watch it, Greg, fucking hell. You're getting it everywhere."

Greg looked down in time to see the third slosh of water spattering over the floor, then steadied his hand accordingly, ropes of hair spilling from behind his ear as lowered his head to concentrate.

"Oh yeah... God forbid one of us slips and breaks our neck, wouldn't that be a tragedy?"

The girl glared at him, cutting his mumbling off.

"I'll clean it," said the older woman as she crossed paths with Greg. He stooped and handed the cup to Aaron, who took it with both hands and started to gulp it hungrily.

"Slow down, take your time," the girl said. "Plenty more where that came from. That's one thing we've got, at least. Thanks, Greg. Sorry. I didn't mean-"

"It's fine."

Aaron looked up as he continued to drink, meeting Greg's eyes and blinking his silent gratitude. Once he'd drained the cup, he placed it on the floor and wiped the water from his lips.

"What the fuck's going on?" Aaron said to the girl. "Where are we?"

He still couldn't shake the jittery weakness from his voice or slow his arhythmic breathing. It was like having the hiccups; the more he tried to will it away, the more intense

128

and infuriating it became. The girl turned back to look at Greg, then stood and helped Aaron to his feet.

"Come on," she said. "Come over here and have a sit down."

The man with the long beard came to Aaron's side and helped the girl carry him over to the circle of chairs by the window. They both smelled faintly of sweat, and generally stale, though they were still a good deal fresher than Aaron was, still wearing the tracksuit bottoms and boxers he'd been forced to piss in countless times.

They lowered him into an ornate, padded chair, then took their places in the circle. As he waited for the rest of the ragged group to sit down, Aaron looked out of the window and noticed thick, iron bars on the other side of the glass. Whatever the rest of these people were guilty of, they certainly weren't going anywhere unless they were allowed to.

"What's your name?" the girl said, leaning forward to rest her elbows on her knees.

"Aaron. Aaron."

He wasn't sure why he said it twice. It was almost as if his brain was trying to remind him that he was still in his own body, and that this really was happening.

"Ok... Well, I'm Romy," she said, forcing a split-second smile. She started pointing as she went around the circle from her left. "This is Greg, Gazwan, Bayley. And that's Maria over there, doing all the work as usual."

The older woman – Maria – smiled over to them as she finished mopping up the water Greg had spilled. Gazwan was the tall, bearded man, while Bayley was the young lad struggling with the shakes. All of them tried shallow waves as Romy introduced them, but it was plain to see that their spirits were already well on their way to being properly broken.

129

They'd been in this room for a while, Aaron thought. It certainly smelled that way; the open bin smell of the dirty plates piled up in the corner combining with an unmistakable stench from the doorless bathroom. Still, it beat the hell out of being alone in Owlgreave's cellar with his commode chair for company, he thought.

"So do you lot know what's going on?" he said. "How long have you all been here?"

Romy puffed out her cheeks, sat back in her chair, and crossed her legs.

"Varies," she said. "Me and Greg – what – about three weeks now?"

"Yeah," Greg said. "And three days. But who's counting?"

Romy ignored him and continued going around the circle. "Then Gazwan and Maria weren't long after, were you?"

Gazwan nodded. "Maria two days... after."

"Yeah, and then Bayley has only just got here too, really."

"Right," he said, bringing his frayed nail up to his gnashing teeth again. "Sunday night."

Romy and Greg sounded southern to Aaron, and definitely more well-bred than him. Uni students, he thought. If they were at either of the Manchester ones, chances are Aaron could have even sold a bit of weed to them or their mates.

Bayley's accent wasn't far different from Aaron's – definitely Manchester or thereabouts – but the other two, Maria and Gazwan, didn't speak as if English came easy to them. A second language, at least.

"So... what is it. Why are we all here?"

"Well, that's the million-dollar question, isn't it?" said Greg.

Even though Aaron had only been in the room a couple of

minutes, he could already tell that Greg's attempted gallows humour was a mask for his fear. He could see it in the water spill, in his trembling hands each time he messed with his greasy hair. He was terrified.

"Come on, Greg, don't be a dick. You know how fucked up all this is."

"I know, I know, I'm sorry. It's just... that's what it is, isn't it? It's fucked. May as well try and-"

"What is? What is all this?"

Romy looked up at the ceiling and bit her lip.

"This job doesn't get any fucking easier."

"What doesn't? What the fuck-"

Aaron shuffled onto the edge of his seat and waited until she met his gaze again.

"Basically," Romy said, drawing out the word. "We're being held here until they're ready to use us. For the... well, as part of their fucked up game."

"Game?" said Aaron.

"Well, they think it is. We heard about it while back – me and Greg, I mean – but I never really believed it was true until I saw it for myself. That's when they caught us."

"Caught you doing what?"

"Watching... watching what they were doing out there. Hunting."

"Hunting what?" Aaron said, becoming exasperated. "Foxes or something? Or-"

"No," Romy said. "People. That's what they do here; they hunt people."

19

Aaron

Aaron stared at her, open mouthed, as if that would somehow change the words she had just said. He was half expecting them all to burst into laughter, to clap him on the shoulder and admit they were just winding him up, but the solemn silence continued unbroken. This wasn't a prank on the new boy, some kind of sick joke. This was the truth.

"And all of you? Us?"

She nodded. Aaron leant forwards and buried his face in his bound hands.

"Boys can you try and get all that off him?" Romy said. Although Aaron couldn't bring him to look up, he guessed she was talking about his duct tape and rope handcuffs.

After a few moments someone – Gazwan – tapped him gently on the shoulder and set to work with a shard of broken wood, possibly an old chair leg. It didn't take him long to unpick the layers of tape, but the rope seemed like it was taking forever. Each tug and stab at its fibres scratched at Aaron's skin, his wrists raw and bleeding from hours on hours of restriction.

"When?" Aaron said to Gazwan, his voice hushed.

"The hunt?"

Aaron nodded.

"We don't know. Soon, maybe."

"They've not told you? Not said anything?"

Gazwan looked over at Romy. "No," he said.

"They feed us, sometimes," Romy said. "Tell us to shut up, now and again. That's about it."

"They know by now we're broken," said Greg. "That we don't have the balls to try and escape anymore. Or to kill ourselves, or each other. It's just the same every day, unless someone new appears."

"Our chances are better now," Gazwan said. "We have to be strong. Get through this together."

Aaron tried to smile at the man's optimism, though he still wasn't quite sure what 'this' actually was.

Just then the ropes popped open, freeing Aaron's hands for the first time in days. He inhaled through gritted teeth as the fresh air stung his wrists, then turned and thanked Gazwan. Maria appeared at his side with a damp flannel, pressing it against his grazes.

"Cheers," he said, still trying to grunt away the pain.

"Keep them clean," she said, then walked over and sat down on one of the chairs to his left.

"So, what happened to you?" said Greg, touching his finger to his temple. Aaron reached up and touched his own, flinching at the pain that erupted from the spot where the corner of Tess' metal bar had punctured his head.

"Long story," he said.

"Yeah, we've all got those," Greg said. "Give us the short version."

PREY

Aaron looked over at him. Both of his eyebrows were raised, making him look like a teacher waiting find out who'd vandalised his whiteboard. Like he was somehow in a position to demand answers.

"I made a mistake," Aaron said eventually, still dabbing at his wrists with the flannel. "A few mistakes."

He looked up, half expecting one of them to press him further, but all he saw was open, sympathetic faces. Even Greg's patronising expression had softened.

"I had to run from the feds. Lost some money, someone else's money. A right nasty fucker. I need to pay it back before next week or he's gonna hurt... people. People I don't want him to hurt."

"So... how does that get you here?" said Greg.

Aaron exhaled sharply, the rueful grin on his face turning it into a half laugh.

"I tried to rob a house," he said, shaking his head. "Fucked it up, obviously. Like I do with everything."

It was like saying the words out loud suddenly made him realise what he'd done, what he'd been driven to do. What he'd done his whole life.

"So, who brought you here? How did they even-"

"The person I was trying to rob," said Aaron, cutting Greg off. "I had him tied to a chair, then this Frankenstein-looking... bloke came out of nowhere and knocked me out. Not that it makes any difference. I'm here, and if all that shit you've said is true then I'm guessing I'm pretty much fucked anyway. Did you hear that guy, out there? He's right. It's my fault. I deserve it. All I have to do is accept it."

"Well, the good news is you're not the only one that's fucked," said Greg, trying a wry smile. "We're all as fucked as

134

each other."

"You do anything as stupid as me?" Aaron said. He directed the question at Greg, but his eyes flicked across to Romy's as he spoke. He could already tell that whatever he had done, she was probably involved.

"You're still not half as stupid as us. Like Romy said, we knew what was going on here and we came anyway."

"I'm a reporter," Romy said. "Greg was helping me get to the bottom of the rumours about all this. He's a sab, so he-"

"A sab?"

"A saboteur," said Greg, straightening from his slouch. "We disrupt fox hunts, try and stop them from getting away with all that kind of stuff, even though they still do... Anyway, I ended up finding out that there was this tradition – not everyone, but a tight circle of them – who were into this... whatever the hell you call this."

"How long's it been going on?" Aaron said. He immediately started thinking about the exclusive hunting groups that Charles had been part of over the years, of all the high-paying trips to exotic countries. Countries where it was probably even easier to get away with something as insane as this. Maybe his grandfather had done more than just set these things up, he thought. Maybe he'd even gotten involved. If that was true, maybe he was even going to be involved in this one.

"No idea," Greg said, pulling Aaron back from the abyss. "Centuries probably. You know what they're like, these lot. They love their traditions. Their rituals."

"They know people are onto them," Romy said. "I thought it was bullshit at first, just your usual conspiracy theory internet crap, like Pizzagate or Bohemian Grove or something. But then I got speaking to people, like Greg, who said they'd seen things.

135

More I looked into it, more I realised that there's no reason they *couldn't* get away with it. They've got the land, got the money. The power and influence to make people disappear."

"Most importantly, they've got the advantage of not giving a shit about anyone who isn't them," said Greg. "We're nothing as far as they're concerned."

It looked to be involuntary, but Greg's eyes did briefly flick towards Gazwan and Maria when he said this.

Aaron rested the flannel on his left wrist, the most damaged of the two, and leant forwards to get Maria's attention.

"What about you?"

She bowed her head and clasped her hands together in her lap like she wanted to sink into her chair and disappear.

"I made mistake too," she said. "I trust people I should not trust. They say they can help me. Come to UK so I can help my family, send them money. I did not want to leave at first – I was very scared – but my father, he became ill, so I had to go back to them and beg them to bring me here. I risk everything. Now, lose everything."

"It is the same for me," Gazwan said with a shrug, as if it was just an inconvenience. "We gave them all we had just to get across the water. Then they betrayed us anyway."

"Where were you coming from?"

"Syria," Gazwan said. "Damascus. From there, running across Europe all the way to France. Then to here. They caught us soon after we landed. Maybe it was planned that way, I do not know."

"Fuck, man," Aaron said. "What happened to your family? The ones you were with?"

Gazwan looked down at his beaten white trainers, shook his head.

"I don't know," he said. "We have all made mistakes, one way or another."

Aaron nodded solemnly as Gazwan's words seemed to settle over the group like a heavy blanket, sealing in the warmth of their shared remorse. Despite the bone chilling fate that was in front of them, there was a strange kind of comfort that came from knowing that (as Greg put it) they were all "as fucked as each other".

Still, Aaron couldn't help but feel a pang of guilt. After all, Gazwan had been trying to escape what looked on the news to be something like Hell on Earth, while Maria had been trying to help her family, her ailing father. Even Romy and Greg had been trying to do the right thing, putting their own lives at risk to put a stop to whatever this was.

But why was Aaron here? It wasn't his Mum's fault; he was quite sure of that. Yes, she was unpredictable, even volatile at times, but she'd always wanted the best for him, always been honest about her mistakes in the hopes that he didn't make them all over again. Despite that, he'd fallen in with the likes of Eastside Dave, and put himself at the mercy of even worse men like Tommy O'Brien. He'd had the choice to do anything he wanted, but instead took the easiest route, the one that would make him the most money in the shortest amount of time.

He broke away from his thoughts then, and looked over at the youngest of the group, Bayley, who was conspicuous in his silence. He just sat there at the furthest edge of the circle, chewing his nails, his right leg juddering like it was attached to a paint mixer. Romy noticed Aaron noticing him.

"How about you mate?" Aaron said. His voice came out more shrill than he'd wanted it to, like he was talking to a dog or a small child.

"Just grabbed me off the street. Chucked me in a van. Next thing I was here."

"Manchester?" Aaron said. The boy nodded.

"You on something, yeah?"

"Yeah. Not since I got here, obviously."

Aaron leant back in his chair and exhaled again, still struggling to get his head around how that one decision to drop the bag full of O'Brien's gear to help him get away from the police had caused him to end up in this house: in a room full of other, equally doomed, souls.

The more he thought about it, Greg and Romy's point that they were 'all in this together', that they'd all fucked up one way or another, definitely wasn't true. Of course, they'd all trusted the wrong people or made rash decisions, but their intentions had been good across the board, apart from Aaron. Bayley, the poor kid, didn't even get the chance to make any bad decisions, by the sound of it. He was just unlucky enough to be homeless and easy to abduct.

"What do you reckon they're gonna do with us?" Aaron said, standing up and walking into the middle of the empty room.

"Didn't we just go over that?" Greg said. "They're gonna set us loose over there and-"

"No," Aaron said. "I mean after. Say they hunt us and kill us, what do they do with us then? People will come looking for us."

Romy and Greg exchanged a quick glance, but Aaron continued.

"Like... I haven't got a passport or anything, and I guess you two" – Gazwan and Maria –"don't if you've, you know, come over here that way... But surely one of you must have? They can't just make all of us disappear... Every trace that we've been here."

"They have got the power to do whatever they want," said Romy. "Greg and I have found out about multiple missing people and followed the trail all the way and it just... goes cold. We'll be missing people for a while, but do you know how many missing people just aren't found? It's not even far-fetched to think they have a way of doing this by now. They've been at it for so long that it's almost industrial by this point. Have you not seen that place out the back?"

"I had a bag over my head."

"Oh, ok. Well, out the back there's a long brick building," she said. "Like a barn almost, with a big chimney stack on top. We think it's probably some kind of... disposal building. An incinerator."

Romy looked at Greg again, then shuffled forward on her seat.

"There's no record of us being here, no CCTV or anything. I set an email up so it would be sent to my mate who's a lawyer, just for insurance, but God knows if she ever got it. They've probably junked Greg's car already. Basically, until people find out what's going on at places like this – until someone exposes them – they'll keep getting away with it. They just burn all the evidence and deny everything... pay off whoever they need to. That's why we all need to help each other and make sure at least one of us gets the fuck out of here somehow... Then go and tell anyone who'll listen. If we can get my camera back, even better. Either way, we need to try and figure out a way of surviving what comes next."

20

Charles

Once Charles had unpacked his things in the musty bedroom at the far corner of the house's East Wing, he slipped a box of bullets and a few paper targets in his jacket pocket, shouldered his rifle, and headed across the fields and into the woods.

It was his favourite kind of morning in his favourite kind of place; cold and bright and crisp, the sun dappling through the trees each time the wind blew hard enough to ease them apart. Once he found a big enough clearing, about half a mile inside the tree line, he pinned the targets to the trunk of a large fir tree and retreated back to around 100 yards and dropped to one knee, swinging the rifle from his shoulder as he did so.

He fished the box from his pocket, opened it and laid it on the grass, then took a marble-smooth bullet out and fed it into the chamber and slowly slid the bolt into place. He groaned as he lowered himself onto his belly, shuffling himself around until the forestock of the weapon was resting snugly in the crook of his left arm. He peered into the scope, both eyes open, and allowed his fingers to reacquaint themselves with the feel of the varnished walnut grip.

He slowed his breathing as the targets appeared in the crosshairs, the entire world of fading greens and yellows and pale browns around them disappearing for a split second each time he shifted.

Bang on at 100 yards, the boy in the shop had said. Charles inhaled deeply, then slid his finger over the trigger and squeezed it until the rifle erupted, driving sharpened lead into the feeble paper at 3,200 feet per second. Clouds of once-hidden birds clattered out of the trees as the report echoed around the clearing, leaving Charles alone to admire the smoking hole he'd punched at the centre of the target.

* * *

Charles arrived back at the house just before midday, and in that time the entire atmosphere around the house had transformed. Cars lined the driveway and people were gathered on the gravel next to them in tight clusters, all talking excitedly and hugging and slapping one another on the shoulder. He didn't recognise any of them, and some were a good deal closer to Aaron's age than his.

It wasn't until Charles had made his way past them, almost to the steps of the house, that a shrill voice cut through the din like a circular saw.

"Mortimer? Charles is that you?"

He turned to find the speaker, feeling slightly self-conscious as he searched the faces of myriad strangers, most of whom were assessing him right back.

"Over here. Charles?"

Charles caught a blur of colour, and the movement of a waving hand in his peripheral vision, and affected a smile, if only to shut the boy up.

"Matthew," Charles said as he approached. "How are you?"

Matthew Reeves was like a peacock among pigeons, his crushed green velvet jacket and shocking pink cravat making him an easy target to pick out within the circle of dark suits that surrounded him. His dark hair was as much of a bird's nest as usual, and Charles noticed he was currently favouring a sickening pencil moustache, which looked quite outrageous on a man of his age.

He was stood with three other men, all of whom were dwarfed by the gleaming white four-wheel drive monstrosity behind them.

"Charles Mortimer. A good friend of the family and one of the finest groundskeepers ever to set foot on these hallowed hunting grounds," Reeves said, clearly enjoying himself. "Charles, this is John Wheeler and Franklin Ashton, I'm not sure if you've already met?"

"I don't believe so, no. How do you do," Charles said as he dropped Reeves' enthusiastic hand and greeted the two men.

"And this," Reeves said, turning to gesture to the man stood closest to the gigantic car. "Is some of the new blood."

The man was taller than Charles by an inch or so, and broader too, with short ginger hair and a pointed beard that had been groomed so precisely it looked to have been sculpted from marble.

"Tommy O'Brien," the man said, thrusting out a huge paw. Charles took it firmly as he could, O'Brien's layered jewellery clinking as they shook. His inner-city accent was made slightly conspicuous by his company, though he clearly attempted to make up for it my covering himself in as much gold as possible.

"Pleasure," Charles said.

"They never said we'd be up against the pros, eh," O'Brien said with a snigger. "Don't think that's very fair, do you?"

"That was a long time ago," said Charles, his voice measured.

"Will have been, won't it? Question is, can you still shoot?"

"We'll find out soon enough," Charles said. "And what brings you here, Mr O'Brien?"

"Same thing as you, my mate," O'Brien said with a wide grin. "The money and the mayhem."

All of the men – apart from Charles – burst into laugher. He simply let go of O'Brien's hand, subtlety wiping it on his trouser front before slipping it back into his pocket.

"I wish you all the best of luck," Charles said, turning back towards the house.

"Sounds like we'll need it," said O'Brien, still chuckling at his own joke.

"Charles, sorry, can I borrow you for a minute?" Reeves said as he scuttled along at Charles' side. As he approached, Charles noticed he wasn't wearing any socks inside his chequerboard patterned loafers.

"What can I do for you?" Charles said.

"Well, it's nothing really, just a... I don't know what you'd call it, a rumour perhaps. Or something that-"

Charles stopped at the foot the steps and turned to face the younger man, whose forehead was beginning to bead with nervous sweat. His aftershave was applied so liberally that it was almost suffocating at this range. Everyone around was still talking nonchalantly among themselves, stood in their groups as if they were at a summer festival.

"What is it?"

"I had a word with Swire, the 'keeper. This morning... while you were out. I'm sure he didn't want to pry or, you know, overstep the mark, but... he mentioned something about the young lad, your buy-in."

Charles sighed, glanced over at the three men Reeves had left standing by the cars. He had noticed Swire's eyebrows raise when Aaron was unmasked, upstairs in the house, the way he looked across at his underkeeper.

"Because of what the boy called me?" Charles said.

"Well... in a manner of speaking, yes," Reeves said, lowering his voice. "He said he called you 'Grandad'... is that true?"

Charles' jaw clenched as he nodded slowly, imagining the two men gossiping about him like schoolchildren.

"Yes. It's true."

"So... is it something that-"

"It's true that he shares my blood. It's true he was born to my good-for-nothing daughter. I'm his grandfather in name, nothing more. As far as I'm concerned – as far as anyone should be concerned – he is a criminal who broke into my house, held my family and me captive, and attempted to steal from me. That was the truth. Luckily, he failed... like he's failed at everything else, most probably. Regardless, his failures have led him here, and he's no one to blame for that but himself."

Reeves puffed out his cheeks, placed his hands on his hips as if he'd just finished a long-distance run.

"Well, if you're sure you're sure," he said. "I just wanted to check that this wasn't some kind of family dispute that's gotten out of hand, that's all. Wouldn't want all of this to be set in motion, then you get cold feet and-"

"The decision is made," Charles said, his tone sharp and cold. "I'm here because I need the money, not because I'm trying to teach him some kind of lesson. He's already dead to me. If I get the opportunity... I'll take him myself."

21

Aaron

Aaron spent the majority of his time in the room trying to look out of the frosted, barred window, down onto the driveway and the lawns beyond. He'd heard more and more cars pull up, then dozens of people talking easily like they were queuing outside a nightclub. By midday, it looked as if there was as many as twenty cars lined up on the gravel, some of which had been full, by the number of vague figures congregating outside them.

At one point, he thought he heard someone shout Charles' name, though it was impossible to be sure with nothing but blurred shapes and muffled voices to go on.

He finally turned around to see the rest of the group scattered around the room; pacing the floors or trying to sleep on cleverly arranged rows of chairs. Romy was stood in front of the other window, bracing herself on the sill, though she'd clearly given up trying to see anything through the frosted glass.

Aaron walked over and leant against the wall next to her, facing the door.

"You think this is it?" he said, his voice almost a whisper. "You think that's why they're all here?"

She straightened up and met his gaze. She looked tired; her bright blue eyes misted by tears.

"Maybe," she said. "Saying that, I don't know why they'd want so many witnesses. There's gotta be sixty, seventy people out there. Maybe close to a hundred."

"It's not usually like this?"

"No idea. I've only ever seen one – the one when we got caught – but there was nowhere near this many then. And it was different, the... I dunno. The vibe was just different."

Aaron nodded, and looked down at his dirt-soaked socks. He covered one foot with the other, like that would somehow be half as embarrassing.

"You think it's gonna happen today?" he said.

"I dunno," she said. "Just something off about everything. Like... it sounds like they're all here for a fucking laugh, doesn't it? Like they're just setting up their tents at Glasto or something. And so many of them... Maybe it's nothing. Not related to us, I mean. Like-"

"What 'oh, don't mind those people locked upstairs, let's just have a fucking party'?"

Aaron heard Romy sniff quietly, and he looked up to see it was a stifled laugh. He smirked back.

"Maybe," she said. "Maybe it's all a big wind up and they're throwing a massive party for us tonight. All our favourite food and drink, our favourite bands. That's probably all our friends and family parked up out there, all getting to know each other. Maybe our mums are out there right now, swapping recipes for Eton Mess."

Aaron tried to smile as he cocked his head, but it fell flat as

147

soon as he spoke.

"Not my Mum, but... Part of that's not as far-fetched as you might think."

"What?" she said, still half-grinning. "What do you mean?"

"The man who brought me here – the one who's house I tried to rob... It's my Grandad."

"You're taking the piss."

He turned to face her; his eyes opened as wide as he could.

"I wish I was. He's been involved with this lot since he was my age. Fuck knows what he's got up to in his time."

"You knew about all this?" she said.

"Nah, no course not. Just thought it was normal hunting. He was a groundskeeper, here and loads of other places. Even took them on trips abroad and shit, so... maybe it's happening all over."

"Fuck," she said, pushing away from the window. She slid down until she was sat on the wooden floor, then hugged her huge jacket around her legs. "We have to get out of this, even if it's just one of us. One person to tell everyone the truth about what's going on here, to prove it. Do you think, if you got chance to see him again, you might be able to get him to-"

"Let me stop you," Aaron said, lowering himself down to sit next to her. "You don't know him. He's... fucking hell, I dunno how to say it. He doesn't give a fuck. He thinks what he thinks, and he likes you or he don't. He's hard, you know? He's like-"

"Ruthless?"

Aaron smiled. "Yeah, exactly. Ruthless. He ain't gonna listen to me anymore. I had my chance to speak to him and I fucked it up proper. I reckon he's gonna be out there, you know. When it happens."

Romy shrugged her hand out of her baggy sleeve and rested

it on top of Aaron's, causing him to flinch. Her touch was warm, her fingers thin and delicate. She squeezed his hand for a second, then let it go and tucked it back under her armpit.

"Think of it this way," she said. "They're chasing us for a sick thrill, or for money. We'll be running for our lives, just to see another day. Surely, that gives us the advantage, right?"

Aaron stared down for a moment while he considered this, his eyes fixed on the spot where her hand had been.

"Is that what usually happens?" he said. "The people get away?"

Her hopeful expression melted away as he spoke, and he felt a pang of guilt in his stomach. Even so he couldn't bring himself to take it back, to say he was sorry. Having hope was one thing, but the odds were unarguably stacked against them. Hanging onto a fantasy wouldn't do them any favours, he thought. They had to be ruthless, as ruthless as he knew Charles would be.

"No," Romy said eventually, her voice little more than a whisper. "They don't. But we're not them, we're us. We know this is bigger than us, so we can do things they couldn't."

"You really believe that?" Aaron said.

"Yeah," she said. "I have to. And so do you."

Aaron leant forward and squeezed his toes, trying to warm them despite the soaking wet socks that held them.

"How did you even decide to come here?" he said. "Like... get in the car, or whatever, knowing what could happen?"

"Because this has to stop."

"Yeah, I know that, but... why is it you that has to do it, I mean? Couldn't you just tell the feds or whatever? You must have known this is what they'd do to you if they caught you."

Romy sighed. "I guess so. Obviously, I didn't think they'd catch us. We just planned to get up to that ridge, get the

149

pictures, and get out. Get the evidence to take to the police. I still don't even understand how they found us up there. The guy said it was the dogs who smelled us, but... fuck, sorry."

She wiped the tears from her eyes with the sleeve of her jacket and sniffed loudly.

"Shit, no I'm sorry, I shouldn't have said it," Aaron said, bowing his head. "I just meant... I don't understand how you're so brave, you know. To take all these people on, by choice."

"What, a stupid little posh girl?"

Aaron sniggered along with her. "Little posh girl is the bravest one here, by the look of it."

"Brave doesn't mean shit," she said, exhaling sharply to quell the tears. "I could be the bravest person in the world and still end up in that incinerator tomorrow. We don't need to be brave now, we need to be like them... we need to be ruthless."

22

Charles

Charles had attended a number of these kinds of gatherings over his years in the employ of the Reeves family and their proxies, and he always did his best to stay invisible for the duration of them. There was usually some kind of dubious pagan underpinning – a quirk of some of what Charles referred to as the 'inner circle' – and in this case it was Samhain, the end of the harvest and the onset of darkness.

He wasn't even sure whether Sir William actually believed any of what was said at these events, or whether they were simply a thinly veiled excuse for depravity, but both the old man and his contemporaries made sure they always marked the occasion. Even after all these years of being obligated to attend, Charles struggled to distinguish one from the other, as they all usually involved fire, frivolity, and a good deal of alcohol.

The guests at Barden Hall – many of whom were in their late teens and early twenties, by Charles' reckoning – were mostly dressed in formal attire, with some even opting for black tie.

Due to the bite in the evening air and the rain-soaked state of the lawns, almost all of them were forced to deface their smart appearance by layering on heavy coats, scarves, gloves, and wellington boots.

Charles had opted to wear his tweed jacket, with a simple white shirt and deep red cravat, and black trousers which he'd tucked into the tops of his wellingtons. He didn't need to wrap up any more than that, like the rest of them had, as he planned to make his way back inside as soon as the formalities were over.

He stood alone on the lawn at the edge of the crowd, most of whom had encircled the two-storey pile of broken wood in anticipation, plastic cups of spiced mead sloshing out onto the grass as they laughed and jostled one another.

As the swollen orange sun had all but dipped behind the horizon, Sir William finally emerged from the house and began inching his way towards the bonfire area, his one-time valet and current consigliere Christopher Holdsworth, as ever, at his side. Charles caught the unmistakeable scent of petrol being splashed onto wood and used this as a cue to make his way through the crowd so he could see – and be seen by – Sir William as he made his address.

The din of constant chatter had dropped to a few pockets of whispering by the time Sir William reached the makeshift dais. He stood and waited as the last naive few were shushed, clasping both sides of the varnished oak lectern as if he would crumple to the floor without it.

He looked around at the eager faces of the crowd, his smile broad and proud, almost paternal. He was wearing a strange, formless grey woollen suit that buttoned all the way up to his throat, which made him look like an aging communist dictator.

His hair had also thinned so much now that it was little more than a few patches of white peach fuzz on the top of his head.

Charles noticed that men were stood on either side of the dais. Both of them were holding a wooden, cloth-bound club out in front of them, each of which were rippling with fresh flames.

"It is good to see you all," Sir William said, stopping to cough after the first few words. "I see old friends and new friends, all side by side, all gathered here to... Banish the darkness together. To look back on the year we leave behind, and to look ahead. To consider the trials to come.

"As is always the way, we stand here ready to enter the dark months, the void, which is as daunting as ever for us, and for our once-great country. But we must remember, that within the void there is always potential. For growth, for new life."

He paused and looked about again, his wizened face wrinkling back into a smile. If Charles hadn't been so aware of all the things he had done, all of the suffering he had caused, he might have mistaken Sir William for a kindly old man.

"So, with that in mind, I would like to raise my cup, and ask you all to do the same," he creaked around, one hand still on the lectern, and took an engraved ivory cup from Holdsworth's careful grasp. Sir William straightened up, and faced the bonfire again, then raised his cup slowly until it was level with his hooded eyes.

"Here, tonight, together... We banish the dark, just as our ancestors before us, for generations on this sacred land."

He inched the cup higher, and the gathered masses mirrored him, excited murmurs rippling through the crowd.

"Waes hael!" Sir William said.

"Drinc hael," was the roared reply.

Charles took a mouthful of the sweet, sticky mead, then tipped the rest out onto the grass as the cheers echoed across the fields, reflecting back, seconds later, from the distant forest.

Sir William was helped down from the dais by Holdsworth, then – when he was safely on his way back towards the house – the two torch bearers stepped forwards and tossed their flaming clubs onto the wood pile.

The blaze spread instantly, hungrily, surging inside towards the base of the bonfire, before the whole thing whooshed up into the beginnings of an inferno that would burn until the next morning. Charles dropped his plastic cup to the ground and turned and started towards the house, doing his best to ignore the jubilant cries that were bubbling up all around him.

* * *

The whole ritual had been a lot less, for want of a better word, 'pagan' than some of the events Charles had been forced to attend in the past. It was as if Sir William had mellowed somewhat in his old age, realising that the next generation might not be as welcoming to the headdresses and face paint and woollen robes that had been more accepted in the sixties and seventies. Going off the disposition of the youngsters gathered by the bonfire, they seemed happy to be involved while the festivities stayed relatively secular and would most likely continue to attend if it meant social advancement, debauchery, and time to socialise with well-connected members of the opposite sex.

Either way, Charles was glad that he hadn't had to endure

any long, drawn out ceremonies, and within a few minutes he'd even managed to find himself a supply of alcohol that wasn't mead and a dimly lit room within which to enjoy it, undisturbed.

He sat for a while in a battered green armchair next to a modest fire, drinking a quite impressive single malt from an ornate crystal tumbler. The way the room was set up and decorated in dark, textured wallpaper and heavy curtains, it wasn't too far removed from his own sanctuary back at Owlgreave, though it was missing the taxidermy.

Despite his situation now and the situation with Phyllis at home and the unavoidable severity of what was to come in the morning, Charles noticed that he was feeling something almost approaching relaxation. Just then, he was jolted from his repose by a strong double tap on the door frame.

"There you are," Holdsworth said, a wry smile on his weathered face. "Mind if I join you?"

"Of course," Charles said, setting his drink down on a side table and standing to shake his old friend's hand. "Have you been released?"

"Indeed, I have. Sir William has settled in for the night, upstairs. Matthew is with him. Is there any of that left?" Holdsworth gestured towards the decanter on the table, next to Charles' glass.

Charles smiled. "Maybe one or two."

Holdsworth tossed his grey overcoat onto the back of the chair opposite Charles' and sat, waiting patiently as his drink was poured. He was dressed in a black suit and white shirt, though he had chosen a simple grey tie instead of the bow ties favoured by most of the youngsters outside. Like them, he had been forced to tuck his tailored trousers into high, olive green

155

wellingtons.

"How is he?" Charles said as he sat back down.

"Still going strong," said Holdsworth. He paused to take a sip, rolling the whisky around in his mouth as he admired the hue of what was still left in the glass. "Ninety-nine years old and he's still adamant that he stays involved. Insistent that the hunts go ahead every month or so, despite the growing... pressures I suppose you'd call them. And there are these gatherings too, of course. You know about that."

"Indeed."

"He was asking after you, you know."

"After me?"

"Are you surprised?"

"Not surprised," Charles said, taking a sip to give himself time to think. "I wasn't sure if he even knew I was here."

"Oh, he knows," Holdsworth said. "He hasn't changed all that much. He still wants to know... everything, like I said. You saw all those kids out there, I imagine? He knows the names of every single one of them, or their parents at least."

"And their addresses, I imagine," Charles said, somewhat under his breath. Holdsworth smirked, but other than that seemed content to let the remark pass.

"And... how are you?" Holdsworth said.

Charles scowled into the flames. "Surviving," he said eventually.

"Surviving," Holdsworth said, the smirk returning. "That's as well as can be expected, I suppose. More than can be said for other members of your family, so I hear..."

Charles felt snakes of rage coiling in his stomach, before suddenly realising that his old friend was not referring to his grandson, rather than his ailing wife.

"News travels fast," Charles said.

"Well, news like that tends to, yes. How in God's name did-"

"It's not important," said Charles, cutting him off. "What's done is done and it's no one's business but mine."

"I see. That's that then. Well, best of luck to the boy. You never know."

Holdsworth drained the rest of his whisky, then pushed himself out of his chair far enough to lean over and pluck the decanter from Charles' side table. He filled his glass, then leant back over and dribbled the last few drop into Charles'.

They sat like this for some time, slowly drinking and staring into the roaring fire, like a cosier, more exclusive, microcosm of the crowd gathered around the bonfire outside. Occasionally one of them would break the gathering silence by mentioning an anecdote from a previous hunt or resurrect a character or event from the decades they had both toiled – in their own ways – for the seemingly immortal Sir William Reeves.

After a while, a young man burst into the room through the creaking door at the back. The top two buttons of his shirt were undone, and his bow tie was nowhere to be seen. His hairless cheeks were flushed from the cold air and the mead.

"Dad," he said, slightly out of breath. Although Charles was initially shocked that Holdsworth even had a son, let alone one who looked to be at least eighteen, his attention was drawn by how distressed he appeared to be.

"Sorry," he said. "I'm sorry to... interrupt you, but I need to speak... need to tell you something."

"Tell me what?"

The boy's eyes flicked to Charles.

"Anything you need to say to me you can say in front on him," said Holdsworth. "What is it?"

"It's Archie."

"Archie? Matthew's son?"

"Yeah."

"What about him?"

"Well, he's... he's had a bit to drink I think, or... I'm not sure. But I heard him talking with Mille and Daffs and a couple of-"

"Get to the point lad, for God's sake."

"Sorry... Sorry, I just mean I heard him saying... boasting really, about the hunts and stuff. I know it's kind of a-"

"Boasting?"

"Yeah, he was talking about them, upstairs. About what's going to happen to them."

"Bloody hell," said Holdsworth, briefly turning back to Charles. "Matthew Reeves' eldest. He's as stupid as he his arrogant, and has the-"

"Dad, it's not just that," the boy said. "He said he was going to... That his dad would let him take one... For himself."

"Take one?"

"Yeah... of them. The ones upstairs."

"Bloody idiot," Holdsworth said, grunting as he pushed himself up out of the gelatinous softness of the Chesterfield. "Where is he?"

"Archie?"

"Yes, Archie. Who else do you think I'd be talking-"

"Outside, I think... or gone up there, maybe?"

"Up to the room?" Charles said, dismounting the chair with a good deal more grace than Holdsworth had.

"He said he was going to. Said his dad would let them take one out into the woods and... well, you know. He could have been joking but it didn't really-"

"Of course, he wasn't," Holdsworth said. "Jesus Christ.

Right, go and find Matthew, go and tell him. Charles, you come with me. Hopefully we can get up there before him, the little shit."

23

Aaron

The two guards had slid serving plates full of leftovers through the door not long after the blurred flames materialised outside, staining the blackness fire white. The food was a strange mixture of delicate canapés – fingernail-sized portions on cardboard-thin crackers – and hearty slabs of roasted meat, chunks of white bread and piles of pasta salad. According to the long-termers, Romy and Greg, this was by far the biggest meal they'd been given during their whole three-week, three-day stint. That sign alone was enough to reinforce their suspicions. As far as they were concerned, this was the last supper.

The six of them had helped themselves in reverse order of how they'd arrived; Aaron and Bayley diving in like ravenous animals, followed soon after by Gazwan and Maria, albeit less enthusiastically. Romy and Greg hung back while the rest fed, eventually sloping over to pick at what was left.

Just as they were beginning to relax into the feast, one of them occasionally critiquing the state of the salmon or the staleness of the bread as if they were high-end restaurant reviewers, they were silenced by a muffled argument out in the hall.

Aaron and Greg sprinted over to the door and pressed their faces against it, eyes locked on one another.

"I said get lost," a voice said, firm and confident.

"I don't think my father will be happy when he hears how you've spoken to me," said someone else. The voice was considerably younger, and where the first accent had been harsh and regional, the second was definitely more well-to-do.

"I don't care mate," the first voice said. "We answer to Sir William and his lackey, that's it. Now take your little girlfriends and fuck off, the pair of you."

Aaron heard a number of new voices, male and female, all laughing and goading the upper-class boy.

"Listen to me, sir," he said. "I thank you for doing your job correctly but what you need to understand is Sir William is my grandfather, and if you take orders from him then you can take them from me too. Now open that door and let us get what we came for."

"What the fuck are you on about?"

"We're taking one. My grandfather's orders."

"What for?"

"That's our business."

"Is it fuck, not when I'm-"

"Alright, alright," the boy said, shushing the rippling laughter again. "Look, we're not allowed to hunt tomorrow but we still wanted to have a bit of fun and my grandfather – Sir William, to you – said we could take one of them up to the woods for a bit of... well, you know... target practise."

The guard let out a spiteful chuckle. "You are joking?"

161

Neither Greg nor Aaron had blinked for the entire conversation, all they could do was stare at each other, wild-eyed. Aaron tore himself away from the door for a second to glance at the rest of the group as they gathered behind him. From their gaping mouths he assumed that he didn't have to waste any time explaining.

"I certainly am not," the boy said. "My father will pay whatever's necessary, so... can you open the door please, so we can pick one?"

"Pick one? Fucking hell are you deaf?"

"If you want, I can call my father now?" he said. These simple words were like an explosion, and the silence that followed louder by far.

"Is that what you want me to do?" The boy said eventually, his confidence growing. "I can see what he says about all of this, if you like? I think he's putting Sir William to bed, but it shouldn't be a problem to-"

"Alright, alright," said the man. "Jesus. Give us the keys Daz."

"What?"

"Just give 'em here."

Aaron listened carefully to the sound of keys jingling in the hallway but was immediately sent stumbling back from the door by the guard pounding on the other side. "Away from the door," he said. "Move back. I know you're there. Move back now."

Aaron and Greg retreated to stand a few feet back with the rest of the group, all six of them involuntarily coming together like frightened animals cornered by a predator.

The door swung open and the two guards entered, handguns held loosely at their sides. They knew they'd see no resistance

– even Aaron was too mentally exhausted for that now – but it seemed like the men were still keen to instil fear whenever they could.

A tall, clean-shaven boy, probably around seventeen or eighteen years old, followed the two men into the room. He was dressed in a black suit, white shirt, and black bow tie, with a black duffle coat over the top and muddy wellies on his feet. A few others – all a similar age and dressed in the same odd mixture of clothing – peeked into the room from behind him.

The boy was grinning, satisfied that his name-dropping tantrum had got him exactly what he wanted. Aaron sensed this wasn't the first time in life that tactic had worked for him.

"Ok, that's more like it," the boy said, swiping a loose strand of dark hair back from his forehead. "So, what have we got?"

All six of the prisoners were silent, shivering as one. All of the sensation had drained from Aaron's limbs, and he was starting to feel as if he was floating out of his own head. It gave him a strange kind of confidence; a reassurance that nothing bad could come of staring this rich psychopath down, because it barely felt like it was him doing it.

"Are you keen?" the boy said, stepping forward and stooping to try and meet Maria's downcast eyes. "Hello? You speak-a English?"

A few sniggers came from the doorway, but Aaron kept his gaze fixed on the boy. He soon got bored with trying to tear Maria's attention away from the floorboards and moved down the line.

"Jesus, look at this one. Bloody stinks," he said as he passed Bayley.

"Hello... bloody hell look at this one," he said to Romy with a snigger. "Were you a model in your home country?"

163

"I'm in my home country," she said, her teeth bared. "Prick"

"Fucking hell," the boy said, glancing back at his friends. They'd almost edged inside by this point. "You'll do well tomorrow, keep that up."

"What about you?" he said to Greg. "You two a couple?"

Greg stared ahead at the far wall. Despite the fact that he towered above the boy, he looked childlike in his terror, his bottom lip still quivering no matter how hard he fought it. The boy reached up and poked Greg's cheek with his index finger.

"Hello? Are you in there?" he said, snorting. The poking hardened to stabbing, almost forcing Greg backwards. "Come on big boy, let's see what-"

"Fucking leave him alone," said Romy, her bellowed voice echoing around the high ceilings and into the hall. It was enough to distract the boy from terrorising Greg.

"Oh, so you are a couple? Well, I'm very sorry, I wouldn't want to break you up, I mean-"

"Will you hurry up?" said one of the guards. "This isn't rich boy's play time. You shouldn't be in here in the first place. If you're taking one, fucking get on with it."

"Gosh, party pooper or what," the boy said, setting his friends off again. He looked into Aaron's eyes for a few seconds, the smirk still plastered over his face.

"Nah," he said, turning away. "Ok, sod it. We'll take the coloured one. Come on."

He waved dismissively towards Gazwan, whose wide eyes met Aaron as the guards strode over to him.

"No, wait," he said, turning to face them. "You can't... please. I have a family, please."

"You've already tried that one," said the guard. "Come on."

"No, please."

Aaron felt the blood rush to his head as the guards grabbed Gazwan by the arms, the suited partygoers scattering back into the hallway. Even as the men dragged him towards the door, Gazwan somehow held on to his dignity, only struggling slightly under their grip, his complaints barely louder than a murmur.

"Hold on," Aaron said.

"What are you doing?" said Romy.

"Fuck it. No, it's ok," he held Romy at arm's length and followed the guards. "Oi, mate. Leave him. Take me instead. I'll go, leave him."

He had no idea what he was saying. It reminded him of the woman knocking her coffee cup over on the train a lifetime ago; a clumsy, irretrievable mistake. Was there some part of his subconscious that thought he'd have a better chance of escape from a few posh kids than a group of bloodthirsty veteran hunters? Surely, it couldn't have been pure selflessness, he thought.

"Fuck off. Stay back," the guard said, pointing his gun at Aaron's face, freezing him to the spot. Despite that fact he was looking down the barrel of an actual gun, Aaron felt like he had somehow dodged a bullet. He simply held up his hands and stepped back into line, still trying his best to figure out how those words had come out of his mouth.

Just then, as Gazwan was being wrestled over the threshold, the sound of footsteps came thundering down the hallway, turning heads and stopping all three men in their tracks.

24

Charles

Charles jerked his head from side to side as he strode along the hall, attempting to see past the crowd of gawking teenagers to the three men scuffling at the door to the holding room. There was a tall, bearded man in the middle of two thick-set private security guards, each one of his thin arms clamped in a pair of theirs.

"Move, get out of the way," Charles said as he approached, practically scooping all of the suited, mead-weak onlookers to the side with one arm. "What the hell is going on?"

The scuffle subsided, and everyone looked at Charles through masks of confusion.

"Who the fuck are you?" one guard said.

Charles narrowed his eyes and took a firm step towards him. As he spoke, each word was heaved out and dropped at the man's feet like slabs of granite.

"Put him back."

"But he said... He was saying Sir William-"

"Which one?"

The guard nodded towards a slim boy with floppy dark hair and an awkward grin fixed on his face.

"You're Matthew's boy?" Charles said. The boy nodded. "He will deal with you. Leave, all of you. Now."

He barked the last word, causing every one of the gathered teenagers to jump, then scamper down the hall towards the staircase. Charles turned back to the guard.

"You have just been played for a fool," Charles said. "By a drunken child. Put him back in there and-"

Charles' words failed him at the sight of his grandson staring back at him through the open door. His expression wasn't one of shock, or even confusion, but anger.

"What are you doing here?" Aaron said. His voice was shaky, but he was able to retain his composure. The guards looked at Aaron for a second, then back at Charles.

"Put him back," he said to the guard. They obliged, shoved the bearded man back inside where he fell at Aaron's feet, crippled by relief.

"What the fuck are you playing at?" said Aaron, striding towards the door. "Save us today, kill us tomorrow? What the fu-"

The guard slammed the door in Aaron's face and locked it. Although he could still hear Aaron's muffled tirade, Charles struggled to make out anything but noise. He nodded at the guards one by one, then turned on his heel and headed back down the hall.

* * *

Charles had planned to go straight to his room, but just as

he had crossed the landing towards the opposite side of the house, a shout stopped him in his tracks. It was Holdsworth, who was out of breath and flustered after hurrying straight from Sir William's room. He looked over both shoulders as he approached, almost as if he was expecting to be followed.

"What happened?" said Charles

"Sir William was asleep, but I spoke with Matthew. I must admit he wasn't as... outraged as I'd expected."

"Does he have form for this?"

Holdsworth shrugged. "He wouldn't say. He said he'd discipline the boy but he's still not taken away his duties."

"Duties?"

"For tomorrow. The boy's supposed to be filming."

"Filming the hunt?"

Holdsworth nodded, though he couldn't hold back a grimace as he did. "Matthew's idea, as you'd expect. For those that can't attend. They can watch online, place bets, follow the-"

"Good God," Charles said, practically spitting the words. "That's madness, what if the footage is seen by someone?"

"No faces, apparently. We're to cover up if he's around and," he trailed off. "What's the use? You're right, it is madness. But he managed to convince Sir William that it's the way to keep everything moving forward, so that's what we're doing. If there's any luck the little moron will roll his quad and cease to be anyone's problem."

Charles couldn't help but smile at his friend's jest, though he suspected there was a good deal of sincerity behind it. Holdsworth clapped a hand on Charles' shoulder and shook it.

"I wish you well tomorrow, Mortimer. Hopefully, you get what you came here for."

Charles nodded, shook Holdsworth's hand and turned to

leave.

He considered trying to sleep at first, to rest enough to give him some kind of edge on the younger, hungrier men he would have to best in the morning, but it was no use. The sight of Aaron, and the anger in his eyes, had triggered in him a feeling that was too complex to name. He knew the boy deserved his fate – his actions were unforgivable, after all – but the thought that his reckoning was so close was a difficult one to process.

He spent the rest of the evening, and some of the night, stood at the window with a glass of whisky clutched in his hand, his room dark but for the swelling light of the bonfire.

25

Aaron

It felt, to Aaron, like they had been huddled together in the middle of the room for almost an hour; all six of them too afraid to move, too paranoid to let down their guard again. Once they were certain that no one else was going to burst in demanding to take them for target practice, they finally dispersed.

Somehow, Bayley was asleep within minutes, curled up across two chairs with his hood covering most of his gaunt face and his hands tucked away in his sleeves. Maria had gone into the bathroom to rinse off the empty serving plates, which meant that Gazwan, Greg, Romy, and Aaron were the only ones able to sit in the circle and dissect what had just (almost) happened and prepare for what was to come.

"Thank you, my friend," Gazwan said, patting Aaron on the back. Clearly his involuntary heroics hadn't gone unnoticed.

Aaron smiled briefly at him, then leant forward onto his knees, dropping his chin to hide his shame.

"Please tell me, after three weeks in here, you've got a plan," he said to no one in particular.

Romy sighed. "Sort of... well, I've got one and then Gazwan. Then Greg's kind of-"

"Hang on, I've not said anything," said Greg, interrupting. "I just know from when we've got stuck in with these lot in the past – and this was when they were hunting foxes, not people – they don't mess about. They're..."

"I think we've all worked that out by now... anyway, that's not what he was asking," Romy said. She looked back over to Aaron. "My idea is... well, when we were up on that ridge – there's like a big rock face on one side of the grounds, about a hundred foot high – you could see that there's this forest at the back of those fields. It goes all the way around the side and the back of the house. That's the bit they make you run towards, the forest, so I reckon you could start turning right after you've been in there for a while and end up round the back of the house."

"Then what?"

"It's water behind the woods at the back, like a big lake. If we could get across that the dogs wouldn't be able to follow, neither would the horses. By the time they'd get around to the other side we could be gone out the other side. I even think we could get to the road on the far side of-"

"This is what I mean," said Greg. "You're talking about a fucking miracle here. You're gonna somehow find your way through all of those trees, round to the back, then find the lake, then get across, then-"

"For fuck's sake," Romy said, burying her head in her hands. "You can't just shoot it down and not come up with an alternative. It's like with my first one, you're so fucking negative, all the time it's-"

"Oh yeah, the 'first plan'," he said, making air quotes with his index fingers.

"What was the first plan?" said Gazwan.

"Well, it was more of-"

"Suicide," said Greg, interrupting her. "Suicide is what it was. Even this plan seems like a sure thing compared to that one."

Romy opened her mouth to speak, then closed it again, exhausted. Aaron could tell this was most likely not the first, second, or even tenth time they'd had this same argument. As much as he agreed with Greg's assessment, surely it was better to have a bad plan than no plan at all.

"What about you, mate? What you think?" Aaron said to Gazwan.

He shrugged. "I just think that we will be better if we stick together. Maybe, if we do, we can defend ourselves better. I think it is-"

"And again," Greg said, chuckling. "Fighting against shot-guns and rifles with sticks and stones. Hopeless."

"She said it, my friend," Gazwan said, gesturing towards Romy. "If you have a better idea... please. Tell us now."

Greg stood and stormed off towards the dark and doorless bathroom, the only place in the world the six of them could go to be alone.

* * *

"How is he doing that?" Romy said, staring over at Bayley, who had started to snore gently.

"Too dumb to know what's coming," Greg said. He'd only spent a couple of minutes in the dark before he sloped back over to the circle and took his seat again. Romy sighed a little and turned back to face into the circle, hugging her knees to her chest.

"Maybe it is the opposite of that," said Gazwan. "Maybe he knows that it will help him. He can run for longer if he is well-rested."

"We should all try and sleep," said Maria.

"You think any of us are gonna last long enough for that to matter?" said Greg. "The head start they gave to the ones we saw wasn't even 10 minutes. Plus, they were on horses and they had dogs. We'll be lucky if we make it a hundred metres into that forest."

"So, you think we will do better if we are tired?" said Gazwan.

"No, I didn't... I don't," Greg was so exasperated that he was struggling to form the words. "I'm not saying I wouldn't want to sleep if I could; I'm saying I wouldn't be able to... Because I have the sense to know that I'm going to be dead by this time tomorrow. So are you. He couldn't sleep if he really believed that. Was Romy who said it anyway."

Romy's eyes were barely visible under her dark fringe, her mouth buried in her jacket sleeve.

"It doesn't matter how he can do it, or why, I suppose," she said. "He's sleeping. Maybe all he has to do if run faster than any of us, or further... and he might have a chance."

"I told you, we have to stick together," said Gazwan, glancing at Aaron. "If we stick together, we can-"

"What? Become bulletproof?" said Greg. "If we get shot then it-"

"Have you ever seen it? Someone shot?" Gazwan said. It was almost as if his brush with death had emboldened him, pushed him out of his shell.

Greg sighed. "You know I haven't," he said.

"Well, I have. It is not good. And it is not something I would wish on you. Or any of us. We have to help each other for as long as we can. It is the only way. If that means we run for the water, like Romy said... that's what we need to do."

Romy and Greg shared a look.

"What do you think?" Romy said, her blue eyes locking on Aaron's. "You've been quiet. Out there, was that... *you know who*?"

Aaron nodded.

"You know him?" Greg said.

"He's... my Grandad," Aaron said, his chin still cupped in his hands. "The house I tried to rob... it was his. I held a knife to him, locked my Gran and her carer in a room. Tried to get into his safe."

He leant back in his chair and folded his arms, awaiting an onslaught from Greg that never came. Gazwan bowed his head, his new hero toppled within minutes.

"Shit," Greg said, after a few moments. "You really did do the stupidest thing, didn't you?"

Aaron stared at Greg, watching as a grin crept onto his face. To Aaron's surprise, he found himself smirking back, and like conspiratorial children in a school assembly, they began to laugh.

* * *

Despite his bluster, Greg had managed to fall asleep in one corner of the room, the exhaustion of his three weeks finally beating him into submission. Maria and Gazwan had done the same, with similar ease, leaving Romy and Aaron alone at the window, watching the fire outside slowly die.

"Do you think it's gonna work?" Romy said. Aaron turned to face her, but her eyes remained fixed on the darkening world outside.

"What?"

"The plan."

"Maybe," Aaron said. "Either that or we try and fight back, like Gazwan said."

"It's a death wish," said Romy. "The only way is to run."

"Well, I can do that," Aaron said. "Although running's what got me into this shit in the first place."

Romy turned to him them, touched his arm gently as she spoke.

"You think this guy is really gonna do something to your Mum, if you don't get out of here?"

Aaron ground his teeth, his eyes welling up with tears of rage as he pictured the scene over and over. All of the horrendous things Dave and O'Brien might cook up if he thought Aaron had tried to disappear. His Mum's face, contorted in agony.

"I'm not even thinking about it," Aaron said, his voice little more than a crackle. "If you imagine it, there's more chance it might happen. It's exactly how it went down at the house. You plan for shit and... you make it real; you know? I think my brain always knew I was gonna use that knife, that tape. Deep down. When I saw that old house, and the back steps and the kitchen... Nothing had changed. I felt safe again, you know? Like when I used to go there as a kid. I thought it might all work out... but then you panic, and that thing in your head that was just plan B starts to look like a better shout. So, that's what I'd say – fuck plan Bs."

26

Charles

Charles had made sure to check in with Liana and Phyllis every few hours since his arrival at Barden Hall, though very little seemed to change from call to call. Even so, it had softened Charles to hear their voices – Phyllis placid and innocent, Liana firm and maternal – removing him from the emotional turmoil of his current situation, if only for a few minutes.

As soothing as that was, the escapism would do him no favours today.

He rose from the wing chair where he had passed out in the early hours of the morning and stuffed his old mobile phone into his bag, muffling it, along with any more calming thoughts of home. After washing quickly, he dressed in his hunting tweeds and high boots, picked up his weapons and ammunition, and headed downstairs to the atrium.

The house and lawn outside were already teeming with activity after what can only have been a few hours of silence. Charles was surprised to see groundsman and stable boys, rather than maids, clearing up discarded plastic cups and cutlery, paper plates and Styrofoam boxes, and a number of guests were already making their way outside, dressed for the hunt.

Charles stepped outside into the cold, his rifle and his shotgun slung over his shoulder.

He stepped down onto the drive and inhaled the crisp, new November; the powder blue skies above clear but for a few ripples of cloud. He looked over the lawn and noticed a thin veil of smoke still emanating from the husk of the bonfire, the charred wood and debris crumbled to half the size it had been the previous evening.

Out here, Charles gained a better understanding of the scale of the debauchery he'd missed. Cups and cigarette butts and small plastic bags were strewn all around the bonfire, as well as a few items of clothing. More busy groundsmen were weaving past each other on the lawn, instinctive like salmon in a stream, occasionally stopping to stab at the earth with their spear-tipped litter pickers.

A few of the hunters were already gathered at the edge of the drive, talking, smoking, and preparing their weapons. The appetising smells of fresh coffee and toast clashed were soiled by the musk of the open stables. Hounds were already beginning to appear from their kennels around the far side of the house.

"Charles," said Matthew Reeves, his voice tired and hoarse. He was stood with Wheeler, Ashton, and O'Brien again, the same men he encountered here the day before. "We missed you last night," Matthew croaked.

Charles shrugged the guns off his shoulder as he approached and stood them on the gravel in front of him.

"I was inside," Charles said. "Babysitting."

Reeves snorted. "Yes, the fruit of my loins," he said. "I'm dreadfully sorry about that. He described you as the man who put him in his place, and I told him he'd gotten off lightly. Rest assured he's learned his lesson. Thank you, for not... being too hard on him."

Charles nodded, grunted his agreement.

"You look fresher than any of us, mate," O'Brien said, his accent made even more garbled by the alcohol that was still clearly thundering through his veins.

"I had to practically drag this bear from his bed," said Matthew, slapping O'Brien on his thick shoulder. "A damn sight too much of the old man's mead."

O'Brien laughed, though Charles thought he looked almost sheepish for a second. "And the rest. I'll be alright, mate... don't you worry."

"Perhaps you should go back to your bed, Mr O'Brien," said Charles. "Leave the money and the mayhem for the rest of us."

The big man stopped laughing, cocked his head to the side as much as his tree trunk neck would allow.

"Don't you worry pal, I'll be right as rain when it kicks off," he said.

Charles flashed a smile at him and walked over to where Holdsworth was stood, talking to the head 'keeper, Swire.

"Eh, Morty," O'Brien shouted after him. "You better make sure you get to your lad before I do... or he won't be getting shot, he'll be getting his fucking head sawn off."

27

Aaron

The soberness in the room was suffocating. Everyone was now rooted to whichever spot in the room they'd chosen after taking turns to swill water from the bathroom tap and splash a little on their faces. That is, with the exception of Greg, who was on his knees in the corner of the room, retching into an ornate marble plant pot.

Although Aaron had made up his mind that Greg was a dick, it was hard to feel anything but sympathy for him now. In the hours since he'd woken, Greg had been hysterical; pounding at the door and the windows, screaming, and shaking the rest of the group into action, despite the fact that they were all too exhausted to really acknowledge him.

Aaron went to the bathroom to fill a cup with cold water, then tucked the cleanest towel he could find under his arm and sauntered over to Greg. He sat on the floor next to the giant plant pot and waited for Greg to finish throwing up.

"Here you are, mate," Aaron said, handing over the towel. He waited for Greg to wipe his mouth, then swapped him for the water.

"Thanks," Greg said, eagerly bringing the cup to his quivering lips.

Aaron waited for him to drink, then took the cup from him and placed it on the floor next to the soiled towel.

"I just... I can't believe this is happening," said Greg, who was starting to sob. "I can't believe this is how it ends. Like... I just wanted to do something good, you know? Just wanted to help, and they... why would they want to do this to me? Like, to me, personally? They're gonna shoot me like an animal, and for what? For the sheer fucking thrill of it? I just don't understand how this is happening. How is this for real?"

"Never mind all that now, mate," Aaron said, patting Greg's back. "Anyway, it could still work. If we can cover our tracks somehow, maybe we can still find a way out of this."

Greg forced a snide laugh, still apparently suspicious of any show of optimism.

"You've not seen what it's like," Greg said. "You can already hear them out there, there's gonna be a load of them. Horses and dogs. Guns. We haven't got a chance."

"So... what are you gonna do, once it starts?"

Greg tried to pull his mouth into a grin, though it ended up being more of a twitch.

"Who cares?" He said weakly. "Doesn't matter now... how you want to get there, we're all going to the same place. We're all gonna die. If you run, try and hide or fight or... It's useless. You're just delaying the-"

Greg was cut off by the clunking of a key in the door. Everyone stood and fell in line as the two guards entered, pistols in hand again. They each dropped black bin bags onto the floor and kicked them over, spilling their contents into the middle of the room.

"Put those on," the bald guard said. "All of you. Two minutes."

As the door slammed, the six began edging towards the bags. Aaron got there first and knelt down, pulling a tweed jacket from the nearest bag. It was ragged and worn at the elbows, ingrained dirt and something darker than dirt staining the lapels. He looked up to see Maria examining a matching pair of trousers, while Romy pulled a muddy white shirt from the bag.

The texture of the fabric prickled Aaron's fingers, sending shivers up his arms, all the way to his collar bone. It was as if his body needed something this tangible to realise the seriousness of the situation, to begin firing adrenaline through every vein in his body. He felt like he was going to be sick, right there into the bin bag.

"Fuck," Romy said, her voice barely more than a whisper. "This is it. This is what they want you to wear. There's these fucking masks too, these-"

Romy trailed off as Aaron pulled a handful of rubber from the bag and dropped all but one of them to the floor. There was an audible gasp as he unfurled the mask in his hands, and silence as he sat there and stared into the hollow eyes of a fox.

* * *

Bayley and Maria complied straight away, cobbling together the best fitting suit they could find, while the others argued among themselves about how worthwhile it was to follow orders when they would end up dead in a matter of hours either way. Greg's points were made quickly through the gritted teeth of someone fighting back vomit. Even Aaron considered running to the toilet to force himself to do it. Anything to give his body some release from the pins and needles that stabbed at his skin, the shaking and the cold sweat that clung to his face. It wasn't long before the guards and their guns returned and, after the bald one had shown Aaron's his frustration with a sharp knee in the stomach, the rest of the group eventually gave in.

Picking a suit was mostly just a question of measurements – finding trousers that were snug enough not to fall down while running, a jacket that wasn't so tight as to restrict movement – but the whole psychology of the exercise changed when it came to choosing a mask.

It went from being a cold, practical decision, to being something that forced you to have some kind of preference. To pick which mask you'd most like to die in, to decide which animal you wanted to look like as you breathed your last ragged breaths and shit your borrowed tweed trousers.

Aaron did the most automatic thing he could and chose the one he'd first pulled from the bag, the fox. Maria picked up the doe, Gazwan the badger, and Bayley the rat. Romy eventually decided she'd feel the least stupid as the relatively subtle otter, which left Greg with the dramatic-looking horned owl.

Charles

Charles was helping the stable hand adjust the stirrups on his horse when the grim menagerie appeared from the house's main door. As far as he could see, there was definitely three of them tall and broad enough to be men, while two of the three others could have been either. The one bringing up the rear, disguised as a doe, was so small and slight that it could only have been a woman. The longer he watched them trudge along the gravel, assessing their gait and their builds, he was almost certain that the bearded man Archie Reeves almost executed was the badger, which meant that Aaron had either been cast as the wise old owl, or – more fittingly – the cunning, vicious fox. The quintessential country prey.

He was distracted from his assessment by a feeble voice from behind.

"Erm... 'scuse me, Mr Mortimer," it was Archie Reeves, looking decidedly less grown up in a dark fleece and jeans than he did in his tuxedo.

Charles raised an eyebrow as he spoke. "What is it?"

"I just wanted to say that... everything last night. All that with the buy-ins and stuff... I spoke to my Dad and he, erm... I'm sorry, is what I'm trying to say. And thank you for not, you know, taking it any further."

Charles nodded. The boy hung around for a few more seconds, just in case Charles had any more to say, but he did not.

"Happy hunting," he said, and scurried off to stand next to his friend, who was leant on a muddy quad bike and fiddling with a small, handheld video camera.

Charles looked back over to the lawn and saw the prey being lined up, shoulder to shoulder, then forced to their knees.

Aaron

Aaron's breath was loud inside the fox mask, making the rest of the world outside seem silent by comparison. This, along with the softness of the dew-soaked grass and the rolling mist ahead, made him feel as if he was wearing a space suit and walking on an alien planet, with only grotesque animal human hybrids for company. At least they'd given him his trainers back, he thought.

Once they were dressed, they'd been forced to put on the masks at gunpoint, then one of the guards had gone along the line and sealed them in, one by one, with a few passes of duct tape around their necks.

As they stepped out of the house, Aaron glanced at a crowd of people dressed in long coats of bright red and dark blue. Some were holding long rifles, comparing them, while others were stood next to huge thoroughbred horses, the breath of both man and beast turning to steam in the cold morning air.

The guards led them over the grass to a spot around 20 metres from the drive and started forcing them to their knees. He looked across to Romy – the otter – and could see the whites of her eyes trembling through the ragged holes in her mask as they were made to kneel on the ground.

Aaron's whole body was coursing with adrenaline, like angry needles pricking the skin on his arms and thighs and the backs of his hands. He tried to slow his breathing, or regulate it at least, but it was like his lungs were working on a higher level, outside of his control. His legs were juddering automatically too, grinding his knees into the wet grass, inviting the dew to seep into the tweed.

Gazwan was muttering to himself in a language Aaron didn't recognise, most likely praying, he thought. Maria was doing the same. The way she was crossing her chest, Aaron thought she was trying to get hold of the same God that he might have, if he believed it would do any good.

Neither of them was distracted from their whispering when Greg started to shout, standing and turning as he screamed at the guards that were standing behind them. After he realised that any talk of using his parents' money to sway these people was laughable, he started to throw one wild bribe after another their way.

"I'll do anything, I'll help you," he said, his lip juddering as he babbled. "I'll get others here, other sabs. I promise. I can make it up to you, honestly, please you don't have to do this. I can even-"

"Shut the fuck up Greg!" Romy screamed, cutting him off. "They don't care. Just fucking shut up for fuck's sake."

A guard stepped forward, clapped a hand on his shoulder and forced him back onto his knees.

"You get up again, and I'll start cutting bits off you, alright?" he said. "You can still run with no fingers, so listen to her and shut the fuck up. Get some fucking bollocks."

The guard slapped him on the back of the head as he fell back into line, knocking Greg forward onto his elbows.

After a few more moments of near silence, a commotion began to bubble up behind them. Aaron glanced over his shoulder to see two men coming down the house's front steps.

Charles

When Sir William emerged with Holdsworth at his side to steady him, Charles couldn't help but feel a swell of adrenaline that he hadn't experienced for decades. The hunt was near. Just a few formalities – mostly symptoms of Sir William's prehistoric beliefs – and they would be allowed to begin.

"Ok chaps," said Matthew, striding to the front of the

185

hunting party and clapping his hands together. "I'm sure you all know the rules, but just humour me alright?"

The group muttered their assent. Although the 20-strong party was mostly made up of old and familiar faces, Charles was surprised that – along with a handful of new, and possibly unscrupulous, money like O'Brien – there were three relatively young women dressed in livery and armed with rifles. Daughters, he thought, or maybe even wives, of some of the regulars. As far as he knew, no woman had even taken part in one of these hunts, anywhere in the world; at least not while he was helping to organise them.

"First horn is for them, the second is for us," Matthew began. "From then on, we pursue until we come across one or all of them, depending on what they try. As you'd expect, it's first come first served. We pay the killing shot. That means limbs, non-lethal wounds, get you nothing. We're here for the sport, not to torture them. I'm looking at you, Mr O'Brien."

Charles couldn't help but wince as amusement bubbled up around him, O'Brien looking as pleased as any of them at the sound of his own name. Charles had attended and even participated in countless hunts, and he had never, for one second, found it to be a laughing matter.

Servants appeared then with small glasses of brandy balanced on silver platters and began distributing them among the group.

"Also," Matthew said. "And I know this seems obvious, but any actions taken to hinder or assault another hunter is absolutely forbidden. Any issues that transpire out there can be settled back here at the house. Health and safety, for the newbies, really; do just be mindful of the hounds and the quad while you're riding... and be careful as you cross the tree line –

186

it's quite thick and there's plenty in there that can catch you off guard. No sense in spending all this money and being killed by falling from your horse. Alright, good... Now that's out of the way."

He took a brandy and held it aloft, waited for everyone gathered to do the same.

"For those about to die, for those about to take lives, the mantra is the same: we will not relent, we will not stop, until the last drop of blood has been spilled. Until the last drop."

Charles knew they were entering into an unofficial oath by repeating the words, but Sir William's pagan beliefs meant as little to him as any other religion. He raised his glass, out of politeness, much like he would bow his head during prayers at a funeral or remove his shoes before entering a Shinto temple. It meant nothing and neither did the words that followed.

"Until the last drop."

The group all drained their glasses and cheered. Matthew returned his glass and started walking towards the lawn, then stopped and pressed his finger to his lips.

"Oh, sorry, there is one more thing," he said. "The rat, the little one on the end. He's to be left until last. I'll explain more at the time... but no one takes him until I've given the word... That alright?"

Murmurs passed through the crowd, though any joking seemed more reserved this time. Charles simply picked up his guns and walked over to the men and horses waiting at the side of the house.

28

Aaron

It felt like Aaron had been staring at the fields for hours. Now the mist had finally cleared, everything ahead of him looked almost fake in its simplicity, like one of those expensive paintings that seemed like nothing more than a bunch of coloured lines, something even a child could reproduce. Drab green fields leading up to a solid wall of brown and yellow leaves, with only the clear blue of the sky above. Even through the eye holes of his mask, the world looked so massive out here, virtually endless.

The perfection was finally spoiled as two old men came into view: one straight-backed and stern, a lot like Charles, and the other hunched and feeble. They were both dressed differently than the hunters, the younger man in a plain grey suit and the ancient one in all black, his strange jacket buttoned all the way up to his throat.

They came to Gazwan, who was at the far left of the line, and Black Suit touched his forehead and muttered something and moved on to Maria, who was on Aaron's left. He did the same her, and Aaron thought the word he muttered was 'pray'. He could have meant 'prey' instead, Aaron thought, as either made sense. Gazwan and Maria both were still whispering mantras to themselves, almost oblivious of the two men.

Once they were finished with Maria, Grey Suit helped Black Suit over to Aaron, where they stopped and looked on for a few seconds. Aaron raised his head to see Black Suit staring straight at him.

He was so wrinkled that Aaron struggled to find a patch of skin on his face that was smooth. One of his eyes was squinted more than the other, which twisted his thin lips into a kind of permanent smirk, and the last few tufts of white hair on his head looked as sturdy as dandelion seeds.

He raised his stubby right hand, which was balled into a fist with the thumb outstretched. The underside was completely black with what looked like soot or charcoal, or maybe even oily paint. Black Suit pushed his thumb into the forehead of Aaron's mask, then said the word again.

"Prey."

He stepped back and nodded, then moved down the line to Romy to continue this strange ritual.

Suddenly, as Black Suit was assessing his next plaything, voices rose up all around them, causing Aaron first to look back at the crowd, who were all looking back at him. The guards lurched forwards out of their line, towards Greg, who had hauled himself to his feet and broken into a run.

Charles

Charles whipped around to see Owl Mask sprinting past Sir William and Holdsworth and towards the long drive that led back towards the estate's main gate. While everyone else was gasping and laughing and pointing, Charles shrugged his guns off his shoulder; allowing the shotgun to fall to the gravel and snatching the rifle across his body.

"Hang on, what's he playing at?" said O'Brien.

"Shit, sorry, yes," said Matthew. He raised his voice. "A runner's fair game. Wait for Sir William to clear and he's all yours."

Charles thumbed a bullet into the chamber of his Remington and slapped the bolt into place and drove the butt into the shoulder that had welcomed it thousands of times before. Others fell in beside him, cocking and loading and sharing nervous jokes.

Charles' jaw pulsed against the stock as he settled his crosshairs on Owl Mask's back, dead centre of the shoulder blades. He was zig zagging wildly, but the adrenaline had clearly turned his legs to jelly. Charles glanced away from the scope to watch the guards hurrying the prey and Sir William back towards the house, but there was some kind of problem with one or two of the former tangling with the guards.

A piercing crack came from Charles' right. It was O'Brien, his smoking rifle still held firmly in firing position. He pulled the trigger again and again, his semi-automatic weapon allowing him to fire without manually reloading like Charles would have to.

Although O'Brien's shots were numerous, the dirt they kicked up showed that he was a novice marksman at best. Dropping a moving target at 100 yards was difficult enough, and Owl Mask would soon be well past that if Sir William's sluggishness continued to stall the other, more sensible, hunters.

"Enough," said Matthew, taking hold of the stock of

O'Brien's rifle. "Let the guards get him. He's going nowhere."

A few others fired off speculative shots, but Matthew raised his voice again.

"It's alright, it's done. They'll get on the quad and grab him and we'll get back on schedule in a moment. Charles?"

Charles hadn't moved, and still had his rifle pointed at the fleeing owl, who was now almost 200 yards away. He held on longer still, until he saw Holdsworth and Sir William make it onto the gravel, then took a step forward and sighted again.

He would have liked to go prone at this distance, or even drop to one knee, but Owl Mask was now running downhill towards the path and it would have made the shot even more difficult than it already was. He watched for a few more seconds, trusting the advertised dip of the bullet – *three inches of drop at 200 yards* – and slowly squeezed the trigger.

The rifle snapped, then the filling burst from Owl Mask's jacket where the lead punched into his back, sending him staggering forwards into the wet grass. Gun smoke filled Charles' nostrils as he lowered the rifle, keeping his eyes fixed on the path of the bullet. Instead of admiring the shot, like those around him, Charles ejected the shell casing and quickly reloaded while Owl Mask got shakily to his feet and turned to face them.

This time there wasn't the added the difficulty of leading a moving target, so Charles simply sighted again and fired. The round connected solidly with the owl's head, putting him down for good. Even if he wasn't dead by the time that he'd hit the ground, he wouldn't last longer than a minute or two. Charles imagined him, staring up at the open sky through the holes in his rubber mask, the eyes wide within as he felt the strength drain from his body.

191

"Fuck me," O'Brien said, adding a long whistle for comic effect. "They said you were a pro, didn't they, but... fucking hell. How far is-"

"Just under 200 yards," said Charles, lowering the rifle. He turned to Matthew, who was standing open mouthed behind them. "What's he worth, the runner?"

"Jesus, I don't... Erm I'm not 100 percent sure. Of course, there's-"

"Minimum," Charles said, ejecting the spent cartridge and stooping to pick them both off the ground.

"At least a quarter mil' I suppose. Good morning's work, eh?"

The crowd's shock turned to gentle laughter, though Charles could sense that this was the first death some of them had seen. A woman with a mass of bleach-blonde hair tucked underneath her riding helmet and the scrawny man next to her both looked as if they were ready to vomit.

"Good," Charles said. "Was it him?"

Matthew looked startled, glancing around at the others as if Charles had let slip some candid secret.

"I... I'm not sure. I can check, if-"

"No, don't bother. Makes no difference."

"Ok... alright then," Matthew turned to face the rest of them. "Right, everyone get yourselves mounted up and we'll try this again, shall we? So much for the wise old owl, eh?"

29

Aaron

The group were eventually moved back onto the lawn as a handful of groundsmen were sent in a Land Rover to fetch Greg's body. As soon as Greg had decided to run, Grey Suit had yelled at the guards not to give chase, or to fire on Greg as he sprinted away. He had looked ridiculous as he ran towards the long, snaking driveway; his out-of-time, flailing limbs somehow working together to keep him on his feet until the first bullet hit.

Aaron had felt it too, that second shot. Not just the shock from Charles' rifle, but the audible crack as it connected with Greg's skull. It had taken all of his self-control not to vomit inside his cloying rubber mask.

"You will run through the fields and head for that tree line, on the sounding of the first horn," Grey Suit said, pointing towards the forest. "The hunt will begin on the sounding of the second. Then you're on your own. If you have any more preparations to make, or prayers to say, I suggest you do so in the next minute."

He disappeared with that, leaving the six of them on their knees, staring at the rolling fields ahead. Aaron looked to his left, then his right, for some kind of cue as to how the others were processing what was about to happen, but everyone seemed to be lost in their own thoughts, oblivious to anything or anyone but the lawn and the forest and the sky in front of them.

Aaron was still juddering on the spot, looking up at the blue, then down and the green, then ahead. There was nothing to think about yet, no plan A, B, or C to make. All they had to do was run. He could run, he knew he could, and he was quite confident of those by his side. The one he'd worried for most, in terms of their physical stamina, was Greg. Clearly, that was a worry he no longer needed.

He looked over his shoulder to see the red and blue coated hunters mounting their horses, being handed rifles and shot-guns by submissive stable hands. The dogs were straining at their masters' leashes, barking hungrily, then a boy stepped out onto the drive and put a shining brass horn to his lips and blew a long, searing note.

* * *

The whole world began to thunder and shake as Aaron lurched to his feet and broke into the most desperate sprint of his life. Every fibre of his being was focussed on the tree line, all other sound drowned out by the ragged, rasping breaths trapped inside his mask.

A few seconds after he had gotten up to speed, the tiny frame of Bayley in his rat's head mask came streaking into his peripheral vision. He didn't even seem to be moving his legs much faster than Aaron was, but the way he ate up the ground made it look as if he was running along an airport Trav-O-Lator.

He clambered over the first wooden fence without breaking stride and was already off across the next field by the time Aaron reached it. He took hold of the top beam and hauled himself over, his jelly legs making the whole thing take much longer than it should have. He caught a glimpse of the rest of the group as he dropped down into the next field, Gazwan a towering figure in his badger mask next to the two women.

Aaron didn't wait for them, turning on his heel and sprinting after Bayley, who'd taken a diagonal route across the field so he could jump the iron gate instead of trying to battle over or through the thick hedgerow at the far end.

Aaron followed Bayley's lead, and once he cleared the second obstacle, he saw that the tree line was painfully close. Just one more fence and it was a clear run across the final field, whose slope would help them when they needed it most. His lungs and his limbs were both threatening to give up, but everything looked more real now than it had before and was even more inviting as a result. It wasn't just a wall of trees anymore, but a deep, tangled mess of bracken and bushes and brambles, guarded by a few rows of tall pines. It looked like sanctuary.

There looked to be some kind of path over to the right; worn tyre tracks with grass tufting up in between them, the trees parting to let them through. Bayley was already aware, sprinting straight for it, apparently unfazed by the jagged half mile they'd already ran. Aaron could sense the others at his back, as far away from him as he was from Bayley, their desperate feet sucking and slipping over the sodden grass.

195

The morning light was snuffed out as soon as they burst over the tree line, the undergrowth so thick that it held the cold inside, making the forest feel more like a walk-in fridge. Bayley was still sprinting ahead, his light feet barely touching the potholed path, while Gazwan was now close behind, followed by Romy, then Maria.

There was a small clearing up ahead where the canopy of the forest was open, creating a kind of tree-lined courtyard. Just as Bayley was illuminated by the light from above, Aaron heard a snap and a stumble, followed by a shriek of agony, which caused him to stop in his tracks.

As he was turning, Gazwan slammed into him, sending them both tumbling into a wheezing heap on the floor. The smell of damp earth was so strong that it surprised Aaron, as if any odour that hadn't been held inside that stuffy room was somehow brand new to him.

He rolled sideways and looked down the path to see Romy doing her best to haul Maria to her feet, though Maria was so concerned with her left ankle that she seemed oblivious to the rest of them shouting her name.

"Come on, Maria, get up," Romy said, trying drag her through the mud. A thin string of blood was dribbling from the left eye hole of Maria's mask.

"Stop, stop please. My ankle, please get off me, stop."

Gazwan pushed himself to his feet and went over to help, tearing off the tape, then his mask as he went and hurling it into the bracken. Aaron looked towards the clearing as he stood, quickly realising that Bayley was long gone.

"Little fucker," he said in between gasps.

He sat up, then tore the tape from his own neck and ripped the fox mask off, the cold air stinging his face. As he reached

196

his three tangled companions, Aaron couldn't help but hear their time ticking away with every failed attempt to get Maria to her feet. He noticed a particularly gnarled tree root in the path behind her, its thickest part like a wooden elbow poking up out of the mud. The longer he looked, the more amazed he was that the rest of them had managed to miss it.

"What's wrong with her?" He said. "Come on, just pick her up."

"It's her ankle, look," said Romy. Aaron winced as he saw that Maria's foot looked almost as twisted as the tree root itself. "She won't move,"

Although Gazwan had hold of Maria's other arm, it wasn't doing much to resolve the problem.

"Come on Maria, for fuck's sake," said Romy. "We haven't got time for this, come on."

"Wait, move back, I'll do it. Please, wait," said Gazwan, gently easing Romy out of the way so he could stoop and haul Maria to her one good foot. Her groaning was muffled by her mask as he took her weight and straightened up, though his own face was already sheened with sweat.

"Are you serious?" Romy said. "We'll never make it with her like that."

Gazwan glanced at Aaron, his brow furrowed, then back at Romy. If they were in any other situation, it would have been impossible to take Romy seriously with her otter head still in place, but Aaron could almost feel Charles' presence at his back with each passing second.

"What else can we do?" said Gazwan. "We can't leave her."

"We can," said Romy, starting towards Aaron. "We have to."

"What? What do you mean?" said Maria through moans.

197

Romy started working on her duct tape collar then, while Gazwan looked between them all, looking more and more frantic with each movement of his head. Maria was still trying to convince Gazwan to let her sit back down, but he ignored her, keeping his eyes fixed on Romy as she finally unmasked.

"Don't," he said, his voice barely more than a whisper. "We have to stick together. Romy you said that-"

"Just look at Greg. He did something stupid and now he's... fucking... Look we don't have time for this. Come on."

"She's right," said Aaron. "Mate, I'm sorry but she's right. We're all dead if you're carrying her like that. It's shit but-"

"Aaron," Gazwan said.

"Aaron," Romy this time, even more insistent. "Come on. He won't listen, I know he won't. We can still do this if we go now."

She stuffed her mask and the ball of tape in the inside pocket of her tweed jacket, then set off running towards the clearing. Aaron looked at Gazwan, his pleading eyes and the wounded doe leaning on his shoulder.

"Aaron, come *on*," said Romy, her voice splintering now.

The forest was silent but for Maria's moans and the sound of their collective wheezing. Aaron met Gazwan's gaze and was about to speak when the next piercing note came from the horn back at the house. The sound of it was as loud and clear as if the boy was just a few feet away from them. Aaron's stomach lurched.

"I'm sorry," he said.

He looked at Gazwan and Maria for a second longer, then stuffed the mask in his pocket and turned on his heel and sprinted after Romy.

30

Charles

As soon as the second horn sounded, it felt to Charles as if the morning had recoiled in fear. Horses lurched forward and hounds darted in between them and shot off across the lawn like missiles towards the woods. Masters and keepers drew level on quad bikes, their acrid exhaust fumes polluting the cold, crisp air. Matthew's son, Archie, was at the head of the convoy with his friend clutching a camera with one hand and the back of the quad with the other.

Charles squared his jaw and focussed on getting to the head of the pack, easing past the other riders with a combination of poise and determination. It was the first time he'd ridden in almost a decade, and the half tonne of horse he was attempting to control felt unwieldy beneath him.

The rest of the hunters were bantering with each other as they picked up speed. O'Brien, Wheeler, and Matthew were galloping hard out in front, and laughing even harder, as they approached the first fence.

All three of them cleared it with ease and somehow Charles

matched them, though he felt the landing shake his bones and twinge muscles he'd almost forgotten existed. The hounds poured from the open gate to their left, drawn over the ground by the lingering scent of their quarry preserved by the cold morning air.

After a hedge, then another low fence, the charge approached the treeline. Archie and the other quads broke off to the left, presumably to use a separate path, while the horses and hounds fell into single file and surged through the same entrance that the prey had used a few minutes before.

The thundering of hooves was muffled as they ducked under the canopy one by one, replaced by the sound of wet leaves and undergrowth being whipped aside. Around 300 yards into the forest, the barking up ahead intensified and the horses came to a stop. Charles craned his neck to see past Wheeler, towards Matthew and O'Brien at the head of the line.

He saw Matthew dismount and go digging around in the bracken, one hand steadying the rifle still slung around his shoulder. He shooed a pair of agitated hounds out of his way, then reached down and picked up the discarded badger mask. He turned towards them with a grin, holding it up like the severed head of a vanquished foe.

"Yep, this is them alright," he said. "They always bloody come the same way. It's almost too easy sometimes, eh?"

He strutted over and stuffed the mask into the flap of his saddle. Just as he was about to swing himself back up, his hand already on the pommel, his attention seemed to be taken by the hounds, which had come a few yards back down the path, level with O'Brien.

"Reeves," he said, becoming increasingly concerned as the hounds weaved through the legs of his horse. "Can you sort these out or what?"

"Just try to stay still," Matthew said as he approached. "What on earth are you-"

He stopped mid-sentence as the hounds dispersed, staring open-mouthed at the spot that had so interested them.

"What is it?" said Charles.

"Blood."

"Blood?" echoed O'Brien, still struggling to keep his horse in check. "They fallen out already?"

"Or injured," said Charles.

Matthew stood and laughed. "I hope not," he said. "Could end up being a very short morning. Either way, if the hounds didn't have their scent before, they've certainly got it now."

Gazwan

Gazwan tried to focus on forward motion and they stumbled on, rather than the dead weight of Maria dragging him down to the forest floor. Her ankle had already swollen up to twice its size, and her forehead was still streaming blood from where it had slammed into the ground. With every shuffling step, the mulch sucked hungrily at their shoes, conspiring to hold them until the hunters came to take them.

Although Gazwan had forced himself to chant a steady stream of encouragement as he set off carrying Maria, his depleting energy had eventually stilled his tongue. Now, every sinew of his body was straining just to put one foot in front of the other.

The trees that had been so close and welcoming when the group first entered the forest were now spaced far apart like strangers, indifferent to the two foreigners struggling to find a path on their own. It was like the trees had their backs turned; an awkward silence settled between them. Every so often a bird would call out from somewhere unseen, loud as gunfire, sending both Gazwan and Maria's heads twisting from side to side like frightened mice.

"Stop," Maria said. "Please, just stop... I can't."

"Maria," Gazwan tried to hold on to her arm but she struggled free and slumped onto her backside.

"Romy was right," she said, staring at her useless ankle. "This won't work. You know it. You have to leave me."

"This is crazy, don't do this. You'll never-"

"It doesn't matter. I can't go any more. It's too painful."

"They will be here soon; they will kill you."

Maria looked up at him and forced a sad smile through her tears.

"I died the moment I agreed to get on the plane," she said.

Gazwan dropped to his knees and pulled her into his chest. He lowered his face into her hair and closed his eyes. She had always done her best to wash daily, to maintain her routine in despite their situation, but her hair felt greasy now against his skin. Smelled stale, musty, just like the room and its moth-eaten furniture.

"I cannot do this to you."

"You have to," she said, gently easing them apart. "The only way these people will stop is if somebody stops them. What if my sister comes over here next, or your brothers? What if the same people bring them to this house? I believe Romy. She can stop this."

"She left us," said Gazwan. "She cares only about herself."

"She knows that her story is the only way to beat these people. If she gets away, she can tell the world and they will listen. Who would believe us, even if we do survive? No, it has to be her. We have to help her."

"Help her? How?"

"Run," Maria said. She nodded firmly as she spoke, shaking tears free from her glistening cheeks. "Run as far as you can, for as long as you can. If they are chasing you, they are not chasing her. Please, Gazwan... do this for me. Please."

Gazwan clenched his jaw as he considered this, pushed himself up and surveyed the forest. Although there was very little to help him in terms of landmarks, he did notice what looked to be some kind of natural irrigation ditch or stream running down the left-hand side of the forest. He thought for a moment, trying to balance the risk, but the faint sound of barking in the distance spurred him into action.

"Ok, stand up, come on. Stand," he said, helping Maria to her feet. "I will go, but first I will help you hide. Over there, behind those bushes, there is a ditch. If there is water, it might cover the smell. Maybe they will follow me instead, if the smell is stronger. Come on, I will take you."

31

Charles

The hunting party followed the path through a clearing, then into the forest proper, the horses slowing to make sense of the uneven ground. The hounds had been reenergised at the smell and taste of fresh blood, sniffing every pine needle and fallen leaf as they surged through the trees as relentless as a tidal wave.

The crisp morning had barely been allowed to permeate the canopy, meaning the air they had to breathe now seemed older, more intense. An ancient, earthy odour that felt like it had been preserved inside a cavernous vault of bark and branches and leaves. It almost made Charles feel some empathy for Sir William's anachronistic beliefs. After all, with this kind of portal into the past on his doorstep, who wouldn't begin to become dwarfed by the thought of how many years this country and its wilds had existed independent of man?

Despite his flamboyant assurances prior to the hunt, O'Brien was clearly uncomfortable on a horse, on this type of terrain at least. This meant they were having to slow the pace to accommodate him, but it had the added advantage of keeping him quiet now he was having to concentrate on preventing his mount from throwing him into a nearby tree.

Charles eased past him at a canter to draw level with Matthew, who smiled broadly to acknowledge him.

"We're close," Matthew said. "Even I can smell it now, Mortimer. You can tell the masters to send the hounds back home."

Charles ignored Matthew's excitement. He had no interest in making what was to come seem anything other than what it was. He simply came to the front, so he'd have the best chance of getting the first sight of their prey.

Matthew was about to begin boasting again when the hounds' chatter suddenly intensified to a chorus of full-throated barks. They appeared to be converging on the same spot around 300 yards ahead, and from the way they were being forced to jump from one point to another, Charles guessed it must have been some kind of shallow ditch.

"Here we go," said Matthew, raising his voice to the trailing hunters. "Give each other a wide berth, ready your weapons. Looks like we've got one."

The hounds were surging in and out of the ditch now, clearly feeling far more confident around whatever or whoever they had found in there. Charles shrugged his rifle off his shoulder and laid it across his lap, still unloaded and with the safety still on. He squinted to try to discern what was happening in amongst the rippling wave of black and tan fur, but if there really was someone down there, they had clearly decided to gamble on being ignored. Unfortunately for them, it would pay someone at least a quarter of a million pounds to trust the hounds' noses.

205

The party finally approached the ditch in a rough kind of pincer movement, just in case whoever was in there decided to make a last-minute dash for freedom like the not-so-wise old owl. Charles thumbed a round into the chamber, loaded it, and nudged the safety off as his horse slowed to a stop.

Matthew dismounted as he did, while many of the others behind were content to stay on their horses and watch. A handful of them will turn tail and run before long, Charles thought. He could practically hear their stomachs lurching at the thought of what was to come.

A pair of men appeared on quad bikes from the back of the pack and began calling the hounds back to them, out of the line of fire.

"What's the procedure?" Charles said as they strode towards the ditch.

"Let's see what we've got first, shall we?" Matthew said, a strange glint in his eye.

Charles shouldered his rifle as the hounds surged in the opposite direction, brushing his legs as they hurried back towards their waiting masters. He planted a solid foot on the edge of the ditch, then slowly leant forward until his eyes met those of a startled woman, who was lying on her back under a patchwork blanket of brown and gold leaves.

"Well, well," said Matthew, lowering his rifle. He turned to the rest. "The doe, I believe."

The woman wasn't wearing her mask anymore but given how slight she was it seemed to Charles to be the most logical conclusion. Another two quads arrived as they stepped away; one driven by Archie with his cameraman friend on the back, and the other transporting the head 'keeper, John Swire, and his underkeeper, Danny Lees.

"Just the chaps," Matthew said, waving the two 'keepers over. "Can I borrow you two for a minute?"

Lees hopped off the back of the quad while Swire cut the engine. They both sauntered over, their eyes narrow with suspicion.

"It's alright, nothing messy," Matthew said with a snort. "Just grab her out of there would you? Thank you, splendid."

Matthew turned and walked towards the crowd as the two men slid down the banking to retrieve the doe, who was now shrieking her protests at an alarming pitch. Once they'd dragged her out, they dropped her onto the mud in a heap. A weeping wound on her forehead confirmed to Charles that it had been her blood the hounds had gotten a taste for on the path.

"She's injured," Swire said, pointing at the woman's leg. "That ankle."

"Shit. Ok," Matthew said, clapping his hands together again. "So, we've reached a bit of an impasse, it seems. I was going to turn this into another shootout, but if our doe has lost the ability to run then... that's that. Any suggestions? Who's interested?"

Charles turned to scan the faces of those gathered, many of whom recoiled in disgust at Matthew's question, just as Charles had suspected. He even noticed a few at the back of the group begin to whisper among themselves, itching to leave before the bloodletting began.

"I can't," said the woman who'd looked unwell back on the drive. "I'm... I can't. Please."

The man next to her did his best to reassure her while his horse began to become agitated at the softness of the forest floor, picking up its hooves and backing away. The man got

Matthew's attention with a shallow wave.

"I think we're going to... adjourn, Matthew, if that's alright? Perhaps the hors d'oeuvre last night, you know."

"Yes, us too," said another man. "Apologies."

The two couples smiled politely, turned their horses, and left as quickly as the terrain would allow.

"Well, it's not for everyone I suppose," said Matthew.

This got a laugh from those remaining.

"So," he continued. "Any takers?"

Charles raised his hand, as did O'Brien, Wheeler, and three others. Every one of them meant it too, Charles thought. Maybe none of them knew what it felt like to take a human life, or maybe they were all seasoned killers, but either way Charles knew he was going to have a fight on his hands.

"Alright, maybe we should-"

"She's mine," Charles said, turning his hard stare on each man with his hand raised. "Anyone that disagrees is welcome to settle it with me back at the house, in any way you see fit, but I'm taking her now."

The woman started to mumble again to herself, most likely in prayer, Charles thought. She had already given up. He snatched up his rifle and walked towards her, sending Swire and Lees retreating back towards the edge of the ditch.

"Hang on," said O'Brien, hopping down from his horse. "Hang on, hang on. Why does he get to do that? Why can't I do that?"

"Because you'll have to settle this with me," Charles said, turning back to him.

"Alright old timer, I know you're a good shot but let's not get silly, yeah? You know who I am?"

"I've no interest whatsoever in who you are. Stand back."

208

Charles levelled his rifle at O'Brien's chest, sending a ripples of disapproving sneers through the mounted hunters.

"Charles, Charles," said Matthew, lunging in between the two men. "Come on now... let's not get-"

"Stand down," Charles said again his eyes and his barrel both trained on O'Brien.

"What the fuck, mate? I'll have you fucking murdered in your sleep, you old-"

"Stand. Down. Now. I won't ask you again."

"Charles, that's enough, please."

"Alright, alright," said O'Brien, backing away with the palms of his hands on show. "Fucking hell grandad, you got a screw loose? You not done enough of 'em in your day?"

"I'm here for the money," said Charles, eventually lowering his weapon. "Nothing more, nothing less."

O'Brien flashed his teeth. "Is that right?"

Charles nodded.

"Tell you what then, and this is my word, yeah? I'll shake on it. What's she worth Reevesy lad?"

Matthew frowned. "Same as the other, I suppose. Around two-fifty."

"Alright, I'll take the hit," said O'Brien. "I'll pay you the two-fifty."

Charles' expression remained unmoved. "For what?"

"If that means she's mine. No rules."

"You think I'd trust *your* word on that much?" Charles said, looking O'Brien up and down.

"Look," Matthew said. "I can understand why you're... reluctant. Emotions are running high, we've all gotten a bit carried away with the, you know... It's totally understandable. But the longer we mess about, the more complicated all of this

209

is going to get. The rest of them could be bloody miles away by now, you know that. What do you say? Will you shake on it? You have my word this is as good as done. On my honour."

Matthew laid his hand gently over his own heart, as if that somehow gave legitimacy to his words. The way he was pandering to this thug, O'Brien, and whatever his foul intentions were, was beginning to turn Charles' stomach. He clenched his jaw as he thought, looking over at the doe, who was sobbing again quietly after finishing her prayers. Water was starting to drip from the canopy, cold on Charles' forehead. The start of a downpour outside the protection of the forest. He wiped the salty sweat from his upper lip with the back of his hand, then held it out towards O'Brien, who smirked and shook it gleefully.

"That's two hundred and fifty thousand, on top of the money from the first?" Charles said, turning to Matthew. The younger man popped out his lower lip and gave a curt nod.

"Then I'm done," Charles said, ejecting the shell from his rifle and slipping it into his jacket pocket.

"Done?" said Matthew.

"Yes. Half a million is more than enough for my needs, and this is turning into circus already. I don't know what you've advertised this as to these, people... But I want no more part of it. I'll wait at the house for my money."

Charles slung his rifle over his shoulder, hauled himself up onto his horse, and turned it to face the way they'd already come.

"Give my grandson my regards."

Charles yanked on the reins to start his horse cantering back towards the path. The commotion faded as he drew away from the crowd, though it was eventually drowned out by the blood-curdling cries of the injured woman's ordeal beginning. The screams continued to echo through the woods long after Charles had left, though he never once heard the sound of a mercy giving gunshot to silence them.

32

Aaron

"Aaron, hold on," Romy said, doubling over before she'd even finished speaking.

They had turned off the main path a few hundred yards after the clearing, still travelling at a jog despite the distance they'd already sprinted. Aaron felt as if he was breathing sulphur now instead of air, the capillaries in his lungs burning like seams of molten lava. Romy looked like she was ready to collapse, grasping her knees to stay standing as her back heaved and her lungs wheezed.

"What's wrong?" Aaron said, turning to face her with his hands on his hips.

"That's far enough," she said. "Just hold on a sec, while I just... fucking hell."

She managed to straighten up but was still sheened with sweat and struggling for breath, her once-perfect fringe now ragged and pasted to her forehead.

"Come on, you can rest when we're out of here," Aaron said, going to take hold of her arm.

"No," she said, stepping away from him. "No this is far

enough. We need to head back now."

"What are you on about? Back where?"

"To the house. Back the way we came."

Aaron let out a strange, high pitched laugh in confusion. He looked around, as if he was hoping to see cameras finally confirming this was all one big wind up.

"Why the fuck would we do that?"

"Because," said Romy, still breathing deeply. "That's the plan. Always has been."

"What plan, I thought we were-"

"Water was plan B, and Greg was right... it's a shit plan. We'll only end up getting lost and turned around and the dogs will lead them right to us. No, now Greg's... gone... We can go back to my first plan. The better one."

"The one he said was suicide?"

Romy smirked enough to flash her pearl-white canines at him for a second. He couldn't help but smile back.

"What are you-"

"Look, every plan is stupid if we're out here for long enough that the dogs find us, right? So, I thought the way to beat that was to somehow go back the way we came, over our own tracks, and head back to the house. If we can get there, maybe we can steal a car or hide long enough that an opportunity comes up."

"You're taking the piss."

"You really think so? It makes perfect sense, doesn't it? They'll just assume the trail is from us coming in here... they'll never believe we'd intentionally go back up there, to the house."

"Yeah, who'd be that thick?"

"Come on, Aaron. Don't be like that, you sound like him.... I just thought as soon as Maria fell... like it's shit for her but it's perfect for us. Now we've split up, and it seems to me like they've headed after her, we can just turn around now and go back. Alright? Then make a new plan once we find somewhere to hide?"

"Fuck," Aaron said, rubbing his hands over his face before clasping them on top of his head. He paced back and forth for a few seconds, whispering a stream of obscenities into the forest canopy, then turned back to face her. "You're serious, right?"

"Yeah... fucking hell Aaron there's not really time to have a debate... Are you coming or not?"

She took a step back towards the path, then turned and held her hand back for him. He allowed himself to meet her glacial gaze. Greg had never trusted her, and now he was dead. Gazwan most likely the same. Aaron would certainly be joining them soon if he tried to head deeper into the forest and execute Romy's plan B without her.

The way he saw it, trusting his own intuitions had got him into this mess, so maybe – if he really did want to survive the rest of the day – he would have to start trusting someone else's to get out. So much the better if that person was as assured as Romy. This mysterious girl, so determined to expose evil, even if she had to make herself ruthless to do it.

He swore again under his breath, took her hand, and nodded.

"Thank fuck for that," she said, squeezing his hand before letting it drop. "Come on, and keep your eyes open."

"Yes boss."

* * *

The path had been chewed up to mud by heavy horses and

frantic dogs since they'd last set foot on it, the faint, musty smell of the animals still lingering in the air as they emerged from the dripping wet undergrowth.

Aaron could feel his pulse throbbing in the ends of his fingers, the arteries in the side of his neck, and his temples. He wanted nothing more than to strip off the heavy tweed jacket and waistcoat, but the last thing they needed was to give any more clues to the dogs than they already had.

Romy had slowed to a brisk walk now, trading off some of her speed in favour of stealth. She glanced back at Aaron every minute or so, as if she expected him to have silently abandoned her. Each time he gave a weak smile or a half-thumbs-up to reassure her, but she was a mess of nerves again, now the plan was in action.

Just as the light from the first clearing began to appear up ahead, Aaron heard what he thought was a faint rumbling. He froze to the spot and hissed Romy's name.

"What are you doing?" she said, her eyes wide and accusing.

"Listen," he said, pointing up at nothing in particular.

As they waited, the sound of hooves gradually intensified, like someone slowly rolling up the volume on a sound system.

"Shit," she said. "Where's that coming from?"

"That way," Aaron said, pointing behind them. He grabbed a handful of Romy's jacket and went headlong into a chest-high thicket of bracken, smashing a path for her to follow. Their forward momentum was redirected as Aaron's foot was snagged by a fallen tree branch, and they both stumbled into the mulch of the forest floor.

"They'll find us here," said Romy, her voice raspy. "We need to run."

"Listen," Aaron said, keeping his hand on the top of her back.

215

"No dogs. Listen."

Her eyes glazed as she tuned into the nearing thunder, then nodded and burrowed herself as far as she could into the earth. They were too low to see much more than the tops of the four riders' helmets as they bobbed past, oblivious, but Aaron was sure one of the voices belonged to a woman.

Once the sound had faded completely, Aaron and Romy met eyes again and they silently agreed it was safe to stand as one. Aaron held the bracken to one side for Romy to step out onto the path, but as she did, they were held still by fear yet again.

Romy glared back at Aaron, as if she was accusing him of having somehow conjured the single horse that was now galloping their way, much faster than the ones that had just passed.

"Shit," she said, pushing him back into their hiding place.

As Aaron stumbled back, he caught a glance of the horse that was baring down on them; its rider tall, straight-backed, regal; like he was built for it and it for him.

"The fuck," he said as the dropped to the ground again.

"What?"

"It's him."

"What, you mean-"

"Yeah. What the fuck."

He leant up on his elbows, looked around the cluttered undergrowth, eventually spotting the long, poleaxe of a tree branch that they'd stumbled over a few moments earlier.

"Aaron, no," Romy said, her eyes darting between him and his potential weapon.

"What?"

"It's not worth it. Look what he did to Greg. He will fucking kill you."

"Nah, fuck it," he said, his breath quickening. "Nah, he's having it."

He sprung to his feet, snatching the branch up as he went.

"Aaron, no!"

33

Charles

Charles was barely able to focus on the ride back to the house, his mind ricocheting between the doe's screams and the crack of the shot that put the owl on his back. He'd taken one life this morning and condemned another to unimaginable suffering and he would profit handsomely from them both.

His horse seemed to know where it was going, even as he occasionally forgot, perhaps following the scent of his stablemates who'd made tracks only a few minutes before. He felt like he was catching them up by the time he reached the narrow track out of the forest, maybe he'd even end up running into them before they made it across the fields. He hoped they would all still be too shellshocked from what they saw to make any kind of small talk with him.

He'd seen their like at plenty of these events over the years. Those who are tricked into thinking the hunts are all about adventure; about pitting oneself against what is so often romanticised as being the most dangerous game. Others simply afflicted by a morbid fascination with death and the money to indulge it. Whatever the reason, Charles had seen scores of them come and go in his time; all dressed in their livery, clutching rifles that spent the majority of their existence in safes, happy to laugh and joke about death until they see it for themselves. Until they are engulfed by the smells of blood and faeces and fresh vomit on their lapels.

Once the track evened up, Charles kicked the horse into a canter, the low sun illuminating the clearing up ahead like service station on a dark motorway. He was almost there when he noticed a burst of movement in the undergrowth to his left, which caused him to automatically pull back on the reins.

As the horse slowed, Charles let go of the reins with his right hand to reach back and pull the rifle down from his shoulder, but all that did was serve to unbalance him when Aaron leapt from the bracken and swung a huge tree limb at him like a battle axe. Although it was a thick lump of wood, the branch let out a resounding snap as the end crunched squarely into the side of Charles' face, sending him tumbling from his saddle.

The next thing he knew, everything was upside down and the forest floor had appeared at his back to drive his chin into his chest, his neck bent almost at a right angle by the awkwardness of the fall. Charles was sure he heard his neck pop, but he couldn't be sure if that was from breaking bones or simply the internal noise caused by a septuagenarian body being slammed into the ground.

He could taste hot, metallic blood in his mouth, and smell the musty, downtrodden mud that was suddenly his entire world.

Aaron's tweed-clad legs appeared in front of him and were soon joined by another pair; a woman's. Charles rocked his weight to the left and managed to roll onto his front, but the cold barrel of his rifle drove him back down as he attempted to stand.

"It's not loaded," Charles said into the mud.

"You reckon?" Aaron said.

He bent down next to Charles and picked something up, then came the unmistakable clunk and snap of a bullet being loaded into the chamber of his Remington. Aaron and the woman – the girl – took a few steps back, allowed Charles to push himself up and, after much groaning and grunting, stand.

Geysers of pain were erupting all over Charles' body, but his lower back and the back of his neck felt more like volcanos. He straightened, as much as he could, and stared at his grandson through narrowed, mud-spattered eyes.

Aaron

"How did you do that?" said Charles, gesturing at the rifle clutched in Aaron's shaking hands. "How did you know?"

"You didn't remember, did you," Aaron said. "About teaching me to shoot, in the garden. I knew you didn't."

Charles grunted.

Romy sniggered but Aaron was deadly serious, just like he had been when he half-drunkenly boasted to Charles about joining him on a hunt, back at Owlgreave what seemed like a lifetime ago. He'd never forgotten what the old man had taught him, never let go of that feeling of acceptance, despite the fact that it had clearly meant nothing to Charles.

One man's trash is another man's treasure.

Aaron stuffed the rest of the spilled bullets into his jacket pocket and aimed the rifle back at Charles, who had turned and was now walking away from them.

"Where you going?" Aaron said, his cheek flat against the cold rifle stock.

Charles winced as he pressed his hand to his ribs. "Back to the house."

"Alone?"

Charles nodded. His horse had stopped after a few riderless yards and was now wandering around the path, apparently waiting for the conversation to finish.

"Why?" said Romy. She was clearly getting as worked up as Aaron, probably as she came to realise that this was the same man who had put two bullets into her friend not long before.

"Back to the house. I'm leaving," Charles said. "As soon as I have my money."

"Money?" said Romy. "Is that really what all this is about? These hunts? Money?"

"For me, yes," he said. "Others, like that thug, O'Brien, have their own motives, apparently."

"O'Brien?" Aaron said, allowing the rifle to drop slightly so he could stare Charles squarely in the face.

"Yes," Charles said. "Tommy O'Brien. Some kind of-"

"He's my boss," said Aaron, turning slightly to Romy. "Well, my boss' boss, if it's him... Big, ginger beard and-"

"Yes."

"Fuck," said Romy under her breath.

"What did he do?" Aaron said.

"It was the young woman. The doe. I don't know what he did exactly, but he wasn't quick about it. She was... in a lot of pain, by the sounds of it."

"Jesus Christ, I feel sick," said Romy, pressing her fingers to her lips. "What the fuck."

"This is the man who's threatening you?" Charles said.

221

"Yeah... well, sort of. Not directly but... yeah," Aaron said. "Why are you bothered anyway? Thought you didn't give a shit?"

"I don't," Charles said. His voice was as deep and measured as ever. Somehow, he still seemed in control of the situation, despite being injured, outnumbered, and on the wrong side of his own rifle.

Aaron glanced at Romy but, for once, she had no orders to give him. He drove the butt of the rifle harder into his shoulder, pointing the barrel at Charles' heaving chest.

"Look, we need to squash this, now," he said. "We need to make this work."

"What on earth are you talking about?"

"You and me. I fucked you over, you got out of it. You fucked me over, I got out of it. Sounds to me like we're even, yeah?"

"You came into my home under false pretences, tied me to a chair, put a knife in my face, trapped my ailing wife-"

"You brought me here to die!" Aaron said, his voice shrill and childlike. "To be fucking... hunted like an animal, for money. You know what? I don't even know why I'm trying to sort this out, you were happy to kill me so-"

"Aaron," Romy said, shooting out a hand to stop him as he took a step towards Charles. "No. You're right. Come on, we can help each other."

"What about Greg?" Aaron said.

"Greg's gone... what are we gonna gain by lashing out now? We can't bring him back, so we need to look forwards, not backwards. We still have a chance, we just have to make this work... all three of us."

She turned to Charles. "Look, Aaron's told me what happened... obviously you two aren't in each other's good books, but you can work this out another time. If anyone finds us here, we're dead, and if you refuse to help us... well, I don't know. He's the one with the gun."

Aaron noticed Charles looking over at the horse. Although he was tall, strong, and relatively nimble for a man of his age, there was no way he was making a sprint for it, even without his injuries. Aaron decided to press his advantage.

"How much money are you waiting on?"

Charles growled. "You will not get a penny from me; I can assure you. It's too important. That money is to secure the rest of mine and your grandmother's lives. It will pay for the house, for Liana. And more besides."

Aaron softened slightly at the mention of Phyllis and Liana, at the crumbling home he'd invaded, until Charles added: "You won't survive out here that long anyway."

"We weren't planning to," said Romy, unafraid. "We were on our way back to the house too."

Charles' flashed his wolf's grin. "To do what? Fight your way through the house? There are five armed guards in there, four more on the front gate, patrols all around the perimeter, even ghillies out on the water... and that's without the hounds and hunters in there."

Romy's head dropped slightly. Even with Greg no longer around, she still wasn't short of men keen to poke holes in her plans.

"Alright then," said Aaron. "Help me take him out."

Charles cocked his eyebrow, and looked over at Romy, who was equally as shocked.

"O'Brien?"

"Yeah, why not? You won't give me the money – you need it, for Gran or whatever – fine, you can help me another way.

We get rid of him then there's no meeting with him and Dave, no talk of me losing the money. Everything's fixed."

Charles shook his head, his jaw clenching in frustration.

"It's impossible," he said. "It's against the rules. Everything will be forfeit, including the money. It can't be done. Not without killing everyone on this estate to a man."

Aaron exhaled with frustration. The fact that a place like this, where people like Greg could be gunned down like pests, could have rules was like the final insult.

"So, you won't help me with the money, and you won't help me with him... why shouldn't I just finish this, then, eh? Take you with us?"

Aaron shook the gun at Charles, his teeth gritted, but the old man didn't budge. He reached up and rubbed the back of his neck, wincing as he did so, then went into his jacket pocket and fished out another handful of bullets.

"Please yourself," he said, sprinkling the shells into the mud at Aaron's feet. "You can keep the rifle; I won't be needing it anymore. Call it payment for sparing me."

He turned and started limping towards his waiting horse, so indifferent to Aaron and Romy now that it was as if they had vanished into thin air.

"What are you doing? I never said I was sparing anything... you can't just-"

Aaron strode after Charles with the rifle still levelled at him, keeping the crosshairs on his back as he heaved himself up and onto his saddle, groaning all the while. Aaron imagined pulling the trigger – the kick and the crack and the smell of burning metal – but his fingers didn't allow him to do anything more than that. He swore and lowered the weapon, disgusted by his own weakness, then stood and watched as the horse turned on the spot until it was sideways on, blocking the path.

Charles took hold of the reins, rolled his shoulders, and did his best to recapture his solid, regal posture.

"Aaron," he said. "If you are so ignorant as to think shooting bottles in our garden has equipped you to go after O'Brien and the rest, at least take my advice; keep your distance, and make sure you finish him... I'll leave the side door to the horse box open, just in case you do. Try and survive long enough to use it."

He tugged the reins and the horse pointed itself towards the clearing and set off at a canter. Even with a gun aimed at his back, Charles held himself as if he expected any shot would be so insignificant as to just bounce off and fall to the ground, no more than the fleeting touch of a falling acorn. Aaron swore under his breath again, then turned back to face Romy's fresh scrutiny.

34

Gazwan

Gazwan had been able to hear Maria's cries over the squelch of his shoes and the wheezing of his tightening lungs, her pain echoing all around him, haunting his every footstep like some malevolent forest spirit. He assumed it would end after a few seconds, but it did not. After a while it engulfed him, becoming so unbearable that he started to talk to himself as he ran, to try and drown out her screams with his own apologies.

When Maria's straining voice was eventually silenced, a new terror prickled Gazwan's skin; the realisation that they were done with her now, and it wouldn't be long before they had their turn with him.

He tried to shake it off, to focus on his task; outrun these animals for long enough that Romy and Aaron had time to get to safety, to potentially avoid the brutality that had already been inflicted on a third of their group.

Just as the ground evened out and he was able to pick up speed, a shaky voice called to him from the crest of a rocky hill to his right.

"Gaz," came the voice. "Gaz, up here."

Gazwan skidded to a stop and looked up to see Bayley peeking from behind a cluster of boulders, still – somewhat bizarrely – wearing his rat's head mask. He gave a half-hearted wave, then beckoned Gazwan over.

Gazwan was struggling to believe this was anything but a mirage, a figment of his terror-spiked imagination. This boy was the most defenceless of all of them yet, perhaps, the one who had done the best in escaping the hunters' initial charge. He was selfish in his actions, in Gazwan's opinion, but his application could not be faulted.

"Bayley?"

"Yeah, come on. I found a good place."

From what Gazwan could remember – and this was quite monumentally interrupted by Maria's fall and the subsequent separation of their group – Bayley had sprinted straight through the clearing and into the forest proper. That would explain why they hadn't yet seen him, as well as how he'd had the time to find this particularly well-fortified spot. There even appeared to be some kind of narrow cave in the rock face behind him.

Gazwan jogged over and scrambled up the hill, then dropped to his knees and cowered behind the same boulder as Bayley, though his six-foot-four frame made it a more difficult proposition for him than it did for the boy.

"Why are you still wearing that?" said Gazwan, struggling to speak in between ragged breaths. "Can you breathe?"

"Yeah, it's fine. Didn't want to waste any time."

"Do you want me to take it off for you? The tape?"

"Nah, no need."

Gazwan opened his mouth to protest, but the sight of Bayley's droopy eyes inside the unmoving rat's head was so unnerving that he struggled to find to the words. He wrinkled his nose as the tang of fresh faeces drifted over from the nearby rocks, as if the boy had relieved himself only moments before.

"Was that you?"

"Yeah, man," he said, the rat's head bobbing as he spoke. "Couldn't help it, stomach is doing flips."

"We have to keep running," said Gazwan. "The dogs... they will find us here."

"Nah," said Bayley, pointing over towards the fissure in the rock. "We can hide in there."

Gazwan followed the boy's bony finger. To call it a cave was an exaggeration, to say the least. The hole itself probably was big enough for Bayley to squeeze through, and it did look as if it opened up inside, but there was no way Gazwan could contort himself to get through. The idea of both of them doing so was almost laughable.

"It will not work," Gazwan said, taking hold of Bayley's tweed-clad shoulder. "We have to run. We can help each other, but not here. We have to go, now."

Bayley cocked his head to one side, a rat-like mannerism in itself.

"Just wait here a bit longer," he said. "I... I don't know what to do."

"I told you, come on."

Gazwan tried to pick him up but Bayley snatched his arm away.

"Bayley, please. There is no time. Just come with me and-"

Gazwan trailed off as the sound of ferocious barking rippled across the forest, closely followed by the rhythmic thudding of countless hooves. He dropped onto his stomach and crawled in the direction of the noise, peeking over the edge of the hill a millimetre at a time.

He saw at least five horses weaving through the trees, their riders all in bright red coats and high leather boots, long rifles resting on their laps. A pair of quad bikes buzzed around behind them, one carrying two gamekeepers and another with two young men; the same young men who had tried to take Gazwan into the woods for 'target practice' the night before.

He rested his forehead on his hands and began whispering a prayer into the damp earth, when Bayley tapped him on the shoulder.

"You want to try the cave?"

"Get down, boy," Gazwan said, his voice trembling. "On your belly, please. They will see you."

Gazwan heard him shuffle around, turned to see him standing up and waving at the approaching hunters with both arms above his head, like he was signalling to a passing aircraft.

"Over here," he said, the sound of his shrill voice bouncing chaotically from tree to tree like a pinball. "One over here, down here."

He was now pointing to Gazwan with one hand and still waving with the other. Gazwan felt vomit bubble up into his throat, taking hold of Bayley's trouser leg in an attempt to pull him down.

"Get down, Bayley! What are you doing? What are you-"

Gazwan was cut off by a loud crack as bullets bit into the rocks just above their heads, sending fragments of stone spraying over their backs. More rifles snapped in the distance a split second later, followed by a chorus of shouting men and barking dogs.

Instead of burying his face into the dirt, like Gazwan, Bayley jumped to one side, then skittered down the hill like the rat they'd dressed him as. Gazwan watched as he sprinted, quite bizarrely, in the direction of the hunters. If he wasn't in mortal danger, Gazwan might have even found it amusing how strange Bayley looked in his tweed suit and rat's head, waving his arms as he ran like a mascot at the side of a football pitch.

Gazwan screwed his eyes shut as he waited for the next shot and subsequent screams, but neither came. He peeked over the rocks again to see Bayley approaching the line of horses and having some kind of conversation.

Another volley of bullets made Gazwan shrivel back into the ground again, this time a little lower down, a little closer. He could even feel the air being displaced just above his back and his buttocks as they flew over him. The smell of burning metal was everywhere now, overpowering even the musk of the wet earth that was being forced into his nostrils.

He knew that this position wouldn't protect him for much longer, but at least he had the advantage of knowing where the shots were coming from. He knew where he needed the cover to be.

He grunted as he twisted his neck around to look back at his feet, at where the rocky hill dropped away sharply behind him. Even if he managed to avoid the shots that would come as soon as he moved, he considered how much hurling himself down such a hill could cause some kind of injury, maybe even one that could hamper his ability to run.

He peered over at the hunters, who still hadn't moved, then back at the drop. Another flurry of shots came, breaking loose jagged shards of rock that slicing into Gazwan's cheek like petrified hail. He gasped at the pain, then pushed himself up onto his knees, turned, and propelled himself off the back of the hill, headfirst.

His body tumbled down the hill, rag-doll arms and legs flailing, until he thudded into the hard-packed mud at the bottom. The final impact knocked the wind out of his lungs, leaving him on his back while he held his right hand up to inspect its little finger, which was splayed unnaturally out to the side at a sickening angle. He lifted his other trembling hand to touch it but pulled it away as the pain surged all the way up to his right elbow.

He got to his feet, his legs thankfully unharmed by his ugly descent, and staggered into a run, making sure he kept the hill at his back for cover, hugging the right-hand side of the forest.

He began to cry as he ran, the tears burning the open wounds on his cheeks, his mangled hand useless at his side. The hooves and the barking started up again as they gave chase, the sound rising to a crescendo in mere seconds.

All Gazwan could see was row upon row of trees, endlessly queuing to reach a faint light, dappling through the trees on the horizon. He thought of his homeland, of his family, most of whom were already waiting for him in that light and warmth he was now running towards.

The noise behind him was monstrous now, like a tidal wave about to break and swallow him whole. He had to reach the light first, he had to draw them for as long as his broken body would allow.

A dog ran past his left leg, then two more on his right almost tripping him. They were circling him, their drooping ears flapping from side to side as they shook their heads, eyes vacant and oblivious. They had no idea how much pain they had caused already.

Another shot whipped past Gazwan's head, splitting the bark

231

of a nearby tree, then another past his arm. The third, a barely audible snap, caught him between the shoulder blades almost knocking him onto his knees. He continued to shamble on, though his limbs were numb, and his lungs had become hives of angry bees.

One more bullet zipped by his ear, but the shot to his back had now become too much. He had been running for so long – from war, from persecution, and now from death itself – but his body was now finally tired enough to stop. He slowed, then dropped to his knees, the stinging taste of warm blood on his tongue as it tricked out onto cracked lips, matted his beard.

He looked ahead at the glow of the light, at the patient trees in their ceaseless procession, and was finally at peace. He closed his eyes, and waited for world to fade.

35

Aaron

"He'll kill you," Romy said, her stare burning Aaron's cheeks. "This O'Brien, whoever he is, is here because he likes killing people, end of. I know you think you can shoot, because of your Grandad or whatever, but it's not the same thing. You know it's not. He'll fucking kill you and if he doesn't one of the others will."

Aaron avoided her stare by assessing the rifle, which was feeling heavier in his grip by the second. He ran his hand along the grain of the wood, turned it over and shouldered it to check the scope again. Despite his concentration, he wasn't really sure what he was looking for.

"Aaron? Please tell me you're not considering this."

Aaron sighed and lowered the gun.

"No... not really. I don't know, man, it's fucked either way isn't it? Why not try and take that fucker with us?"

"Because you won't," said Romy. "You'll just be walking into their hands. They'll probably love it, the sick bastards. Like an animal trying to fight back. It'll just make them want

233

to kill you even more."

"So, what, just sneak back to the house over the fields? Somehow I don't think-"

"He said something about leaving a horse box open, right? Your Grandad?"

"Yeah," said Aaron. "That's what he brought me here in. Like a big trailer you use for-"

"I know what a horse box is," Romy said, half-laughing. She stepped forward and took hold of the hem of his jacket, tugging on it as she spoke. "But if he's said he's leaving it open for us, then he must think it's possible for us to make it back without getting spotted. Maybe he's changed his mind, finally, you know? Maybe he's decided you don't actually deserve this after all... Maybe he's seen you're worth more than this."

Aaron smiled. "It's not just him, it's O'Brien. I've got a chance to... I mean, if I can stop him now, then there's no way he can-"

"The way to stop O'Brien isn't by taking him on with guns in a forest, some kind of pre-emptive revenge. We nail him the same way we nail everyone else; by exposing the truth of what's going on here."

Aaron ran his hands over the stubble on the back of his head, the grease and dirt and sweat slick under his fingers. She was so close to him now that her eyes were unavoidable, their crystal-clear blue even more striking against her mud-smudged face. He swallowed hard, and was about to nod, when a flurry of gunshots crackled from within the forest like distant fireworks, sending nesting birds clattering and squawking into the air.

"Shit," said Romy. "Was that-"

"Yeah... that means..."

Aaron trailed off as the shooting started again, growing more frustrated and chaotic as it went on, like the rifles were trying to shout over each other to be heard. Aaron imagined Gazwan and Bayley fleeing the hunters and their weapons, the forest being torn apart by flying lead, Maria cowering somewhere just waiting to be found by the dogs or, even worse, by the men.

The fire eventually ceased, though the echoes still lingered for a few moments in the still air. The woods breathed a sigh of relief. The slaughter was over, for now.

* * *

Aaron and Romy had sprinted from the forest as soon as the gunfire died, certain that most, if not all of, the rest were dead now, apart from them. It was only a matter of minutes before the hunters would break from the trail of Maria's blood and be back on their heels, eager to finish the job, and begin whatever strange rituals followed a successful day's killing.

The slope of the fields meant that they were concealed from the main house until they had to clamber over the final gate. Until that point, they'd hugged the hedgerows as much as possible, their heads constantly swivelling in all directions, watching for any sign of red coats and wild-eyed dogs and half-tonne horses.

They crouched either side of the final gate and peered through the gaps in the metal bars. Aaron could see the top two thirds of the house, but that meant they were still almost as blind as they were when they first burst from the treeline. He stood slightly and tried to use the rifle's scope to zoom in on some kind of detail, but it was no use. He swore as he dropped back to his haunches.

"Can you see anything?" he whispered to Romy. She shook her head. "Fuck. There's nothing between here and the drive, no cover. I don't even know which way is... fuck's sake."

"We're just gonna have to run for it," Romy said.

"Are you serious?" Aaron said, his breath flapping erratically inside his chest like a newly caged bird. "How was this your fucking plan?"

"You really wanna do this now?"

"When do you want to talk about it? We could be fucking dead in the next two minutes... may as well fucking-"

"Aaron, listen," she said, wafting her hands to try and calm him down. "We're almost there. We could be safe in the next two minutes... think of that."

"Fuck," Aaron slumped back against the gate, letting the rifle rest against him, and raked his fingers over his head until they wove together at the back of his neck.

Romy scurried across to his side, cupped his cheek to bring his eyes level with hers. "We can't go back in there now, and we can't wait here. The only place we can go is that way, and the only time we can go is now. Any other choice and we're done. Come on, we can do this, I promise you. I can't be responsible for any more death... if you don't come with me now... come on, stand up."

Aaron took her hand and stood slowly, careful to stay hunched over enough that he never broke the line of the hedge.

"Alright," he said, closing his eyes for a second as the word reverberated in his ears. "Ok, let's go."

The gate clanked in its frame as Romy mounted it, sounding as loud as church bells to Aaron's adrenaline-charged ears. She was off as soon as she dropped down into the soft grass on the other side, forcing Aaron to take hold of the top rail and clear the gate in one movement just to keep up with her.

The rifle banged against his hip as they ran, almost doubled over, across the last field. Each time he looked up at the house, it seemed to grow taller and wider, rising from the ground like an ancient monster woken from aeons of slumber.

Aaron followed Romy's arcing path, toeing the line between getting too close to the house and too close to the driveway. When the ground floor and the gravel in front of it finally appeared, there was no one to be seen; no hunters milling around on the drive, no gamekeepers or dogs prowling the lawn. In that moment, everything – anything – seemed possible.

There were still at least a dozen vehicles lined up in front of the house, though none of them were Charles' battered Land Rover. Despite this setback, they were close now, close enough to read the cars' license plates, to see the air fresheners hanging from their rear-view mirrors.

"It's not here," Aaron said, trying to keep his voice as weak as possible.

Romy didn't stop, didn't turn to acknowledge him, practically throwing herself into the last few steps. She slammed into the grass banking a few inches short of the wide chrome grin of a parked Bentley, then turned to wave him in like an aircraft marshaller.

He thudded down next to her, his chest burning, sweat soaking him from the nape of his neck to the small of his back. They rolled onto their backs and lay next to one another for a few moments, sucking at the air like they'd just been pulled from the sea into a passing trawler.

"There's some more over there," Romy said.

237

She pointed to their left, and the handful of vehicles parked on the opposite side of the main driveway that had been Greg's poorly chosen escape route. Aaron sat up slightly and followed Romy's finger, then partially stood to get a better look.

"Be careful," she hissed.

"It's ok," he said, sitting back down onto the grass. "It's alright... it's there."

It felt ridiculous to smile, given the context, but he couldn't help it. She grinned back for a second, then swallowed and gave a firm nod.

Aaron went first, darting from one car to the next. Each time he crossed one of the gaps between them, he felt as if he was stepping over a bottomless mountain crevasse, death breathing on his neck every second he was in the open.

He thought he heard the sound of conversation spilling out of the wide-open main door, but he didn't care to hang around and see who it was, focusing instead on skimming across the gravel with the fewest possible footsteps. It was like he was back in PE lessons again by the last three strides – hop, step, jump – skidding to his knees along the grass, tearing it free.

He dropped to the wet ground again in front of the Land Rover, and once Romy had caught up, he stood, then slipped around the bonnet and along the door to reach the large, red and white horse box.

As Charles promised, there was indeed a small side door, almost like the half-and-half kind found on an old caravan, with an even smaller metal handle. Aaron shrugged the rifle higher up onto his shoulder, then met Romy's gaze as he pressed down slowly, his face grimacing as if he expected it to explode at any minute. The squeaking continued until, at once, the handle clicked, and the door swung open to welcome them.

36

Charles

Charles had spent almost an hour soaking his aching bones in the free-standing bath in his room's en suite, alone in this wing of the house but for a few scurrying staff. He guessed that the simple act of riding for that long – particularly after so many years out of the saddle – would have been enough to hurt hum for a few days anyway, but being clubbed from his horse into a heap on the floor had introduced him to a whole new world of pain. He was quite sure nothing was broken, but his neck and his left shoulder were already so sore he could barely move them.

Part of him worried about whether he would be able to drive home effectively that evening with more whisky in his system, but the thought of a stiff drink to ease his suffering was too tempting to resist. He poured himself a large Scotch from the half-empty decanter on the drinks trolley, then took his place in the same chair in which he'd fallen asleep the night before, watching the day's light fade through his window.

As dusk was falling, Charles was stirred by the sound of

hooves rumbling across the fields. He levered himself out of the chair with the help of his fully functioning arm – moving a little easier now, thanks to the whisky – and hobbled over to peer out from behind the curtain.

The remaining hunters slowed to a canter as they reached the driveway, then made their way around to the side of the house where olive drab-clad groomsmen were already waiting. They were all talking quite heatedly between one another, and the quad bikes carrying the 'keepers and the camera-wielding teenagers were conspicuously absent.

Charles took a step sideways to see the group better, which allowed him to single out Matthew and O'Brien, who were the most vocal of the bunch. The latter was spattered with blood, some of it still caked in his beard.

Charles set his drink on the nearby table and unlatched the window and opened it a couple of inches, the smell of the cold evening air rushing in at the slightest invitation.

Matthew handed his reins to a groomsman and started striding towards the house's main door, when O'Brien caught him up and stopped him with a firm hand on the shoulder.

"Oi, I wasn't finished mate," O'Brien said, spinning Matthew around to face him. "I paid a lot of money to come here – a lot more than the rest of these posh fuckers – and I want what I paid for."

"Get your bloody hands off me man," said Matthew, finally showing the disdain for O'Brien that Charles had long suspected.

"No one walks away from me... I don't care who your pappy is."

The rest of the hunters were still stood where they had dismounted, happy to wait out the awkward confrontation by whispering among themselves. Lingering near the back of the group, Charles noticed a young boy dressed in the dirty tweeds of the prey. By his frame, it could only have been the one who'd worn the rat's head mask, the one Matthew had asked them to leave until last.

Only a few hours before, this boy had been on his knees with the rest of the condemned, and now he was rubbing shoulders with the very same people who had been after his blood. Had he been spared? Or was it some kind of ploy to make sure all of the prey stayed within the bounds of the forest, some kind of hunt shill? If the latter was true, it didn't sound like it had worked.

"We'll find them, alright?" Matthew said, distracting Charles from his scrutiny of the boy. "Until then you're just going to have to... be patient. Go inside and have a drink or-"

"I can have a fucking drink anywhere," said O'Brien, forcing the words through gritted teeth. "I came here for a reason."

"I know, I know. We all did. Look, every spare man we have is patrolling the perimeter, we've got the ghillies out on the water, the quads are already out lamping... It's only a matter of time before we find them. Plus, once the hounds have-"

"Oh yeah, the fucking dogs... Jesus. They're fucking useless, mate. How do you even manage to lose two people with that many fucking dogs?" said O'Brien with a snort.

Two people missing. If Aaron had done the sensible thing and snuck back to the house, that meant that he and the girl were both hiding in his horse box at this very moment. He peeled the other curtain to one side with his index and middle finger, stared intently at the crimson and white trailer.

"They need putting down, the lot of 'em," snarled O'Brien, still cursing the hounds. "Fucking bollocks mate."

O'Brien leant in towards Matthew then, and the pair of them whispered for a few moments before O'Brien pushed past and stomped off towards the main door, leaving the younger man to stare helplessly after him like a jilted lover. Matthew turned to face the rest of the party, who were now approaching, rubbing at the back of his neck sheepishly as he addressed them.

"Ok, everyone. Thank you, again, for your patience. I know that was a bit of a mixed bag... matter of fact I'm struggling to think of a part of it that *did* go to plan," he paused to let out a nervous laugh though no one joined him. "Nasty business, all that with... erm. Anyway... we'll have to wait for now and see what the 'keepers come up with. Any of you that do fancy coming back out to finish the job – either tonight or tomorrow morning – just let one of us know and you'll get the call as soon as we have them. Oh, and well-done to you, Mr Wheeler, on that last one. Hell of a shot, that. Moving target. Well done."

"Very kind of you, Mr Reeves," said Wheeler, doffing his riding helmet. "Shame not everyone was as... gracious."

"Ah, never mind all that, old boy," said Matthew, shaking Wheeler's hand. "You got there first, fair and square. Plus, you've a fine slice of the pie to take back down south with you, so congratulations, sir. Everyone, go inside and help yourselves to a drink, you've more than earned it today."

The party dispersed, leaving Matthew alone on the driveway. His shoulders slumped as the last hunter entered the house, and he let out a long sigh of relief. Clearly, they had been fooled by his mask of calmness, by the pretence that two of their prey vanishing into thin air was par for the course.

As far as Charles could remember, it had never happened, not even on the more remote reserves they'd hunted on in South

243

Africa in the 1970s and '80s; the ones that seemed to go on forever. One might slip through the net now and again, last a few hours longer than the bulk of the pack, but never longer than that.

This was unprecedented, potentially even more damaging to the institution of the hunts than the introduction of new money thugs like O'Brien. Charles felt as if he was partly to blame. He looked back over at the horse box, weighing his grandson's life in his hands yet again.

Aaron

Every movement, even the shuffling of a cold-numbed back-side, boomed inside the horse box so loudly that Aaron and Romy had agreed to stay still for as long as humanly possible. They decided to sit pressed together, side by side, so any essential communication could go straight from one person's lips to the other's ear, so as not to give the box any more sounds to work with than it already had.

The smell of hay and horse piss was immediately familiar to Aaron, though he found it strange how small the box actually was, now he could see it with his own, uncovered eyes. When he had been swaying back and forth in here, tied to the cold metal bar on the way from Owlgreave, the whole world outside of the bag on his head had felt formless and infinitely vast, terrifying in its vagueness. Now, with Romy by his side, he felt as close to safe as it was possible to be on this estate of the damned.

They heard the hunt return eventually, though they couldn't make out any detail aside from that. Aaron guessed they'd be confused, maybe even angry, that the pair of them had somehow disappeared, and he was sure someone would end up paying for it.

Romy had become restless after the noise died away, even standing up and pacing the floor at one point despite Aaron's hissed pleas.

"It's not enough," she had said, a little too loud for Aaron's liking.

"What isn't?"

She crouched in front of him and lowered her voice again.

"This," she said, gesturing at their new home. "Just... Surviving. We need more. Our word is gonna mean nothing. We have to... do something."

"Something like what?"

"My stuff. My camera. We have to get it back."

Aaron couldn't help but snigger, his eyes following her as she stood again and walked over to the far corner of the box.

"You're joking, right?" he said, standing to join her. "We make it out of this... whatever the fuck that was out there... and your mate's shot dead and so are the rest, probably, and you want to go back out there?"

She nodded and Aaron snorted again, tilting his head back to stare up at the unpainted metal roof. If he didn't look into her eyes, she couldn't turn him to play dough with her words. He just wouldn't look.

"Aaron," she took hold of his lapel and, as if she had heard his worst fears, brought his gaze back down meet to hers. "This isn't enough. Us getting out of here won't bring Greg back, or Gazwan or Maria or Bayley, but it can stop this from ever happening again... but only if we have something to show for it."

"So, what, you want to sneak in there tonight? In the house?

Go from room to room until-"

"No," she said, forcing a smile. "The barn, out back. The incinerator. That's where they'll be taking all our shit, to burn it. That's where it will be, I promise you. There's no way they'll be worried about guarding it if they think we're out there somewhere, getting close to finding our way out."

"Fuck's sake," he sighed. He tried looking down this time, a different tactic, but it was just as useless. He looked up at her, and finally allowed himself to give in.

37

Charles

Charles limped out onto the landing just in time to catch Matthew at the top of the stairs, presumably on his way towards his father's bedroom. He looked pale, the closest to genuinely emotional that Charles had ever seen him.

"Matthew," he said, doing his best to keep his voice steady despite the pain and the whisky.

Matthew turned, but didn't bother to mask his unease with one of his trademark smirks. He nodded curtly.

"Mortimer," he said, frowning as he assessed Charles' lopsided gait, his left arm tucked in feebly at his side. He might have tried to cover his aches better, but the blooming bruise on his temple was impossible to disguise. "What happened to you?"

Charles waved the comment away, trying out his own false smile. "Bloody horse threw me as I was coming out of the forest. Something must have... unsettled him."

"You looked to be pretty in control of it to me," Matthew said. All Charles could offer in return was a one-armed shrug.

From the sounds of muted laughter and clinking glasses drifting up from the ground floor, Charles guessed that the hunting party had quickly gotten over their disappointment and were instead looking forward to another night of debauchery. Matthew exhaled loudly as Charles finally reached him, glancing at the corridor leading to Sir William's room like a man late for his train.

"Something bothering you?" Charles said. "I thought you'd be downstairs toasting the hunt."

"Well," Matthew said, sucking air through his teeth. "Therein lies the rub. Seems that two of our little pups have slipped their leash."

"I'm sorry?"

"The otter and the fox. They've disappeared into thin air. Hounds have run out of ideas and inclination and, well, so has everyone else. We've tightened up the perimeter and sent out some quads to try lamping but not heard a peep from them yet. Not exactly the done thing, is it?"

Charles frowned. "The fox... is that-"

Matthew winced slightly, then nodded. "Think so. Obviously, there's nothing you could have done about that... just bad luck I suppose. Well, unless you've secretly been training him all this time to provide us a real challenge for once?"

He laughed to himself, while Charles did his best to appear surprised.

"What about the other, the rat?"

"Oh that," Matthew said. "Yes, a bit of a ruse on our part. These days... sometimes we draft someone in to ensure the group doesn't get too far, a bit of a failsafe, you know? He did half his job, but obviously... well.... He'll be suitably punished. I expect he won't make the same mistake again."

"I'm sure. And the money?" Charles said. "Does that mean everything is still... undecided?"

Matthew popped out his bottom lip and shrugged. "Maybe... I'm not altogether sure. One of the reasons I'm going to see the old man right now. Was there something in particular you wanted to discuss?"

"No, no," Charles gestured in the direction of Sir William's room with his functional arm. "We can discuss it later. Please just give Sir William my best."

"Of course, thank you, Charles. You're a good man."

Charles turned to hobble back towards his room when Matthew called after him.

"Oh and, Charles, with the arm and... all that; do you need us to get the local sawbones up here, Dr Curry? I'm sure he wouldn't mind, very discreet..."

"No, thank you. Just a rest and some peace and quiet. If I hadn't had me fill of this before, I certainly have now."

* * *

Charles had switched from whisky to tea while he sat at the window, willing the time to pass to so he could collect his money and leave this place once and for all. He was just about to drift off into sleep when a loud thumping at the door snatched him back into the waking world.

"Yes? Who is it?"

"It's me," said Matthew, still sounding sheepish. Charles heaved himself to his feet and started towards the door when Matthew added: "And Mr O'Brien. We need to have a word."

Charles stopped dead and stared suspiciously at the huge

slab of varnished oak, picturing that brute on the other side. He looked around the room for a weapon, just in case. Although his shotgun was only in its bag in the corner of the room, it seemed excessive, and the more he considered it, the less he thought he'd even be able to shoulder the thing.

He thumbed the cork into the bottle of whisky, then picked it up by its neck and walked over to unlock the door. He opened it enough to see them both, but kept his right hand and the bottle it grasped hidden.

"Yes, what is it?"

Matthew could only hold Charles' gaze for a second before his eyes darted to O'Brien, who was standing there with his face screwed up in discomfort, like a dog who'd eaten its master's slippers and spent the rest of the following day passing them.

"Me and you," he said, his accent as grating as ever. "We need to sort this cash out. For the girl."

Charles narrowed his eyes, scrutinising both men in turn. "The deal was done. You wanted her, so you agreed to pay me, then we shook."

"Yeah, after you'd finished pointing a fucking gun at my chest."

"Look, we don't need to draw this out," Matthew said, apparently playing peacemaker. "Mr O'Brien claims he was under duress when he made the deal, so he feels that-"

"I don't care how Mr O'Brien feels," said Charles. "I understand you're... dissatisfied with your performance today, or with what you'd come to expect... But a deal is a deal. Now please don't bother me again unless it's-"

Charles went to close the door, but O'Brien shot out a paw to force it back open. The wood thudded into Charles' good shoulder, but even that was enough to trigger explosions of pain all over his body, like a misstep in a minefield. He gritted his teeth and tried his best not to groan.

"I don't think so, Grandad," said O'Brien, keeping his chubby hand pressed flat against the door. Charles could smell the pungent aftershave he'd clearly drowned himself in to cover the sweat of a day's riding. "I've had a chat with Reevesy and the old man and they've said there's a quick way to sort it."

Matthew bit his lip, apparently fixated on Charles' shoes. Charles gave up on trying to get his attention and looked back at O'Brien, who was now grinning a school bully's grin.

"Pistols, I expect," Charles said. "He suggested pistols."

Sir William had long favoured settling any disputes on his grounds with old fashioned means. The weapons and rules varied over the years, depending on his particular interests at the time, but he had always liked the idea that he was a gentleman among gentlemen; and gentlemen settled serious grievances in one way – pistols at dawn. First blood.

O'Brien nodded slowly, the satisfaction on his face plain to see. It unsettled Charles that he was so eager, so poised to face him. After all, there was no doubt Charles was the superior marksman, and he had even duelled a handful of times over the years, though usually as more of an exhibition than anything serious.

Still, O'Brien looked enthusiastic. This, combined with Matthew's sheepishness, set Charles' hackles on edge. They hadn't known about his injuries when they were whispering on the drive, Charles thought, but did that mean that they hadn't planned some other kind of advantage for O'Brien?

"As you wish. I will have Holdsworth as my second," Charles said. If he could at least have his old friend at his side, it would compensate for his half-broken body.

Matthew sucked air through his teeth, the wince of a bad news-bearer now glued to his face. "He's looking after my father, I'm afraid. He's not feeling too well... But I can be your second, if you like? Shouldn't make too much difference... We've all done this before. Mr O'Brien has already chosen his."

"It sounds like you've done all my thinking for me," said Charles.

The two men in the doorway shared a satisfied glance.

"So... are we in agreement? First light?" said Matthew. "If the two strays don't turn up in the meantime, of course."

"If you think that will give you satisfaction," Charles said. "Fine."

"There you go," said O'Brien, practically smacking his lips. "I've been wanting to wipe that look off your face since the second I saw you. I can't fucking wait."

Charles waited until they turned to leave, then called after Matthew.

"Matthew... The money, for the owl and the doe. Everything I'm owed. Have it ready for me, first thing, on the lawn. I don't want to stay a second longer than I have to. Is that understood?"

Matthew and O'Brien shared a puzzled look, then the former gave a nod of assent. Charles nodded back, then closed the door slowly. Once he was alone, he staggered over to the armchair, pulled on his boots and put on his jacket.

If this was to be the way of things, then he could still try his best to even the odds.

38

Aaron

Aaron and Romy waited until the night was completely still before sneaking out of the horse box's small door and scuttling over to right-hand corner of the main house, so as to avoid the kennels and stables on the opposite side. They kept one hand against the rough stone as they slipped through the darkness, occasionally having to drop face-first into the gravel when a motion-sensitive light flooded the courtyard with gleaming white.

The unintelligible thrum of conversation spilled from every one of the house's open windows and doors. Aaron only heard snatches of banter as they ducked past, but he was sure some of it seemed to be about Romy and him. Talk of 'those two' and the 'search effort' and 'extra security'.

Romy turned to glare at Aaron every time they heard some-thing interesting, though she never hung around long enough to find out anything concrete. Aaron thought this was odd, given her obsession with exposing these people for what they were, but he soon realised that all she could think about was retrieving her things from the barn. All the overheard conversations in the world meant nothing if she had no way of proving them.

They reached the back corner of the house and set eyes on the barn for the first time. Unlike the rest of the house, which was all clean lines in light sandstone, the barn was dirty and ramshackle. Its sloping roof was made from corrugated iron and looked like it had been thrown on by builders who were in a hurry to get to somewhere else. The building itself was made of the same material, but had been painted in a dark, earthy red that made it seem as if it was more rust than metal. The main double doors were slightly ajar, and there was a faint light coming from inside, the occasional billow of steam.

Once Romy and Aaron were satisfied that there was no one hanging around the house's back doors for a cigarette or private conversation, they scurried across the back lawn towards the barn. As soon as they were out of range of the house's ambient glow, they were concealed again by the moonless night, even confident enough to stand tall and break into a full sprint for the first time since they had left the forest that afternoon. They slowed again as they approached the structure, and Aaron tapped Romy on the shoulder.

"Over there," he said, pointing at the left-hand corner of the building, where a shard of light was slicing out from a gap in the stained metal at around knee height.

Aaron crouched low and leaned in, then immediately jerked his head away as he was assaulted by a complex combination of smells; first a wave of tangy rot, like an open bin on a hot summer day, then a sweeter, sickly overtone that reminded him of blackcurrant cordial left to coagulate on a kitchen worktop. All of this was underpinned by something like raw meat; that cold, iron smell of a butcher's shop.

He pulled his t-shirt out from the collar of his borrowed shirt and pressed it over his nose, then leant back in and peered inside the barn.

He could see rows of deep, wheeled trolleys, like the kind hotel maids would stuff with soiled bedding, and bare metal tables lined up end to end. He could feel the heat from inside now, warming his forehead as he moved from side to side, taking in every detail he could. The source of the heat – a bell-shaped iron furnace – had its doors closed, but the white light that was pulsing in the cracks suggested a raging fire within.

It was then that he saw a figure cross from one side of the room towards the furnace, a heavy parcel in their arms. They were short, but heavy set, with a wide back and high, pronounced traps. As the figure dumped the parcel on one of the metal tables and turned, Aaron noticed the flick of two tight plaits at the base of their neck.

"You're taking the piss," he whispered.

"What?" Romy knelt by his side.

He signalled for her to make her own t-shirt mask, then moved aside to let her look. After a few seconds, he cupped his hand around his mouth and leant in towards Romy's ear.

"You remember I said about the Frankenstein-looking bloke that knocked me out back at the house?" he said.

She nodded.

"Well... That's her."

Romy turned to him with a raised eyebrow, then looked back into the light.

"She's on her own," she said.

"I think so, yeah."

Aaron let the rifle slip off his shoulder, then brought it tight into his chest and took a step towards the barn door, still hunched over to keep himself small.

"What are you doing?" Romy said, tugging on the frayed tail of his jacket.

Aaron's eyes were wide, gleaming white in the near darkness.

"Trust me," he said. "I'll be fine. I owe her one."

Romy let the fabric drop and he carried on, keeping his breathing shallow as he edged towards the light spilling from the gap in the doors. The stench was getting stronger with every careful step, almost overwhelming him, the sweet tang sawing through the acrid musk like a rusty blade.

He took his right hand off the rifle's stock and peeled the door back as gently as he could, wincing in preparation for a giveaway, haunted house creak that never came. He eased himself around and into the steamy warmth of the barn, and fixed his eyes on Tess, who was little more than a silhouette against the dim light pulsing from the furnace.

She was unloading more parcels from one of the deep wheeled tubs and dumping them onto the metal table in front of her, each one landing with a faint wet slap as if whatever was inside the brown paper was wet through. Despite her obvious strength, she was grunting as she lifted each of the parcels, leading Aaron to guess that they must have weighed at least 30kg apiece.

The loose hay strewn over the mud floor was enough to cover the sound of his steps, and he continued to creep forward until he was within a few feet of her. He wiped the sweat from his hands onto the front of his jacket, balancing the rifle in the crook of each elbow as he did so, then locked it in a white-knuckle grip and stood.

"Pssst."

Tess' head whipped around, sending her plaits lashing like

scorpion's tails. Aaron had already started his swing, though he was able to savour the shock in her eyes for a split second before the flat of the rifle's butt crunched into her temple, sending her stumbling into the side of the nearest bin.

She quickly crumpled to her knees but was able to stay solid on all fours instead of passing straight out like Aaron had after she clocked him at Owlgreave. He stepped over to her and reset himself, then gritted his teeth and swung the butt again, this time in a vicious downward arc. The solid walnut stock connected with the same side of her head, just above her ear, driving her face down into the mud and hay. Aaron watched, listened to her snoring for a few moments until he was satisfied that she was out cold, his own chest heaving from the effort of the second blow.

"Sweet dreams bitch."

Aaron laid the rifle on the table next the parcels, then bent down and rolled her over onto her back. The single push told him she was closer to Charles' weight than his, and he immediately began to panic when he realised that he'd not made any plans other than paying her back for that metal bar around the head.

As his eyes continued to adjust to the light in the barn, he realised that Tess' apron was drenched in deep red blood, as were the elbow-length rubber gloves she was wearing. He looked across to the parcels and realised the wetness seeping from within the brown paper was of a similar shade, then glanced at the other bins that were full of the same cargo.

His attention was taken by Romy, who was lingering in the doorway, somehow appearing shocked at his actions despite the hell she'd been through already.

"Is she alive?"

257

"Sleeping like a baby," Aaron said, giving Tess' shin a sharp kick for good measure. "She fucking knew."

"Knew what?"

"When I last saw her," he said. "When I was tied up in that cellar... she said she'd see me again. Or 'bits of me'. I didn't know what the fuck she was talking about at the time, but she must have said it because she knew I was coming here. Because she thought she'd be doing... *this* to me."

Aaron stared at Tess and listened to Romy's gasps as she connected the same blood-red dots that he had a moment earlier.

"Oh my God, is that-"

"I don't know," Aaron said, cutting her off. "And it doesn't matter. Remember what you said, we can't bring them back... we need to have something to show for it. Alright?"

"I know, but... is he... fucking hell, I think I'm gonna be sick."

Romy lurched outside and gave in to the nausea that Aaron was fighting with every ounce of strength he had left. It was almost certain that some of the parcels, if not all of them, used to be their companions. They had names, voices, laughs, and fears, and now they were chopped into pieces and wrapped in brown butcher's paper. Aaron could feel cold sweat dribbling down the side of his head, onto his cheeks, feel the heat of the furnace at his back.

After a few audible heaves from outside, Romy slunk back in, still wiping her mouth with the back of her hand.

"You alright?" Aaron said. She nodded curtly, then walked over to the bins and started going through them, presumably in the hope of finding her things.

Aaron picked up Tess by her boots, then dragged her to the far corner of the barn and wheeled over an empty bin to conceal her sleeping body. It wasn't perfect, but it was the best he could do, he thought.

Romy was still looking through a pile of incinerator-bound clothes and bags and shoes; every possession that each one of them had when they were taken. Aaron joined her and started rooting through until he caught sight of his jacket and his black rucksack. He took them out, pocketed his cigarette pack and lighter, then unzipped the bag's main compartment and took out his knife, his remaining duct tape, and a few zip ties. There was no sign of either of his phones.

He walked back over to Tess and crouched and yanked the rubber gloves from her hands, smearing his own with blood, then bound her hands and feet with ties and tape, and taped over her mouth for good measure. He stared at her for a few moments longer, then snatched the fox mask from his inside jacket pocket and pulled it over her head.

By the time he was done, Romy was already at the door.

"You ok?"

She turned back towards him, a quivering smile on her blood-smeared face and a black camera bag clutched tightly under her arm.

"Yeah."

"Ok, let's get fucking gone then."

"Hang on," said Romy, unbuckling the bag and pulling out a weighty digital camera.

"What are you doing?" Aaron said. "We've got what we came for."

"Not yet we haven't."

She dropped the bag onto the floor, then flicked the camera on and walked over to the pile of bloody parcels.

* * *

Once Romy was satisfied she'd gathered enough evidence, they rushed back across the grass the way they came, a fresh dump of adrenaline pumping new life into their exhausted limbs. They took their time over the gravel, keeping one hand on the wall again, but it was dark now, and silent – all of the hunters presumably passed out on expensive sofas and four-poster beds, thousand-pound brandy still clutched in their wizened fingers.

The white of the horse box was still easily visible in the gloom, and once they were sure the coast was clear, they crept back to their headquarters, mission accomplished.

Romy pressed against the side of the box to let Aaron past and open the door, but just as he felt the cold handle under his fingers, a familiar voice rumbled in the darkness.

39

Charles

"And where on Earth have you been?" said Charles, freezing Aaron and the girl in place like startled rabbits.

He was leant against the bonnet of the Land Rover, his thick arms folded across his chest. He pushed himself off and stepped towards them, the gravel complaining as it was crushed beneath his heavy boots.

"We... erm... I don't."

"And what is that?" Charles said, pointing at the girl's bag.

Aaron opened his mouth, presumably to make a case for her, but even with a rifle in his hands he looked too guilty to offer any kind of resistance. The girl pushed past him.

"Look, I know you're not gonna like this... but this is why I came here," she said, squeezing the bag against her side. It was only then that he caught the stench of death on them, noticed the blood smeared on their hands and faces. The barn.

"What is it?" Charles said.

"It's... my camera. I'm a journalist."

"What kind of journalist?" Charles took another step closer, causing them to shy away. He held up his hands to try and placate them. "Look, just try and calm yourselves down. We're no longer in a position to fear one another. I've already burned my bridges with these people, and if they knew I'd helped you escape I'd be on my knees alongside you first thing tomorrow morning. Do you understand?"

They both nodded.

"Good," Charles said. "Now please answer the question."

"Ok... well, basically we already knew what was going on here... before we came, I mean. Me and the boy I came with, the one who you–"

"The owl."

"Yeah, him," she said, her head dipping slightly at the mention of her friend and his final mistake. "Well, we came here a few weeks ago, the last hunt... and they caught us. We were up on the ridge there, taking photos."

"Of what?"

"Just... them. Getting ready to start. All the red coats and the horses... then the others in their masks... running."

"Faces?"

"Some, yeah," she said. "The old man. His valet."

Charles growled under his breath. Sir William still hadn't deigned to give him an audience, and while he wasn't petty enough to use this as grounds for betrayal, it did make him even more suspicious of the duel to come. A bit of ammunition to use against the old man wouldn't go amiss, if things got particularly desperate.

"Mine?" Charles asked.

"No," she said, her turn to show the palms of her hands. "No, we're even. You did what you had to do, I guess. It fucking sucks but... if you didn't do it, someone else would have. Greg knew the risks of coming here. We both did."

Aaron had been staring at Charles throughout the conversation, as if he was hanging his future on every word.

"So, you went to the barn?"

"Yeah," Aaron said. "Caught up with your mate."

"Excuse me?"

"The butcher girl. Paid her back for this, with interest," he said, pointing at the bruise on his temple from Tess' knockout blow.

"Is she alive?"

"I reckon so," he said. "Tied her up and hid her at the back, she was still spark out when we left. Everyone's in bed now anyway, apart from you."

Charles clenched his jaw. "She was coming here to work with her father, but I can't be sure why."

"You don't wanna know," said Aaron. "Trust me,"

"Well I suppose I'll have to for now.... in the meantime, I need you to do something for me."

He went on to explain – in as little detail as possible – the confrontation with O'Brien and his subsequent ultimatum, as well as his suspicions that he and Matthew had come up with a way of rigging the duel itself.

"I've heard of it happening before," Charles said. "Blank rounds in the gun, tampered sights... I wouldn't discount it, considering how I've left the situation with them."

"So... what do you need us to do?" said Aaron, sharing a worried glance with the girl.

"I need you to cover me, just in case."

"Cover you?" said the girl.

"Yes. You said you know your way around a weapon, so now you can prove it."

"You want me to take out O'Brien... with this?" Aaron said,

holding up the rifle.

"Give it to me," Charles said, holding out his hand.

Aaron hesitated, waited for a nod from the girl before he relinquished the weapon. Charles slung it over his shoulder while he fished around in his pocket for the suppressor he had taken out of the rifle bag while he was waiting. He made the weapon safe and began screwing the black metal tube onto the end of the rifle's barrel.

"This is a suppressor," he explained as he worked. "I don't have subsonic ammunition, but it should be quiet enough, if we time it right."

"What?" Aaron said, as if Charles had started speaking in some alien language.

"Well, if they are planning to hobble me somehow, you can be my insurance... with this. I'll wait three seconds to fire after I've levelled the pistol – one one thousand, two one thousand, three one thousand, fire. That should give you time to take aim," he pointed to his sternum, "here... the centre of mass. I'll make sure the duel happens there on the lawn, no more than 100 yards away, so wherever you put those crosshairs, that's where the bullet will go, do you understand?"

Aaron nodded.

"Say it back to me," said Charles, handing the rifle back to his grandson.

"You aim, I aim – centre mass – one one thousand, two one thousand, three one thousand, shoot."

"Good... Good boy."

Charles couldn't be sure in the dark, but he thought he saw Aaron try to suppress a smile at his words.

"Hold on," said the girl. "Where are you thinking he's gonna shoot from?"

Charles nodded at the horse box.

"In there?" Aaron said.

"Yes, there's a small flap at the top, right there in the middle, which looks out over the roof of the cab. It will give you enough leeway for the barrel and the scope. Take the shot, then get back in and close it as quickly and as quietly as possible."

"Surely someone will hear it? Or feel it, or something?" said the girl, her voice still whisper quiet. Aaron leant forwards to get a look at the flap on the horse box.

"Hopefully not with the suppressor," Charles said. "The duelling pistols they tend to use are called Brownings, and they make a fair racket... with the sound reflecting off the ridge and the glass and the house, the woods... should create enough noise to cover the sound of yours. Is that all understood?"

Aaron stepped back into place beside the girl, and eventually they both nodded.

"Good," said Charles, brushing past them. "I've left some food and water in there for you. If you can sleep, make sure you take turns so you don't miss us coming out in the morning."

Charles stopped and turned then, and after a few seconds of hesitation, clapped his hand onto Aaron's shoulder and stared into his eyes.

"We've wronged each other, and we've spared each other. Now is the time to help each other."

For the first time in the conversation, he saw doubt in Aaron's eyes.

"What if I can't do it?" he said. "What if I fuck it up?"

Charles shook his shoulder, then let his hand drop. "Then get in the driver's seat and keep your foot down until you smash through those gates."

265

Aaron

Charles had left them two plastic bottles of Buxton spring water, two muffins, and two posh looking cereal bars all stacked by the door; probably thanks to his room's coffee and tea station. Once they had found them with the help of Aaron's lighter, they sat in the pitch black of the horse box and inhaled everything that was on offer, the whole world silent but for the smacking of lips and rustling of wrapping.

When they were finished, Aaron wanted nothing more than to light up a cigarette – or maybe even one of the battered one-skin joints – and take a few moments to relax, but Romy managed to persuade him that if he'd waited this long already, it wasn't worth the risk.

They shuffled next to each other again and looked over the pictures Romy had taken from up on the ridge the day she was captured; the last moments of four people whose names they'd never know, whose faces they'd never see. Every time the image on the screen changed, it reminded Aaron of their own ordeal; the deafening sound of his wheezing in that mask, the searing pain in his limbs.

"It's enough," Romy had said when she finally killed the LED screen, plunging them back into darkness. "If we do somehow get out of here."

She slipped the camera back into its bag and slid it to one side, then leant back next to Aaron. "Do you think we will? Get out of here, I mean?"

Aaron puffed out his cheeks. "I haven't got a fucking clue. Part of me still thinks this is some kind of nightmare. A really long, really consistent nightmare."

They both sniggered, though Romy sounded sincere when

she eventually spoke again.

"When would it have started? If it is a nightmare?"

"Shit... That's a question, innit."

"Well, yeah," she said. It sounded as if she was smiling. "That's kind of the point."

"Right, ok. If you say so," said Aaron, exhaling for a while as he pondered the question. "I guess it would be losing that money. That's what started all this."

"What happened?"

"It was me and another lad... We were taking the money from one place to another and the Feds just came out of nowhere. Like they knew we were gonna be there, right then. We ran, first into an alley then started jumping walls, running through peoples' gardens, and the strap got caught on the top. I jumped down and the bag fell on the other side. I had to decide; climb back up and risk getting caught, or just keep running."

"And you ran?"

Aaron nodded. "So... yeah. I guess if I hadn't dropped that bag and run, I wouldn't owe the money that made me try to rob my own fucking Grandad. Then... well, you know the rest."

"Yeah... but if you weren't working for that guy then you would have never been in a position to lose it in the first place."

"I suppose... but you asked about the nightmare. Before all that I've never really had any bad shit working for Dave. It's not like I'm a full-on hitman or something... I just shift a bit of weed so I can do what I want the rest of the time. Bit of powder sometimes, but... yeah usually lowkey, you know?"

Romy didn't reply. Aaron imagined her biting her lip, tucking her hair behind her ear while she tried not to judge him.

"You think I deserved this too, don't you?" he said. "Like I don't deserve to get away with it when the rest didn't-"

"No," she said, jabbing her fist into his thigh. "You daft bugger. Course not... I just... I dunno, I don't like the idea that you'd be going back to all that again, after this. What if something else happens?"

"Shit happens to everyone," Aaron said. "Greg was a good guy, right? Look what happened to him. Gazwan and Maria, they were fucking... angels, compared to me. The world don't give a fuck, man. Eats up good people, eats up bad people."

"Not the people in there," she said, presumably imagining the hunters sleeping off their brandy in the house. "They're immune."

"Nah," Aaron said.

"Oh really?"

"Yeah, man. Maybe before, but not for long. Not once you're finished with 'em. Get your pictures out there, write your story... Game over. Good guys win, for once."

"As simple as that, yeah?" Romy said. She dropped her hand, knuckle down, onto his thigh and left it there. After a second's hesitation, Aaron found it, and entwined his fingers in hers.

"Yeah, it is."

40

Charles

Charles had avoided speaking to Phyllis on the morning of the hunt because he was afraid it would soften him, yet now – hours away from facing almost certain death – it was the only thing that he imagined would give him strength.

Liana was dutiful as always, passing the phone to Phyllis after a short summary of their depressing daily routine and the promise that she would stay by his wife's side no matter how long it was until his return.

"Hello?" Phyllis said, her voice confused but, as ever, polite.

"Phyllis? It's Charles."

"Oh... hello there. What a surprise... How are you?"

"I'm fine. I wanted to speak with you before I... Well, to let you know that I have to do something... something quite unsafe."

"Oh goodness, well I'm very sorry to hear that. Well, do be careful, won't you?"

"Of course, thank you. As soon as it's over I'll be back to see you. Later today, hopefully."

"Oh how lovely. Well, I do hope it all goes well for you."

"So do I. Thank you, Phyllis. It was good to talk with you."

"Oh yes, and you. And give my best to the family, won't you? Alright, see you soon. Bye bye."

* * *

As usual, nothing could happen until Sir William awoke, leaving everyone on the house's lawn – including Death himself, if he was there – waiting for the old man to appear on the front steps. Matthew, despite allegedly serving as Charles' second, spent most of his time engrossed in a very animated conversation with O'Brien and his second, the head 'keeper, John Swire; lots of pointing and nodding and slaps on each other's shoulders. O'Brien was puffing out his cheeks and hopping on the spot as if he was about to sprint for Olympic gold.

Charles kept his distance. He'd already loaded everything he'd need into the Land Rover, with the exception of the leather overnight bag that sat on a small table. It had been brought out from the house by one of the servants, and inside it was his money, as well as the cash disputed by O'Brien – £465,984 in total, according to Matthew. As soon as this was over, he could take it and leave this place and these people for ever.

A number of hunters were massing on the driveway, all dressed up in their red coats and riding boots, ready to head out as soon as the duel was over and search for Aaron's ghost. Charles' eyes drifted from the hunters over to the horse box and back again, and a wry smile crept onto his lips.

He'd taken off his tweed jacket and folded it over the side of an empty stone planter and was buttoning his rolled-up sleeves when Sir William finally emerged, with Holdsworth at his side. Instead of demurring, as he had since his arrival, Charles finished with his sleeve and strode over, meeting them just as they reached the edge of the lawn.

"Good morning, Charles," said Holdsworth.

"Holdsworth. Sir William."

The old man had been focussed on putting one rubber-soled foot in front of the other, but now he looked up to meet Charles' stare with a weak smile on his time-scarred face. It had been years, decades, since Charles had stood this close to him, and it shocked him to see how feeble the once-great man had become. His eyes were hooded with heavy, swollen lids, blue veins visible at the few points where his skin was still tight enough to cling to his skull. The strong hum of liniment was like an aura around him.

"Charles," Sir William said eventually. "Good to see you, old boy. Was quite a shot, yesterday."

"I had assumed you didn't know it was me," said Charles. "I had half expected an-"

"Ah, come Charles. I know everything that it is possible to know, especially on this... my estate."

"So, you've found them then?" Charles said, directing the question more at Holdsworth.

"Not yet," Holdsworth said. He seemed to have the same impulse with the old man as Liana had with Phyllis, that constant need to crane over and check that they were still awake, even while standing. "But we will, today... I have no doubt."

"Are you not staying to finish the job, Charles?" said Sir William. Charles waited until the old man's coughing subsided before answering.

271

"My job *is* done, almost," he said. "All I have left to do is teach your son's new playmate a lesson, then take my money and leave."

Sir William grinned, one eye closing completely as his piled skin bunched up at the corner.

"And so, you came crawling back just to go and wash your hands of us all over again, Matthew tells me. Such a shame, given your years of loyalty. All of the great things we've accomplished. You will still have your memories though... that is a great gift. Hopefully many more years of making memories with your family, your lovely wife. Tell me, how is Phyllis, these days?"

Charles' jaw pulsed as he ground his teeth. He couldn't be sure whether Sir William was genuine, or if he was somehow aware of Phyllis' dementia and attempting to unsettle him before the duel. Given the old man's form, spite seemed a more appropriate instinct. Charles took one last look at him, then at Holdsworth, then turned and took his place on the lawn.

Aaron

Aaron and Romy had decided that the only way he was going to be able to get up high enough to shoot from the small window, as Charles suggested, was to stand on Romy's back when the time was right.

They practised a few times with the flap closed and no rifle, and although Aaron was slight, he was still so much larger than Romy that he felt as if he was crushing her narrow shoulders every second that he was stood on top of them. Once they were satisfied, they stood and waited as the grey morning light bled in, and tired voices began to bubble up on the driveway.

Aaron opened the flap and pulled himself up to look through, and saw Charles stood alone, rolling up his sleeves, while other groups of people talked quietly to one another, apparently keen to get back out on their horses and chase their own shadows in the woods all day.

"It's gotta be soon," said Aaron as he quietly climbed down.

"Is that loaded, yeah?" Romy said, inclining her head towards the rifle propped up in the corner.

Aaron took it, checked the bullet Charles had loaded was still there, and that the suppressor was still firmly screwed on. He nodded at Romy, then thumbed the safety off and got into position.

Charles

The underkeeper, Lees, presented Charles with his gun on a silver platter, as if he was serving hors d'oeuvre at a glamorous dinner party. It was a black Browning M1911, as Charles had expected; the textured grip seemed as if it had been used only a handful of times in the decades it had existed. Although Charles did not think he had seen this particular weapon before, he had used many like it over the years, quite often as a mercy giver to fallen prey while out on the hunt.

He ejected the magazine and inspected it, and once he was satisfied that the rounds appeared to be live, he slid it back in with the heel of his hand and loaded it. He sighted it with his right arm outstretched, his injured left shoulder still useless, and the iron sights looked to be in good shape. He looked back at the horse box for a second then, and noticed the flap was open.

273

Charles hesitated for a moment as he imagined what would happen if Aaron's position was revealed. If they all saw that he had helped them to beat the hunt, then used them to interfere with an ostensibly fair duel. He looked again at the gun, heavy in his cold hands, and tried to come up with another way that they could have tampered with it.

"Mr Mortimer," said Matthew as he approached. "Happy with your weapon?"

Charles growled his assent.

"Good, let's get this show on the road then, shall we?"

Matthew showed him over to the spot on the lawn they'd chosen, where O'Brien was waiting with his gun in hand. His face was pale, expressionless. It was the first time Charles had thought it looked impossible for him to force his reptile grin. He looked terrified.

"You can still avoid this," Charles said, raising his voice as he took his place opposite. "It's not too late."

O'Brien pretended he hadn't heard him. They were around 20 feet apart now, no need for pacing out or dropping handkerchiefs like their ancestors might have. This was as cold and as procedural as a life and death fight could possibly be, almost impersonal in its observation of the rules.

"To first blood, yes?" said Matthew, checking with both men. They both nodded. "Alright then. Mr O'Brien, as the aggrieved... you may call it."

"Heads," said O'Brien. He spat out the words like someone attempting to hold back a tide of vomit.

Matthew flipped a coin, slapped it down onto the back of his opposite hand. He raised a fearful glance at O'Brien, then looked over at Charles and nodded. "Charles... looks like you're shooting first."

Aaron

With the coin toss won, Charles straightened up and stared across at O'Brien, and Aaron guessed that he would be smiling. Aaron swore and snatched up the rifle, then stepped up onto Romy's shoulders and rested the barrel of the rifle on the sill of the flap. He put his eye to the scope, and after a few moments of disorientating black and green, he managed to steady the crosshairs on Charles.

"Ok, just try and hold it there. Don't move," he whispered, though he felt like he was talking to himself as much as Romy. "Shit, ok... Right, come on."

He watched as Charles pulled the gun's slide back, then extended his arm and raised it to fire.

"One one thousand."

Charles was solid, his left arm tucked behind his back and his right gripping the gun, throttling it. Aaron could practically see the veins bulging in his muscle-bound forearms.

"Two one thousand."

He allowed the scope to drift them, to follow the path of Charles' pistol until the crosshairs came to rest over O'Brien's heaving chest. Aaron thought about how many times he'd taken shots like this and made them, only at empty wine bottles instead of the real thing. How different could it be? How different could it feel to take a life, when it was a life as evil as O'Brien's?

"Three one thousand."

Aaron inhaled and pulled the trigger, the metallic spit of the suppressor drowned out by the explosion from Charles' gun.

41

Charles

O'Brien clutched at his chest, still waddling backwards while the sound of the shot lingered in the cold morning air. The horses at the corner of the house whinnied, masters fought to control their startled hounds, onlookers gasped as O'Brien gasped, his lungs filling with blood until it overflowed and trickled from his disbelieving mouth.

Charles couldn't be sure whether he was suffering from the common shock of someone recognising their imminent death, or whether that shock was compounded by the fact that he had been assured Charles' shot would miss.

In truth, he had aimed for the exact point on his shirt that was now spurting with thick, dark blood. Whether it was his pistol or Aaron's rifle that did the damage he couldn't be sure, but one thing was certain; O'Brien would not be alive for long enough to find out.

He stumbled backwards, his usually solid arms buckling underneath him as his attempt to sit down found him lying flat on his back. Swire and Matthew fell to their knees on either side of him, the former ripping open O'Brien's shirt as the latter felt for a pulse at his neck.

Charles stepped closer until he could see O'Brien's greying face; cold sweat on his cheeks and wide-open eyes staring in wonder at nothing, and everything, all at once. The wide open blue sky. His leg began to twitch as his bowels emptied, prompting grumbles from Swire as he recoiled.

"Call that first blood," said Charles, prompting Matthew to look up at him in terror.

"Charles, he can't die," Matthew said, pressing with all his might at the sucking chest wound. "You don't understand, he can't... we'll never... Dr Curry? Where is he? Is he-"

"He's gone to fetch his things, Mr Reeves, sir," said Lees.

"Someone go and help... go and hurry him up, Mr-"

Charles turned away as the panic intensified, dropped the pistol to the floor and took his jacket from where he'd left it on the planter and put it on. He walked over to the money, then – meeting Holdsworth and Sir William's approving smiles – picked up the bag and limped back towards the Land Rover.

Aaron

Aaron had dropped the flap and stepped down from Romy's back as soon as the bullet punched through O'Brien's clean white shirt. He couldn't be sure whose shot it was that connected, but he could see the fear in O'Brien's usually smug face even in that split second. He knew he was done.

Aaron made the rifle safe, then leant it in the corner, the cloying gun smoke still hanging in the air, charring the hairs on the inside of his nose. He turned back to see Romy on her feet, flexing her aching shoulders, though she stopped as soon as their eyes met, lunging forwards and clenching her arms around Aaron's waist.

He pulled her in close, burying his face into her hair, matting it with fresh, salty tears. He could feel the relief, the elation, surging through his body like a spark into dry grass. They stayed this way for what seemed like hours, Romy apparently as content as Aaron to stay locked in each other's arms for fear that they had somehow misunderstood; that this wasn't truly the end of their ordeal.

They both jumped at the sound of the Land Rover door opening, then slamming shut. They stared into each other's eyes and listened as the engine started, then braced themselves against the metal wall as the box began to move from side to side before, eventually, growing to a steady rumble.

* * *

Bright sunlight was pouring through the horse box's translucent windows when they finally came to a stop. Though Aaron had assumed it was just another junction at first, the engine soon cut, and he heard the sound of heavy, uneven footsteps on gravel, coming slowly around to the large ramp door at the back.

Romy shuffled over to his side, and while Aaron hugged her in, he glanced over at the rifle. It was as if the base line paranoia he'd been forced to adopt over the past few days was now trying to convince him that this was going to be yet another betrayal; the door dropping to reveal red-coated hunters licking their lips as they salivated over another chance at tasting blood.

He did his best to stuff the negative thoughts down and took a deep breath before the door dropped and the sun rushed in to blind them. Aaron eventually peered through the cracks between his fingers to see Charles stood at the foot of the ramp, blue skies all around him.

Aaron stood, then helped Romy to her feet, taking her arm as they both edged unsteadily onto the gravel drive, the shadowy form of Owlgreave blocking the sun to their left. The three of them exchanged glances for a few seconds, listening to the birds chattering oblivious as they flitted from one skeletal tree to another.

"So... you did it then," Aaron said, pointing at the leather bag gripped in Charles' right fist. "You got him."

Charles looked down at the bag, then nodded. "One of us did. At least. I suppose we'll never know."

Aaron handed the rifle back to Charles, who took it and slung it awkwardly over his good shoulder.

"Thank you," he said, before noticing the bag under Romy's arm. "The camera... you said there is nothing of me on there... is that the truth?"

"It is," Romy said. "Obviously others are... and the boy I was with. I'm gonna use his name, his picture... to show the sacrifice he made. But I won't use your name... It won't make any difference. I just need to make sure it was all for a good reason."

"That good with you?" Aaron said to Charles.

Charles grunted slightly, then looked back at the house. "Yes," he said. "But these people aren't to be taken lightly. A few pictures won't be enough... and they won't be impressed when they find out. These are incredibly powerful people you're trying to challenge."

"They're monsters," said Romy, defiant. "And they're gonna pay for everything they've done, every person they've hurt. Their time's over, I'll make sure of it."

Charles smiled with what Aaron chose to believe was grudging respect. Two ideological enemies finally calling a truce.

"You think he's dead?" Aaron said. "O'Brien?"

"More than likely," said Charles. "And if he isn't–"

He dropped the bag to the floor and bent down, groaning in pain as he unzipped it and pulled out two stacks of £50 notes, bundled together with a thin strip of paper.

"You should use this, to clear your debts," he said, offering the stacks to Aaron. "£20,000. More than enough for anything you owe, and... your mother, perhaps."

Aaron stared at Romy, the pair of them open-mouthed, though Aaron could see something else in her eyes. Maybe Greg's blood on his newly gifted money. He pocketed the stacks and took hold of Romy's shoulder, did his best to give her an apologetic look, though he was sure his relief far outshined it. He hoped she'd forgive him.

"Thanks," said Aaron, reaching over to shake his grandfather's outstretched hand. "Do you mind if I call her quickly? My Mum? Just to make sure she's alright?"

* * *

Charles went inside to make sure Liana and Phyllis were both safely cloistered away in the sitting room, and after a while he reappeared and waved Aaron inside, directing him to the corded phone that sat on a small table at the end of the hallway. Despite wanting to say goodbye to his Gran, Aaron understood Charles' point that having to introduce them yet again was not worth the distress to either of them, or the questions it would provoke from Liana.

Charles left Aaron alone to dial, though he had to stand there for a few minutes, staring at the pale green textured wallpaper until his Mum's number materialised in his sleep-deprived, adrenaline-pickled brain.

"Hello?" Michelle said after four rings, her voice weak with sleep.

"Hiya Mum."

"Jesus, Aaron? What time is it?"

"Erm, I dunno... Morning still, probably."

The line rustled while Michelle complained under her breath, presumably hauling herself into a seated position in bed. Aaron looked over his shoulder at the front door to make sure Romy hadn't decided to hover there.

"You alright love?" Michelle said. Aaron felt guilty for being surprised by the question.

"Me?" he said. "Yeah, I'm... alright actually, yeah. You?"

"Will be when this bloody headache's gone. Darren opened the bastard rum, didn't he."

Aaron couldn't help but snigger. "Fair play. So, you staying there? Thought you said you didn't want to, you know..."

"I changed my mind," she said. "You sounded... scared. On the phone. Like a little lad. Made me scared too. Even more than I was already. Decided I didn't care if I was in the way here. He could like it or lump it."

"Cool. Well, that's... good."

"Yeah, it's been alright. Darren's a good bloke. I know you don't like him but-"

"I don't know him."

"Well, whatever. You don't know him, then."

"It doesn't matter. If you're happy, safe... I'm happy."

"Yeah, well... you know," her voice trailed off, Aaron listened as flint of a lighter sparked, then tobacco crackled under its flame. He'd not smoked for days, and the mere sound of someone else lighting up on the other side of the phone was enough to turbo-charge his cravings.

"What about you?" Michelle said, stopping to exhale. "Have you sorted it? Whatever you needed to sort out."

"Almost, yeah. This time tomorrow, I reckon."

"Good. Yeah, you sound better, actually. Happier."

"Not like a little lad anymore, yeah?"

They both laughed then, together. Aaron couldn't remember the last time he'd experienced it with her, so he stood there for a second, enjoying how it felt.

"Alright, I'll let you go anyway, Mum."

"Alright then."

"I'll come up and see you soon, like we said. If you want?"

"Yeah, that'd be nice. Just let me know."

"Ok," he went to replace the phone on its moulded plastic base, then caught himself halfway through the movement and put it back to his ear. "Love you... Mum."

She hesitated for a second. Aaron imagined she might have fallen off the bed in disbelief.

"You too... Take care love, see you soon."

42

Aaron – Two Weeks Later

Aaron had his hands stuffed in his jacket pockets as he approached the crumbling block of flats, his breath billowing clouds in the frozen morning air. He pressed the buzzer, then shuffled on the spot as he waited for the whine to subside.

"Alright... It's me."

"Ah shit. You're early," came Romy's voice through the tinny speaker.

Aaron sniggered. "Yeah, you still in bed?"

"No, no. Just... Gimme a sec."

Aaron listened as frantic shuffling replaced Romy's voice, half heard swearing off in the distance.

"Come on, man, I'm freezing my tits off here."

"Sorry," she said, a strange up and down melody to her voice. "Ok, we're good. Come on up."

The buzzer whined again, and Aaron snatched the door open and slipped inside, drawn by the promise of warmth in the stairwell. He took down his hood and pulled off his beanie and gloves as he climbed the stairs, the melting frost under his soles squeaking and slipping on the lino as he rounded each new corner.

By the time he reached the fourth floor, sweat was already pooling under his arms and at the small of his back, the vapours rising from the rattly old heaters practically boiling the air around him.

He thumped on the door to Romy's flat and she opened it almost instantly. Her head was cocked to one side as she tried to wring out her damp hair. Aaron guessed, from her water-speckled sweat pants and jumper, that the commotion had been her rushing around to get dressed.

"What took you so long? Sick of waiting for you," she said, throwing a grin back at him as she headed for the kitchen.

Aaron smiled, shut the door carefully behind him, and shrugged off his jacket and hoody, then flopped onto the wide pink sofa next to the window. Romy's laptop was open on the coffee table with the Skype app filling the screen.

"You fancy a brew?" Romy said, reaching over piled plates to flip on the kettle. Although the place was self-contained, its cramped layout and the clutter on every surface reminded Aaron of the student flats he used to deliver weed to in a past life.

"Does the pope shit in the woods?" he said.

"What?"

Aaron sat and enjoyed her confused smirk for a few seconds, then gave her an exaggerated nod. "Yes please, Romy."

"Weirdo... Coffee isn't it?"

"Yeah, three sugars, too. If that's alright."

Romy continued to smile to herself as she took two cups straight from the draining board and clapped them onto the kitchen counter.

"You know," she said. "If you need three sugars in a coffee, then you probably don't like coffee, right?"

"You said that last time," Aaron said, folding his jacket and hoody and placing them in his lap like a cushion.

"I can get you a Fruit Shoot if you want, sweetie?"

Aaron clamped his teeth over his bottom lip and pretended to shake with laughter, though his performance was soon interrupted by a shrill ringing from the laptop. The screen showed that the incoming call was from 'Mark @ Guardian'.

"Shit, he's early too," Romy said, switching the kettle off mid-boil and gliding over to the sofa, trying to tuck as much of her hair behind her ears as she could.

She settled herself next to Aaron, took a deep breath, and hit the space bar, revealing a balding, ginger man on the screen, who was slurping from a tall mug. He was pale and had a chinstrap beard, and his post-sip smile revealed a mouthful of small, crooked teeth.

"Oh, there you are, sorry," he said, setting the mug down and sliding it out of the shot. He was sat in a room lined with other computer screens and bland MDF desks, though he appeared to be alone. Given that they were speaking on a Sunday morning, Aaron wasn't that surprised.

"No, no, not at all," Romy said, forcing a laugh. "Caught us by surprise."

She held out a strand of damp hair and they all shared an awkward laugh.

Aaron waved to the camera. "I'm Aaron... I dunno if-"

"Course, yeah, we know all about you. It's good to 'e-meet' you, I guess, yeah," said the man, making the air quotes sign with his fingers. "I'm Mark by the way. Mark Conroy. I'm one of the senior news editors here... I'm sure Romy's told you already."

"Yeah, yeah," said Aaron. "Thanks for speaking with us, you know, about all this... Obviously it's a bit-"

"A bit crazy yeah," Mark said, laughing a little too hard. "Totally crazy. I couldn't believe what I was hearing, actually, but... yeah. Thank God you're both alright, too, I mean... Yeah, it's mad. Can't wait to hear your version of it all."

Aaron and Romy shared a quick glance, her posture straightening as she began to speak.

"So, firstly, thanks for doing this on here," said Romy, gesturing towards the camera. "I know it's not ideal, but you saw the screenshots and stuff I sent over, right?"

"Yeah, yeah," said Mark. "Course. I totally understand... Like we said it's a crazy situation so I can understand if you're paranoid or whatever and, it's like... You don't want to go through all that and then, you know, fall at the last hurdle or whatever... yeah, I get it, totally. Saves us going out in this bloody weather as well, right?"

He seemed distracted, his eyes constantly flicking towards the bottom left of his screen.

"Yeah," said Romy. "Thanks Mark, cheers."

"And yeah, I saw the images – kept them to myself, obviously, you know... but yeah, really harrowing stuff. But really important too. We'll certainly do our best to help you get it out there, to the widest audience, you know? Have you decided whether you're happy with the fee?"

Aaron saw Romy hesitate in the tiny window at the bottom of the screen, her eyes darting from his and back to Mark's.

"Yeah, that's great," she said. "Though, obviously, it's not really about the fee, it's-"

"Oh, yeah, yeah, course," said Mark. "Course it's about the

truth yeah. But you're happy with the fee, yeah?"

She nodded.

"Great," he said, and reached over to one side. "And you've said you wanted crypto, right?"

"Yeah, if that's ok," she said. "Better safe than sorry."

"Cool... ok, good. Woman after my own heart, yeah. And you said you're at home now, at your flat, right?" Mark said.

Aaron turned to Romy, whose eyes were already fixed on his. Aaron shrugged.

"Erm, yeah... we are," she said. "I thought you said that was alright?"

"Course, course. I just... sorry, just bear with me a sec."

Mark's head tilted further down and to the left again, as if he was using something just off screen. Aaron felt Romy's clammy palm on the back of his hand. She was still staring at him.

"What is it?" he said. "Are you alright?"

"Aaron..." she said, her voice trailing off just as the door to the flat burst open. She screamed. Aaron stood just in time to see masked men rushing through the hallway like a black wave surging through the bowels of a sinking ship.

43

Charles

They had come for Charles while he slept. His eyes had snapped open at glass smashing downstairs, but by the time he'd stumbled over to the bedroom door they were already on top of him.

The sound of Phyllis' confused shrieks had given him a late burst of vigour, but it was never going to be enough. They were so much stronger than him, so much more aggressive. Within a matter of seconds, he was bound and hooded and marched downstairs, thrown in the back of a car like the frail old man he had somehow become.

If the very nature of being abducted in the night wasn't enough of a clue as to his destination, the duration of the drive confirmed it. He had travelled to Barden Hall enough times to know the road by heart; though this time he was certain he would not be allowed to leave so easily. Certainly not with his grandson and a bag full of money to accompany him.

The car eventually ground to a halt and the blaring music cut off, and Charles was hauled out onto the gravel driveway

and marched inside. They passed through the house's main
hallway and carried on until they took a hard right turn,
towards what he knew to be the house's ballroom. The same
room where he'd spent so many carefree nights, usually leant
against the bar with Holdsworth.

The room was quiet and cold when they entered, noticeably
devoid of the music and mirth that usually filled it. He could
hear booted footsteps alongside the gentle slaps of his bare
feet on the tiles. Despite the life-or-death situation he was in,
he felt a strange pang of embarrassment at being dressed in
his pyjamas in public, so far away from home.

Rough hands jerked him to a stop, and he was forced to his
knees, stiff joints sending shocks of pain up his thighs and into
his hips.

One of the men plucked away his hood, revealing him to the
room like the main course at a banquet.

"Mortimer," said Sir William, who was still wearing his
strange, high-collared suit. The spite in his tone was fitting,
given the ominous surroundings.

The only light came from a jewelled, multi-ring chandelier
in the centre of the room, illuminating little more than the
Reeves family crest mosaic on the floor beneath it; a dragon
and lion facing off either side of a pyramid, with outstretched
wings above and crossed swords below.

Sir William was stood at the periphery of the chandelier's
glow, Holdsworth, as ever, at his side.

"What do you want?" said Charles. "Does that thug O'Brien
want his money back?"

"This isn't about money, Charles," said Holdsworth. "And
even if it was, I don't think Mr O'Brien is in a position to collect,
thanks to you and your grandson."

Charles couldn't help but furrow his brow, though neither Sir William nor Holdsworth seemed convinced.

"Don't play coy Mortimer," said Sir William, grinning. "We've heard the full story, straight from the horse's mouth."

"What on Earth are you-"

"That idiot boy of yours," the old man said. "He and his little bitch journalist went blabbing straight to the papers, told them all about your heroics. Was like something from a bad novel. You think she'd know better, wouldn't you?"

"Aaron," Charles scolded his grandson under his breath as he bowed his head.

Charles tried the bindings at his wrists, but they were zipped tight. He doubted he had the strength to wriggle out of them even if they weren't.

"So, what do you want? You want me to bring him to you?"

"Oh, we're past all that," Sir William said, gesturing at a shape in the darkness.

One of the main double doors swung open and a pair of hooded figures were wrestled inside. Two familiar voices spewed obscenities at the masked men throwing them to the floor.

They took Aaron's hood off first, then the journalist's. Both of them had been beaten and were bleeding from their ears, and there was a large gash at the corner of Aaron's eye.

"Grandad?" he said, though the girl was more concerned with her captors.

"Aaron, what the fuck is going on? What is this? Who the fuck are you?"

The girl's questions went unanswered by Sir William and Holdsworth. All Aaron could do was stare at Charles, the realisation dawning across his bloodied face.

A masked man strode over and dragged the girl to one side, while two more men appeared through the door with another hostage in hand.

As soon as Charles noticed the difference in the guards' demeanour, he felt his stomach lurch. The person in between the two men was short, frail. They looked to be helping her along, rather than dragging her in kicking and screaming like they had with Aaron and the girl. Almost like they were taking pity on her.

"Reeves!" Charles shouted. "Holdsworth... What are you doing? What is she—"

Charles was knocked back to the floor as he tried to rise, but he just growled and pushed himself back up.

"Reeves, you can't—"

The guard slammed him down again, this time driving a knee into the small of his back to keep him in place.

"Just stay there, alright?" said the guard. It was a woman's voice. She smelled of blood, of cold rot. It was a smell he knew all too well.

"Gran!" said Aaron. "What the fuck are you doing with her? Get her the fuck—"

Charles heard Aaron break free, and even manage a few strides across the floor, but he was quickly sent tumbling onto the tiles. The savage metallic crunching of the blow suggested he'd been felled with the butt of a pistol or rifle.

"Enough," said Sir William, with as much weight as his feeble voice could manage. "We're not here to offer you another chance to cause trouble. We're here to finish what was started."

Charles looked up from where the woman – who could only be Tess – had him pinned against the Reeves crest mosaic. Holdsworth had helped Sir William forwards, so he was practically within touching distance. He attempted to kneel but aborted this halfway through and stooped as close as he could to Charles' face.

"Listen to me, old boy. When you used that little shit to buy you in, when you agreed to join the hunt, you swore an oath. Now, tell me, what was that oath, Mortimer? Can you remember?"

"I swore nothing."

"You bloody well did, Charles. I heard you with my own ears," came Matthew's voice from the darkness. Charles shot a poorly aimed scowl in the general direction of his voice, then turned back to Sir William.

"Well," said Sir William. "I'll ask again then. What oath did you swear, old boy?"

Charles grunted, then said: "Until... the last.... drop."

Sir William smiled. "Until the last drop. Very good. Until the last drop of blood has been spilled. This is a tradition we have taken great care to uphold... generations upon generations. We have observed this ritual on every continent this planet has to offer us. Every shade, every caste of man and woman has served as both predator and prey. All ants under the same cosmic wheel. My legacy, my family's legacy, this house... it is all built on blood. The blood we spill in the name of a greater power. Mortimer – Charles – My boy... you have said those immortal words so many times before, and each time you have made good on your word. That is.... until now."

Sir William groaned as he straightened up, began to pace now as he spoke, Holdsworth watching for any sign of a stumble.

"This boy betrayed you," Sir William said. "He betrayed you so grievously. So, you brought him to us for justice and to please the Gods and still you could not bring yourself to do it. To salvage some shred of honour. And now you are here. Both of you, all of you. And-"

"Why?" Charles said, the air being forced from his lungs by Tess' weight. "Why here? If you want me dead, then get on with it. Leave them out of it."

"I never wanted you dead, Mortimer. When you abandoned us, when you came crawling back with this boy in your horse box... even when Matthew begged me to let him sabotage your pistol. I always wanted you to succeed. And – somehow – you always have."

"What then?"

"I want you to succeed again, Mortimer," said Sir William, turning back to face Charles. "End this boy's life here and now – shed his blood on my family's crest – and your debt is paid. You can return home to live out the rest of your days in peace... and your wife will return with you unharmed. You have my word."

Charles sneered at Sir William, baring his teeth like a caged lion. If he believed in anything, in any kind of God, he would have beseeched them for the strength to rise one last time and choke the life out of the vindictive old weasel where he stood.

Charles shrugged his broad shoulders, testing Tess' concentration, but she was as immovable as a boulder on his back.

"Same goes for you, boy," Sir William said to Aaron. "We are here for sport after all. Both women will be freed if you can overpower the old man. That is, if you-"

"You're a fucking psycho!" screamed Aaron, his voice cracking like a schoolboy. "I'm gonna kill you, I'm gonna fuck you up you old-"

Aaron's tirade was ended with a solid kick from one of his

captors.

"Pathetic," said Sir William, turning away from Aaron. "Where is the weapon?"

Holdsworth shuffled over to one of the masked figures in the darkness, who handed him an antique sabre, still sheathed in its chrome and gold scabbard. The metal clinked as Holdsworth's wedding ring knocked against it, then rattled as he removed the blade and laid it on the floor next to his master's feet.

Sir William grinned, slid the sabre into the middle of the crest with a rubber-soled foot, then moved away to a safe distance where he was flanked by masked men, rifles clutched to their chests.

44

Aaron

The weight of disbelief was crushing. Aaron looked on as Charles panted heavily, struggling under the weight of a thickly muscled woman who could have only been Tess, his mouth drooping at the corners in one of the most forlorn expressions Aaron had ever seen.

Phyllis and Romy were a few feet away, whimpering each time one of their handlers shifted their grip on the scruffs of their necks.

Aaron couldn't bring himself to look at them for long, turning back to stare ahead as two of the ring of masked men approached him from behind, wrenched him to his feet, and untied his wrists. Once he was free, he tried to get a look at one of them, but they had already disappeared back into line at the fringes of the room.

The sword snatched his attention back, glinting in the glow of the chandelier, an equal distance between him and his grandfather. It was almost covering a similar looking sword that was part of the crest on the floor.

Tess dismounted Charles and hopped to her feet, her plaited hair swinging down as she pulled off her mask to complete Aaron's dismay. She grinned that vile, gap-toothed grin at him, then winked as she stepped away.

"It's one of you, or both of them," Holdsworth said, pointing towards the two kneeling women. The men behind them had pistols drawn, pointing at the backs of Phyllis and Romy's trembling heads. "If you want to save them, then one of you has to die on this crest. Now get on with it."

Aaron noticed Holdsworth and Charles staring at one another, then saw movement that looked like money changing hands in the shadows behind them. How many men were in the room now... 20, 30? The dim light made it virtually impossible to tell.

"Aaron," Charles said, still struggling to his knees. "Take the sabre and do it."

"What are you–"

"They will kill them... in front of us. Do it, now!"

Charles' voice had somehow ramped up to its booming full strength, echoing from the hard tiles and up into the dark, cavernous ceiling. He lurched forward and picked up the sword, then slid it along the floor towards Aaron.

Aaron stared on, open-mouthed, as Charles straightened up and stabbed at his chest with his index and middle fingers, indicating where the blade should go.

"Here. Do it. Now."

Aaron could feel acid bubbling up in his throat. Words of encouragement started to ripple out from the shadows, gentle at first, steadily building as the men's blood lust grew. Within seconds the shouts had become roars telling him to pick up the blade, telling him to kill the old man, telling him to get it done. It was as loud as a football terrace in the room now, the violence in their voices burning Aaron's ears like airborne acid.

Charles joined them. "Do it, Aaron, for God's sake."

A shriek from Romy cut through the bellowing chants, closely followed by a wailing cry from Phyllis as she shrunk forwards to shelter from the racket. The guards behind them were pushing them closer to the ground, keeping gun barrels pressed to the backs of their heads. They were shouting too.

"Aaron!"

Charles wrenched Aaron to his feet and slapped the sword into his quivering hands, then caught him with an open-handed blow to his cheek. Adrenaline surged from where the strike had landed, rushing around his skull and down to the base of his spine like electricity. Charles took hold of Aaron's hoody and tossed him back to arm's length, beating his chest again where he wanted the blade.

"Look, look at them," he said, pointing at Romy and Phyllis. "Save them. Do it."

Aaron screamed wordlessly as he wrapped both hands around the grip and thrust the gleaming blade between Charles' ribs. He felt it crunch as it sank deeper, the aggression draining from Charles' face almost instantly, leaving a vacant, paper thin stare behind. He made a strange grunting sound and fell to his knees, taking Aaron – hands still frozen around the sword grip – with him.

They knelt there together for a few seconds; Aaron transfixed by Charles' ice blue eyes as they seemed to glaze to grey. Eyes that once stared out so hard that it was impossible to see beyond them. Now they were as fragile as smoke, inscrutable not because of their power, but because there was nothing left for them to hide.

Aaron let go of the blade and lowered his grandfather's body to the floor. The noise on all sides was still deafening, though now there were shouts of triumph alongside the baying for blood. Aaron looked over at Sir William, who was slowly applauding.

"Very good, very good," he seemed to say.

Aaron stood and began to move towards him when the old man's expression changed. He followed Sir William's gaze as he locked eyes with the men holding Romy and Phyllis and gave a deliberate nod.

The men released them, then took a step back and levelled their weapons. Aaron's legs collapsed underneath him as the first shots exploded into the room, silencing the crowd. The man behind Romy stepped forwards then and fired two more shots into her lifeless body. The other man moved past him, stooping to look at Phyllis' face, then straightening back up and firing a final round into the back of her head, blood pouring out of the wound into her cotton white hair.

Aaron tried to scream, but his lungs were empty. He simply sat there on the tiled floor, his face frozen in dumb fear as the two men rounded Romy and Phyllis' bodies, and strode over to him and fired until he stumbled backwards onto the floor.

The chandelier was all he could see as his vision began to fade. Its lights spiralling like a fiery wheel overhead, the dangling crystals glinting like the stars on a baby's mobile. He wanted to reach up to them and feel the smooth glass between his fingers – to be anywhere but bleeding out on the floor of this monster's mansion – but all he could do was stare, listen as the voices bubbled back up out of the cold silence that the gunshots left behind.

His body was useless now. He was merely a passenger,

rattling on to the end of the line. It would be here soon.

He thought of that train then, the one he'd ridden to Owl-greave. The changing scenery that had passed outside his window. The journey that had saved his Mum's life. No matter what had happened, he had done right by her. Her life would go on after his had ended.

He wanted to see her then.

In that moment.

He wanted to go home.

Printed in Great Britain
by Amazon